Past Praise for Mary Connealy

"Brimming with high-stakes action, plot twists, and plenty of shady characters, Connealy's finale captivates. Series fans will be delighted."

Publishers Weekly on *Into the Sunset*

"A propulsive narrative filled with masked gunmen, greedy manipulators, and enough twists to keep Connealy's fans on the edge of their seats. Readers will be captivated from first page to last."

Publishers Weekly on *Toward the Dawn*

"With a vivid setting, compelling characters, and a suspenseful, thought-provoking story, this will please fans of inspirational historical romance."

Booklist on A WESTERN LIGHT series

"Connealy's lively writing keeps the reader fully engaged. A sure bet for readers who enjoy books by such inspirational western authors as Amanda Cabot and Tracie Peterson."

Booklist starred review on *The Laws of Attraction*

"Connealy kicks off the WYOMING SUNRISE series with a spirited, suspenseful romance. . . . [Her] memorable characters—especially tough, gun-toting Mariah—are easy to root for as they propel a richly detailed adventure that captivates till the end. Readers will eagerly await the series' next entry."

Publishers Weekly on *Forged in Love*

Legends of Gold

Books by Mary Connealy

The Kincaid Brides
Out of Control
In Too Deep
Over the Edge

Trouble in Texas
Swept Away
Fired Up
Stuck Together

Wild at Heart
Tried and True
Now and Forever
Fire and Ice

The Cimarron Legacy
No Way Up
Long Time Gone
Too Far Down

High Sierra Sweethearts
The Accidental Guardian
The Reluctant Warrior
The Unexpected Champion

Brides of Hope Mountain
Aiming for Love
Woman of Sunlight
Her Secret Song

Brothers in Arms
Braced for Love
A Man with a Past
Love on the Range

The Lumber Baron's Daughters
The Element of Love
Inventions of the Heart
A Model of Devotion

Wyoming Sunrise
Forged in Love
The Laws of Attraction
Marshaling Her Heart

A Western Light
Chasing the Horizon
Toward the Dawn
Into the Sunset

Golden State Treasure
Whispers of Fortune
Legends of Gold

*The Boden Birthright:
A* Cimarron Legacy *Novella*
(All for Love *Collection*)

Meeting Her Match: A Match Made in Texas *Novella*

Runaway Bride: A Kincaid Brides *and* Trouble in Texas *Novella*
(With This Ring? *Collection*)

*The Tangled Ties That Bind:
A* Kincaid Brides *Novella*
(Hearts Entwined *Collection*)

GOLDEN STATE TREASURE · 2

Legends of Gold

MARY CONNEALY

a division of Baker Publishing Group
Minneapolis, Minnesota

© 2025 by Mary Connealy

Published by Bethany House Publishers
Minneapolis, Minnesota
BethanyHouse.com

Bethany House Publishers is a division of
Baker Publishing Group, Grand Rapids, Michigan

Printed in the United States of America

All rights reserved. No part of this publication may be reproduced, stored in a retrieval system, or transmitted in any form or by any means—for example, electronic, photocopy, recording—without the prior written permission of the publisher. The only exception is brief quotations in printed reviews.

Library of Congress Cataloging-in-Publication Data
Names: Connealy, Mary, author.
Title: Legends of gold / Mary Connealy.
Description: Minneapolis, Minnesota : Bethany House, a division of Baker Publishing Group, 2025. | Series: Golden State Treasure ; 2
Identifiers: LCCN 2024041232 | ISBN 9780764244407 (paperback) | ISBN 9780764244964 (casebound) | ISBN 9781493450732 (ebook)
Subjects: LCGFT: Christian fiction. | Romance fiction. | Novels.
Classification: LCC PS3603.O544 L44 2025 | DDC 813/.6—dc23/eng/20240909
LC record available at https://lccn.loc.gov/2024041232

Scripture quotations are from the King James Version of the Bible.

This is a work of fiction. Names, characters, incidents, and dialogues are products of the author's imagination and are not to be construed as real. Any resemblance to actual events or persons, living or dead, is entirely coincidental.

Cover design by Dan Thornberg, Design Source Creative Services
Cover image © Matilda Delves / Trevillion Images

Baker Publishing Group publications use paper produced from sustainable forestry practices and postconsumer waste whenever possible.

25 26 27 28 29 30 31   7 6 5 4 3 2 1

To my granddaughter Elle

You'll have your driver's license
by the time this book comes out.
God bless you, sweet girl.
Drive safely. Do it for Grandma.
I love you.

ONE

August 1874
Northern California's Central Valley

"I was really surprised the sheriff didn't find an excuse to hang that blackhearted varmint," Josh Hart said as he rode beside Tilda Muirhead on their way home to the Two Harts Ranch near the mining town of Dorada Rio, California.

Josh's big brother, Zane, and Zane's wife, Michelle, who was very near to having her first child, led the way home. Thayne and Lochlan MacKenzie came next, with Josh and Tilda bringing up the rear.

The oldest of three brothers, Brody MacKenzie and his brand-new bride, Josh's little sister, Ellie, had stayed in town after today's wedding because Brody had used up every ounce of his strength to attend the trial of the man who'd shot him only yesterday, breaking his ribs and knocking him insensible.

True, a gold coin had stopped the bullet, saving Brody's life. So Sonny Dykes hadn't killed him but not for lack of trying. He and his outlaw partner, Loyal Kelton, Ellie's one-time fiancé, were both lucky to be spending the rest of their lives in jail instead of being hanged when cold-blooded murder had been their intent.

"I don't like the idea of hanging anyone." Tilda rested her hand on her throat as if she could feel a noose there. "But locking those two outlaws away for the rest of their lives is just good sense. He shot your brother-in-law right in the heart. A life sentence with hard labor should keep your family safe."

They trotted for a time heading home, Tilda on Josh's right. When they reached a rugged stretch, they slowed to let the horses walk. The clop of the hooves was a friendly sound that reminded Josh he'd been away at sea for too long before he'd come home to stay a little over a year ago.

Once, he would have said the sea was in his blood, but now he knew this was the life he wanted. "Have you thought any more about being a teacher?"

Tilda had shown up just today with Zane, Michelle, and a few dozen orphans to live on the Two Harts Ranch. Originally from New York City, she'd come out west searching for Thayne and Lock MacKenzie, who'd ridden here on an orphan train, then vanished into the wilderness after running away from the train and Tilda.

Tilda looked sideways at him. She was not a skilled rider, but then sitting astride a well-broken horse was no great trick. Under careful observation, she'd even handled trotting with just a few pointers from him.

The trail curved ahead, and Josh hadn't really noticed that they'd lagged behind until the MacKenzie boys were out of sight. For the first time since he'd returned home, he rode alongside a woman who wasn't his sister or married. He found himself wanting to talk with Tilda, but not about work and not about orphans. Yet he had a tongue tied in knots and a brain stuffed full of cotton wool.

Searching desperately for something to say, he returned to the subject of her working at the ranch. "You know, Tilda, if you do work for us, you'll be required to sleep with me."

She gasped and spun around to face him, her hair snapping free from its pins and a long, dark braid whipping across her face. "What did you say?" Her eyes flashed with fury and insult.

That's when what he'd just said echoed through his brain. "I-I mean at the school . . . you and I will both sleep at the school and—"

Tilda reined her horse to a stop. "I'll do no such thing." She tugged at one rein as if to turn her horse to ride back to town. Except her horse wanted to go home, and she wasn't handling it right. The horse gave her a mule-stubborn look and seemed to sink right solid into the ground, refusing to let her guide it any farther.

"I'm going back to town. No, wait. I'll get the children first. What kind of place do you run out there?"

"Stop, no. I'm sorry. What I meant was you'll sleep with the orphan girls who live at our school. I'll bed down in the dormitory we have for the boys. There'll be no sleeping together. That sounds so wrong. I have no interest in you at all."

As her eyes widened, he tried to review his words again, not sure what he'd babbled out. Whatever it was, it was clearly wrong. He should probably just go back to sea now.

She wrenched on the reins again, and her horse skittered sideways. Josh reached out to grab the reins before the horse got its dander up, but Tilda slapped at his hand and shrieked as if he were attacking her. He snatched his hand away just in time for her to miss him and slap the horse on the neck. Instantly, the horse kicked out with its back legs, sending Tilda flying.

Nearly as quick, Josh netted her as if she were a fish on the line, and she landed with a thud right in his lap, nose to nose with him. Startled, she quit fighting and shrieking. Their eyes met. He only distantly saw her horse run for home.

"Tilda, I didn't mean to insult you. I just . . . I was only . . . what I meant was . . ."

"What?" She sounded breathless. Maybe it was because she'd just been tossed off a horse's back. But it didn't sound like that. Instead, it sounded like . . . like . . .

He leaned forward, an inch at a time. She didn't fight or shriek or demand to be set down on the ground. She leaned distractingly forward.

"Josh, what happened?" Zane's voice broke in.

Josh jerked away, which wasn't far considering she was sitting on his lap. There was only so far a man could go in those circumstances.

"She got bucked off her horse when she swatted . . . uh, a fly." Right now, Josh felt as low as a bug, so it wasn't far from the truth.

Michelle came next around the curve in the trail, then Thayne.

"Are you all right, Miss Tilda? Seeing your horse come running without a rider scared me."

Thayne looked at Tilda in a way that struck Josh as a bit too mature for his age. Thayne was in many ways a man grown.

It struck Josh that Thayne might have ideas about his pretty teacher. One who'd worried enough about them to travel clear across the country.

"Mr. Hart caught me before I fell." Tilda's eyes glowed as if a white knight on a valiant steed had saved her very life.

Josh probably shouldn't enjoy that so much.

"Where's her horse?"

Lock came around the bend leading it.

Tilda clutched Josh's shirt. So quiet that only he could hear, she said, "Don't put me back on the horse, please. Not alone. I'm afraid."

Josh kept his horse moving forward, even though her hand held the front of his shirt so tight he was in danger of being strangled.

"Tilda's never ridden a horse before. She can ride double with me. We're most of the way home."

Really it wasn't far at all. Holding this pretty little woman in his saddle made him wish the ride were a bit longer.

Michelle came up beside them and rode at Josh's side. "We can't ride fast with Josh carrying double. So we might as well talk. Josh and you MacKenzie boys, tell me more about this treasure hunt of Graham MacKenzie's."

Their treasure-hunting party had discovered fourteen gold coins in a saddlebag when they'd found Grandpa MacKenzie's body. There were old papers too, only they hadn't had time to go over them yet, what with Brody being shot and getting married and attending a trial.

"Did you say there's some Spanish language involved?"

Lock, who probably had his grandfather's whole journal memorized, said, "Yes, several sentences. One that we noticed both in the journal and in the papers with Grandpa's body read, "*Al norte de la Bahia de Los Piños con Capitan Cabrillo en una espesa niebla.*"

Michelle frowned. "All right. That means 'north of Los Piños Bay with Captain Cabrillo in a thick fog.'"

"I've heard of Los Piños Bay," said Josh. "It's called Monterey Bay now, but I've heard of the old name. It's south of San Francisco Bay. Considering the fog that seems to surround San Francisco Bay, maybe what he was writing about was the fog around San Francisco, not the bay."

Lock's jaw went slack. "Why didn't you tell us this before?"

"Why didn't you ask? You know I was a sailor. If you'd asked about a bay, I'd've answered you. Where did you say you found this sentence?"

"Grandpa's journal."

Josh shrugged. "I've never read it. Never even talked with you about that old book."

"But you went on the treasure hunt with us."

"You had a map—or half of one anyway. That's what I was paying attention to."

Josh's sister Ellie, her husband, Brody, and Cord Westbrook were now on a mission to find the other half. Quietly, into the bickering, Tilda said, "I've heard of Captain Cabrillo."

Josh's head pivoted hard to stare down at the woman in his arms. The whole group was looking at her.

"Who is he?" Michelle asked. Michelle liked to know more than everyone, and here she was, not knowing two whole facts about what she'd no doubt flawlessly just translated.

"Juan Cabrillo was with Hernando Cortés, the Spanish conquistador whose expedition led to the fall of Mexico's

Aztec Empire. That was over three hundred years ago. Captain Cabrillo was sent by Cortés to explore the Californian coastline with a small armada of ships. Some say he went as far north as the Columbia River in Washington State. He took very thorough notes, but of course most things had different names back then. Cabrillo tagged names onto them, but not all of his names stuck. There's a record of all the places he found, but he never found San Francisco Bay. Historians have noted that he missed the bay because it was shrouded in a thick fog."

"*En una espesa niebla*," Michelle muttered. "In a thick fog."

"The first European explorer to come upon San Francisco Bay was Don Gaspar de Portola in 1769," Tilda went on. "And he came overland, not by sea."

The whole group was silent, until finally Josh managed to say, "How is it you know so much about the history of California?"

Tilda's cheeks pinked up. "My adoptive father was a history teacher in a big school in New York City. He had a library full of books, and I loved to read. I have always had a fascination with Californian history, especially the stories about Spanish explorers."

Josh studied her. Dark hair, dark eyes. Could she be Spanish maybe?

Michelle's eyes narrowed. "Could it be one of the ships in his armada somehow got separated from the rest of the fleet in the fog? Could they have been left behind in California? Maybe they ran aground and then followed a river inland and became stranded. So they set out to explore, planning to rejoin Captain Cabrillo later, but then their ship sank and they were trapped there. That must be what happened, or something close to it." She looked up, her eyes gleaming. "How fascinating."

"Or maybe they deserted. Jumped ship. Swam to shore." Josh knew sailors who'd done such things. "They could have run off from Cabrillo, done with seafaring, hoping no one would ever find them, especially if they found the bay and the water route inland by accident."

"Cabrillo was the first of his kind to journey up the coast of California." Tilda sure spoke like someone who'd memorized a history book. "But San Francisco Bay wasn't charted for hundreds of years. Whoever left that journal and those coins might have been driven into the fog by a storm. Maybe their ships were wrecked, and they were left to wait for help, which never came. Or maybe it came but they had to leave things behind, like the journal."

Josh shook his head. "A man might abandon a leather book, but he'd take his gold."

"Maybe," said Tilda, "they set out to hike all the way back to Mexico where Cortés was, then looked around at this lush, beautiful land and decided to stay."

"You do know a lot about history." Michelle studied her as if she had her under a microscope.

Tilda shrugged. "I guess my father inspired me. I caught his love of American history, and I read most every history book I could find at the New York City Public Library."

Michelle's eyes sparked. "We need a history teacher at the school. Tilda, you could teach history." Michelle sounded like it was all settled. "Maybe other subjects as well, but history for sure to the older students. Zane's library in the ranch house has quite a few history books. I wonder if Captain Cabrillo is listed in any of them."

Michelle patted Zane on the shoulder. "If we can prove a bunch of Spanish conquistadors traveled inland in California . . ." She paused and looked at Tilda. "When was all this?"

"Cabrillo explored the coast in 1542."

Josh tightened his arms around Tilda and was glad he hadn't returned her to her horse. She probably needed support if she was going to deal with Michelle. Most people did. Not that Michelle didn't have great ideas. They just usually had the relentlessness of an incoming tidal wave about them.

"I want to see that journal." Michelle's eyes lit up, not with the fever to find treasure or gold, but with an interest in something so old.

"I want to see the journal, too." Josh knew Michelle thought she knew everything, but surely he could do a better job of recognizing information that dealt with seafaring than anyone else.

Tilda said quietly, "I'd love a chance to study something connected with Captain Cabrillo and the conquistadors."

The woman really did love history, it seemed. An odd preference to Josh's way of thinking. Better to pay attention to the present, such as if the cows had enough grass and water.

"The journal *itself* is old," Lock said. "But the many pages of *writing* in the journal were all done by Grandpa. He must have *found* it, included in what he called 'a treasure' and used it to take notes, then he mailed it to us. Then he went back to his treasure and died before he could let us know more. The notes we are talking about, including the Spanish about Los Piños and Captain Cabrillo, don't seem to be in Grandpa's words—we think he copied them from somewhere else. For one, he wasn't much of a speller. Never had any schooling,

I don't think. And as far as Brody knows, Grandpa didn't speak a lick of any foreign language, except maybe a few words from his Scottish ancestors."

"Brody called it Gaelic, I think," Thayne noted, guiding his horse alongside Josh as they rode toward the Two Harts. "What about the papers we found with Grandpa's body, Lock? Were those written by Grandpa, too? Or were they written three hundred years ago?"

Thayne scratched his chin. Josh noticed for the first time that Thayne had a fair amount of stubble on his chin. He wondered if the boy knew about shaving yet. Josh should probably teach him. He'd've told Brody to show him, but Brody was gone—and might be for a while, all things considered.

"Let's get back to the ranch and look at that journal."

Zane said, "I need to check how things have been running at the ranch."

Josh felt a bit annoyed by Zane's comment. "The ranch is being run just fine—we know what we're doing."

Zane gave him a sharp look, and Josh wondered what he'd sounded like. He had spent a lot of time away from the ranch the last few days, but it'd been the weekend when they'd gone treasure hunting, and they usually worked lighter days then, especially on Sunday. Today was Monday, and Josh had talked to the men before they'd headed to town with their prisoners. It wasn't time yet to drive the cattle to market, so even though Josh had brought plenty of men along to handle the prisoners, he'd left a crew back at the ranch to keep up with all the chores.

Zane shifted his horse around so he was riding on Josh's left. Thayne was too close on the right, probably to keep an eye on Tilda. Zane clapped Josh on the shoulder and said, "I haven't got a worry in the world about you keeping things running, Josh. I'm just curious. I've been gone for nearly two months. I can't wait to see how the spring calves have grown."

Josh nodded. "I know. I'm anxious to have you around again. You do have a knack for stepping right in to boss this place, though. I know you ran things alone for a long time while I was sailing the seven seas. But I'm back now. And I'm a full partner, not a junior partner, not anymore."

Zane smiled. "Agreed."

Josh heard the words, but he knew Zane and knew his big brother had a bossy streak.

"Let's pick up the pace for home. Josh, if it's too much for your horse, do you mind if we ride ahead? It's only a few minutes more."

Josh looked down to see the alarm on Tilda's face. She needed riding lessons, and Josh was just the one to teach her. "Go on, Zane. We're gonna keep riding at a slower pace."

With that, Zane urged his horse along faster.

Michelle and Lock kept up, Lock leading Tilda's horse. Thayne looked torn. He wanted in on studying the journal with Michelle, but he also seemed to want to ride alongside Tilda. Finally, his treasure-hunting enthusiasm won out, and he kicked his horse into a ground-eating trot. He soon caught up to the others, and before long they were all galloping.

Josh looked down at the armful of woman he carried and remembered his fumbled talk of her staying in the school dormitory with the girls while he stayed with the boys. He clamped his mouth shut so that nothing stupid would come blabbing out again.

Tilda said quietly, "Do you think I'd be doing the right thing to stay out here? I felt like I had a true calling from God to ride on the orphan trains. He put it in my heart to care for orphans after I became one."

Josh stopped losing himself in the pleasure of carrying a woman around and focused on her words. "You're an orphan?"

"Yes, didn't anyone mention that to you? I'm sure Michelle knows." Tilda's brow furrowed. "I did tell her, didn't I?"

"She didn't say a word to me about that."

"And Thayne and Lock know. I talked about it with the orphans." Tilda frowned. "Although those two were such scamps. They might well have not been paying attention."

"That sounds like them. Did your parents die? Do you remember them?"

"No, my earliest memories are of being alone on the streets in New York City. I heard much later that there was an outbreak of fever, and a lot of people died from it. The orphanage I went to live in speculated my parents might've died in that fever. I was left running the streets with so many other children."

"My parents died, too."

Tilda's hand clutched the front of his shirt. "Josh, I didn't know you'd been orphaned as well."

"Truthfully, I was a grown man who'd gone to sea. I came home for a visit and found out then that they'd died. That's not the same as being an orphan. I wasn't left fighting for my life with no food and no roof over my head. But it's mighty sad all the same."

Tilda's eyes brimmed with tears. "I was so busy trying to survive it, I wasn't given much chance to think of how sad it was. I don't remember my parents. I don't even know their names. That all got lost in the cold and hunger." She blinked back her tears, seemingly interested in smoothing out the wrinkles she'd crushed into his shirt. "I was later adopted by a couple whose surname was Muirhead."

Josh patted her hand and felt a few moments of danger that his own eyes might fill with tears. That would never do. Thankfully, they rounded the last corner toward home. "Look," he said, "that's our ranch. See the big white building down from the house, past the barn and bunkhouse?"

Tilda twisted in the saddle to look. "The white building is where the orphans live?"

"Yep, the north side is the girls' living quarters—Michelle calls it a dormitory—and the south side is for the boys. There's no door connecting the two sides on the second floor. The first floor is where the classrooms are. Most of the time I sleep on the boys' side. There's a small private bedroom for each adult who stays with them, one for a man supervising the boys, another for a woman with the girls. Ellie used to do most of the turns on the girls' side, though Annie, my big sister, would fill in for her on occasion. Her daughter—you met them at the wedding, remember?"

"Yes, I sat next to Caroline when we ate. Her pa died, someone said." Tilda's eyes got all moist again.

Josh tried desperately to think of a new topic. "Caroline is school age now. Annie does a lot of teaching now that Caroline goes to classes. Some nights, when Ellie's forced to be away until later, especially now that she's been a nurse to Brody, Annie would put Caroline to bed in the ranch house, then go sleep at the dorm. But that wasn't usual. It was Ellie's job for the most part. Now Ellie's going to want to stay with Brody, I reckon. You'd really help us out if you joined us. You could write to the orphanage in New York and tell them to hire someone else. Lots of folks looking for work in a big city like that. Out here, teachers are scarce."

Tilda nodded silently for a bit. "I do feel a calling to help orphans. God opened the door for me to help with the orphan trains, but now a new door is open." She turned again to look at the Two Harts Ranch. "It really is a beautiful place. So many houses."

"When one of our cowhands gets married, we build them a house. We've got a blacksmith shop and farrier, too. Of course, that's mainly for keeping up with the ironwork at the ranch, shoeing horses and repairing wheels and tools and such. We've always had that. We even got a doctor's office. And Michelle made sure we had a telegraph wire. Anyway, it was a nice, but normal ranch before Zane married Michelle. Michelle's sister Jilly loves to build."

"I met Jilly and Laura, her other sister, in San Fransisco. They came to the mission where I was helping with the children. Jilly loves to build? Really?"

"Yep, she doesn't do all the building herself, but she bosses the work and the workers. She also built a railroad."

Tilda quit looking around and stared at him. "A woman built a railroad?"

"A line up a mountainside. And Michelle is an inventor. She's got several patents. But because she tends to work with molten iron and such, she's set her inventing aside until the baby comes. Their sister Laura is a chemist, with training in dynamite. Michelle and Jilly did a lot of the work organizing our little village. The cabins welcome family men rather than footloose cowpokes. That gives us a steady work crew. We have some single cowhands as well—they live in the bunkhouse."

"You call it a village, but I can't help but compare it to New York City. That's the only town I've ever really known." Tilda studied the ranchland with what sounded like quiet wonder. "I think this is a big improvement."

"Then you'll stay?" Josh tried to act like this was all about needing her help at the ranch and not about how nice Tilda felt in his arms.

"I think I will," she replied. "I'll pray about it, but this place calls to me. I find it very appealing."

Tilda glanced at him for just a moment when she said that, her cheeks faintly flushed, before twisting quickly away to look around the ranch once more.

Two

Tilda was escorted by Josh to a room in a building that echoed with rustling feet and voices. They'd ridden into a large log barn, where Josh tended his horse. They then made their way past a long bunkhouse and two rows of cabins.

Next was the dormitory. The building seemed huge. Not compared to New York's buildings, of course, but compared to the rest of the ranch. The place smelled of savory food and chalk, books and sawdust.

Josh took her upstairs, where he guided her through a warren of small bedrooms, maybe five or more of them. Some doors stood open, and she could see two bunkbeds in each room. Four children shared a room.

Tilda's throat felt thick as she remembered the sleeping quarters of several New York City orphanages. They were miserable and overcrowded, stiflingly hot in the summer and brutally cold in the winter. What food they were given was sparing and none too tasty.

Having to share with only three other children struck her as a luxury. They'd have room for twenty children on this side, and Josh said the other half of this schoolhouse had rooms for the boys.

Tilda had accompanied twenty children to Dorada Rio on the train. Depending on how many children were already at the ranch, they might well have room for all of them to live comfortably here. She thought of Josh telling her she'd have to sleep with him and felt her cheeks heat up. At the same time, a smile curved her lips. She understood now what he'd meant, but the man appeared to have little skill when it came to talking to a woman.

Then he led her to a private room. He swung open the door and gestured for her to enter.

"You won't need to go to work today," he said. "But if you wish it, you can sleep here tonight. Or you're welcome to stay in the ranch house with Annie, Zane, and Michelle. We have a housekeeper's apartment that's empty right now. You'd be comfortable there and also have privacy."

"You don't stay in the ranch house?" Tilda asked.

"I have a room beyond that wall." He pointed at the south wall of the room. "I guess you'd call me a guardian for the boys' rooms. We have a few cowhands who are good with kids, and they're willing to step in if need be. Our foreman, Shad, is the most dependable of the bunch. If you stay here, you'll sleep in a private room next to a dozen or so girls." He paused and added, "There's more than that with the youngsters you brought. They're six years old to sixteen, I'd say. Younger than that, Michelle leaves them in the hands of the Child of God Mission in San Francisco. Older than that, we help them advance their education, if they're interested, or find a job if they're so inclined."

"You help them?"

Josh nodded. "That's right."

Tilda saw a hallway beyond him with doors leading to each child's bedroom. She should have sent him on his way, but she was nervous. Oh, she fooled no one, least of all herself. Truth was, she was flat-out scared. She didn't want to be shoved into this perfectly lovely room and left alone. Her life had taken one strange turn after another since she'd lost the MacKenzie boys on the orphan train.

Now she stood looking at this room she'd be given all to herself. She'd never had something so lovely and spacious before.

"The orphans . . . that is, the boys, did you say they work on the ranch or as lumberjacks?" That didn't make much sense.

"Those are possibilities. We'll employ them if they show an interest in ranching. They can work to gain cowboy skills and take a job here at the ranch since we're always in need of new cowhands, as some move on. Or they can go with the training they received and work on some other ranch. They can train for other things, too. Michelle works with our students to find their special talents and guide them toward training for that talent. We've had one student show an interest in college, maybe to become a doctor. Several of the older girls want to be teachers, and one has taken over Ellie's classes since Ellie started helping Brody. A few have even gone to sea. Being a sailor once, I can talk with those interested and help them figure out how to proceed. I know a few people involved in shipping and can help the boys find jobs."

"I understand why cowpokes, but why lumberjacks?"

"We've got a good connection to the industry. Michelle

is one-third owner of one of the biggest lumber operations in California."

Her eyes narrowed as she tried to remember. "I rode the train from San Francisco to Dorada Rio with Michelle, and she never mentioned that."

Josh shrugged. "No doubt she was busy at the time. And you were too, wrangling all those children."

Tilda smiled. "Good point. We were all really busy. She didn't tell me much about herself. She seemed more inclined to ask about me."

Josh stepped aside and let her enter the room. He stayed outside, as if entering the spacious room with her would be improper.

She saw a good-sized bed with a pretty blue quilt and a chest of drawers with a stack of books on top. On the floor lay an oval rug that picked out the same color of blue as the quilt. There was a window behind the bed. She glanced out the window and could see the ranch house from here. There was a row of hooks on the wall for her clothing, and across from her, an open door revealed what looked like an indoor water closet.

Tilda was amazed at the notion of having her own room. She'd had one at the Muirheads, but she'd had to share it with stacks of packing crates. Yet she couldn't summon the courage to sleep just next door to the children. She supposed that made her a coward. It wouldn't be the first time she'd faced such a truth.

"One of the ranchers' wives is staying here for now. Why don't you come back to the house and eat with us and sleep in the ranch house?"

It was like Josh had read her mind. That might make him

sensitive, and he was paying close attention, or else she'd made some dreadful expression that had displayed her pure terror. Considering what he'd said earlier about sleep, sensitivity seemed doubtful. She suspected she'd pulled a face.

"We'll let Hannah handle the youngsters tonight. She's probably already here, helping get the meal served. The children eat together in the largest classroom downstairs. You'd be a stranger to them, and that may not be comfortable for you. But tomorrow you can meet them and maybe begin to figure out what all you can teach them. You can decide if you're ready to sleep over here after that."

"I think I'd like that. Thank you."

Josh gestured back in the direction they'd come, and she preceded him past the bedroom doors and down a flight of stairs to the ground floor. She heard chatter and the clinking of utensils. The children eating. She remembered all the times she'd been hungry growing up and was so pleased to see these children living and thriving in a land of plenty.

The sun had sunk low in the sky while they'd been inside. As they stepped out into the warm summer evening, the sunset glowed vividly with splashes of blue, red, and purple.

"Wait, stop." Tilda reached out and caught Josh's arm. She was stunned by the beauty around her. "You've got a wonderful place here. The weather is beautiful. Horses and cows, pretty buildings all over. I have a city woman's idea of what a ranch should look like, and the lush grass and all the people around here don't fit that image." She thought of the traffic of New York City. "You can't imagine how this touches me after years of living among the crowds and noise back east."

Red cattle with white faces grazed across gently rolling hills and in a valley broken here and there by outcroppings of rock.

Tilda went on, "Even though I rode out here on the train from San Francisco, this is the first time I've seen such a valley. It goes on forever. I was so busy watching the children and then clinging to my horse, I didn't appreciate the scope of it until now."

A corral with dozens of horses was on the far side of the barn. A few cowhands carried out farm chores in smaller yards that held pigs and chickens. Except for the whitewashed schoolhouse, the buildings were all built of logs.

"Jilly, the redheaded sister, built all of this? And railroad tracks up a mountain?"

"Well, the ranch house was already here, as were the barn and bunkhouse." Josh pointed as he spoke. "We also had the pigpen and chicken coop there and a couple of the cabins. But mostly, with all of us pitching in, yes, of course."

"It's a beautiful place." With all of it set against the lowering sun, it was enough to take her breath away.

Josh swept his arm toward the east, and she turned. She'd hardly noticed the mountains that towered there.

"Out there somewhere is the treasure Thayne and Lock's Grandpa MacKenzie wrote about."

"Out there? In that vast, endless mountain range?"

Josh smiled. "It does seem endless. Any help you could give us would be greatly appreciated. You can study the journal, and maybe your understanding of history will help us get a better idea of what we're looking for."

"Where are the boys?" She realized then that she hadn't seen anyone since they'd hung back from the group they'd ridden from town with. Despite all the buildings, with the exception of a few cowhands, she'd been alone with Josh almost since the moment they'd arrived at the Two Harts.

"Michelle asked them if they wanted to sleep in the ranch house tonight. They slept in the dormitory with the other orphan boys until Brody got here. He was away from home in New York City, going to a medical college in Boston. Unfortunately, once he finished his training and went back to New York, he found his mother dead, his father dying, and his brothers missing. He followed their trail, and it led him here to the Two Harts.

"Once Brody arrived, they settled into the rooms over the doctor's office—two bedrooms and a kitchen. We don't have room for the boys in the dorms, not with the new children. And I'm sure they'd be fine in their regular rooms, but with Brody gone, it didn't seem quite right. I can't believe I was about a year older than Thayne when I went to sea and traveled the world. I sure didn't think I was a kid at the time.

"The two of them ran off from the orphan train in Cheyenne, Wyoming, and made their way to San Francisco with no help. Now we want to protect those poor young rascals, teach them and offer them some adult supervision here at the Two Harts. So Michelle invited them to eat with us and sleep in the house."

Josh looked at her, and their eyes met for a long moment. He smiled, and Tilda returned the smile.

"Anyway," he continued, clearing his throat, "just because they managed to get here alive doesn't mean they have a lick of common sense. They'll stay in the house until Brody gets back. They ran to the doctor's office to change their clothes and wash up. I suppose they're already in the house by now. It's time for supper."

Feeling grateful, Tilda nodded and walked with him the rest of the way to the house.

THREE

Josh led the way into the house to find supper ready and both MacKenzie boys at the table with their journal between them as well as a stack of the papers they'd found when they discovered their grandpa's body. The pair were looking at each other and whispering, clearly not interested in sharing what they were reading.

And since Josh wasn't all that interested either, he let them go on whispering. He pulled out a chair for Tilda in an act of good manners that surprised everyone. Annie, carrying a bowl of what smelled like chicken and noodles to the table, noticed and arched one brow at him before smirking and getting back to serving.

Josh took the seat next to Tilda, across from Thayne and Lock. Michelle was beside Tilda, near Zane, while Annie took the other end of the table, with Caroline around the corner from her, beside Thayne.

"Is that the book you were talking about?" Michelle's eyes were riveted on the old leather book as she set a plate of biscuits on the table before taking a bowl of mashed potatoes from Zane. This was his and Josh's favorite meal, and it took a while to cook up the chickens and make the noodles.

Lock nodded, picked up the journal, and handed it to Michelle. "It's been torn. That's how we found out there was a map glued under the paper on the inside cover of the book. That map's been hidden there all these years. We followed about half of it before we located the cave where we found Grandpa's body."

"You found your grandfather's body in a cave?"

Lock nodded. "Brody recognized his hat and the blanket he had with the MacKenzie clan colors." Lock reached for the bowl of chicken and noodles.

"Let's say a blessing first." Zane beat Josh to suggesting it.

Zane was quick about the prayer, including asking God for His blessing on Ellie's new marriage.

"Were you boys upset about finding his body?" Zane asked.

Thayne and Lock exchanged glances. Thayne said, "I think Brody might've been a little. Grandpa was long gone for years before we were born. It was strange being in a cave with the skeleton, but it didn't seem sad really. Not to us."

Thayne looked at Tilda. "Is that bad, Miss Tilda? We should've spent a bit of time paying our respects, or at least given Brody time for that. Miss Ellie said—"

Lock elbowed him. "It's Mrs. Mackenzie. In fact, she's our sister now. We should call her Ellie." Lock looked around the table. "You're our family, too. It was mostly just Ma and Brody when we were growing up. Pa was gone all the time. We got that journal sent to us from Grandpa thirty years ago. Pa ran off hunting for the treasure. We think Grandpa mailed the book to us at the same time he mailed the other half of the map to Mayhew Westbrook." He nodded at the journal Michelle held.

She'd stopped studying it while Lock and Thayne spoke of their grandpa and having a new family.

"I'm Aunt Michelle now. Do you think we should bring your grandpa's remains here to the ranch? We've got a family graveyard."

She looked at Zane, who said, "That's a good idea."

Thayne nodded. "Brody talked of doing that, but we had to abandon Grandpa and our plans for treasure hunting after the shooting trouble. But we'll go back someday. I agree we should bring Grandpa's body home."

"Except," said Lock, "Brody still plans to move back to Boston." He kept talking as he dished up his food. "I'm sure gonna miss him."

"Ellie's moving to Boston?" Zane sat up straight, frowning.

Josh still hoped Brody could be persuaded to stay, so he set aside that worry and concentrated on the chicken and noodles, which smelled mighty good. Josh dug in while Lock told his story.

"We found more papers with Grandpa." He waved a few old, yellowed papers. "Including the information that this is only half the map. He sent the other half to Mr. Westbrook, who most likely loaned him money. The map was hard to make sense of, and we weren't to the end of it when we were attacked. We ended up abandoning our search because Brody was hurt, and we had outlaws to take to Sheriff Stockwood. But we plan to go out there again."

Now that Josh had eaten a few good bites of his meal, he felt ready to talk. "Brody thinks his grandpa deliberately used confusing words and pictures, almost like a code, in case the journal fell into someone else's hands. He found some kind of treasure, and the journal looks like a part of it. Ellie was sure it wasn't like the normal paper you'd buy in a general store, so we suspected it might be part of his treasure. He had a dozen or so of the gold doubloons, too. It's possible that was all the gold there was, but there must be something left, or why mail the journal off? There was an old knife with Graham, too."

Michelle studied the book. "What's this on the front, an X cut into the leather?"

"That's a *Cruz de Borgoña*," Tilda answered.

Every neck in the room swiveled to look at her.

"Cross of Burgundy? What is that?" Michelle always wanted to know more.

"The Cruz de Borgoña is an old Spanish flag."

Josh nodded. "I've seen it. Some Spanish ships still sail under it. How old is it?" He looked again at the barely visible X etched into the leather.

Tilda shrugged. "The exact date is hard to pin down, but the current flag of Spain was adopted close to one hundred years ago."

"And Captain Cabrillo sailed up the Californian coast how long ago?" Michelle asked. "Was it three hundred years? Spain would have been using the Cruz de Borgoña as a national symbol at that time. Cortés, who stayed in Mexico while Cabrillo sailed the coast, would have done his exploring and conquering under that flag."

A moment of silence descended on the table. Finally, Lock said, "You both need to study the journal, Miss Tilda and Uncle Josh." He grinned when he said the second name. "And

Aunt Michelle, there are other Spanish language phrases in there. You need to study it, too."

Annie, who'd been eating and making sure Caroline finished her meal, looked up and down the table at Zane. "I guess we're not going to get an assignment."

Zane smiled. "I've got a ranch to run. I'm not interested in a treasure hunt."

Annie tilted her head. "I wouldn't mind treasure hunting. It's more interesting than teaching school." She sounded envious. "I suppose Caroline is a little young for treasure hunting, though."

"Tilda, you're meant to be a teacher," Michelle said with urgency. "You know a lot of important history. The children would sense how much you love the subject, and they'd be drawn to want to know more."

Tilda studied Michelle for a moment, then turned her gaze to the book. "I think I'll send a telegraph to Mrs. Worthington, the lady who runs the orphanage I worked for, and tell her I plan to stay out here. If I find I have no skill for teaching, I can see if they need more help at the Child of God Mission where you found me, Michelle."

"Sister Agatha always needs more help. But I very much believe you're going to fit right in at our school."

"Since Beth Ellen got married—" Annie began.

"Who's Beth Ellen?" Lock interrupted.

Annie slapped herself gently on the forehead. "Sorry, that's what we always called Ellie when she was young. I still lapse into it sometimes. Before Ellie got married, she was helping Brody at the doctor's office. We really are shorthanded, Tilda. I teach, and Caroline is of school age, so I can be there all the time. Several of our older students are interested in being teachers, but they're too young still to take it over full time. We'd appreciate the help. And you'll earn a regular teacher's salary, besides having a room and meals provided. Oh, and the position includes seeing that things are in order in the girls' rooms and helping with meals by being an adult presence in the dining room."

Tilda nodded. "How do I send a telegraph?"

"We can send a wire from right here on the ranch." Josh spoke between bites. "We haven't got an official telegraph office, but Michelle knows how to tap out the message."

"Let's send a wire, then. I can assure Mrs. Worthington that the boys are safe and have found a good situation and they've reunited with their older brother." Tilda's eyes narrowed as she looked between Thayne and Lock. "An older brother you never told us about, by the way. You claimed to be orphans."

"We wanted to head west, and we figured we could ride along part of the way with the orphan train without having to buy our own tickets. We didn't have any money."

"I've just realized why you boys would act up every time we'd have adoptive parents come and meet you. You made very sure no one would want to take you. Two healthy, mostly grown boys should have been adopted right away."

Thayne slugged Lock on the arm. "Lock whispered things to anyone who showed interest to scare them."

"What kind of things?"

Lock snickered. Thayne closed his eyes and shook his head and fought to keep the smile off his face.

"Lock! What did you say?" Tilda's voice rose a notch.

"I might've, um, told one of the potential fathers I could

make whiskey. He could help me set up a still, and we'd make a fortune."

Tilda dropped her face into both hands.

"And you asked one very sweet lady how much money she thought they had in the bank and if the man who owned the bank carried a gun with him to work." Thayne slugged him again. "He told another man that he'd run off from his girl back east, so he wouldn't have to—"

"Don't tell her every single thing." Lock hit him back, and his cheeks pinked until Josh had to wonder just what the kid had said. He was only fourteen.

"Basically," said Thayne, "we just said whatever we thought would go over the worst. And you've got to admit, it's just as well no one showed one speck of interest in us. We were going on a treasure hunt."

Tilda shook her head. "And after you ran off from me, you hopped into a baggage car and rode the rails all the way to San Francisco."

"Yep, and we got mighty hungry after a while. But we made it. When we arrived, we went around looking for the kids who'd ended up out on the streets, abandoned for one reason or another, thinking they could help us find food. We found the Child of God Mission, and there was Aunt Michelle hunting up youngsters for her school—which was real close to where we wanted to go."

"So you lied about being orphans." Michelle's eyes flashed. "Lied to adoptive parents in town after town. Lied to Miss Tilda, lied to Sister Agatha at the mission, then lied to me when I asked if you wanted to come to the ranch in search of an education."

Lock looked at Thayne. "That about covers it."

"Not all of it," Thayne said. "We could've just gone home to Pa."

"Is your father still alive?" Tilda asked. "I thought your parents were dead and you had no other family. Then when I got here, I thought you only had Brody."

"Ma died before we left," Lock explained. "Pa was ailing and cranky. We were as good as orphans."

Michelle had a look in her eyes that made most everyone in her vicinity nervous.

Thayne looked a little scared, while Lock didn't show even a speck of worry.

Josh had had his hands full with these two since they'd come here. Once Brody arrived, they'd still been a peck of trouble, but they were Brody's trouble. Now Brody was gone for who could say how long, and they were back to being unrepentant scamps.

"Boys, I had Gretel clean out the room where Ellie slept." Annie was the best of them when it came to taking charge of the children. "You can sleep there. It's at the top of the stairs, end of the hall, on the left. I went to your rooms and gathered your nightshirts and a change of clothes for tomorrow. We all best get some rest. It's been a long day that followed a long weekend exploring in the wilderness. Tomorrow things get back to normal. You've got school."

"No, we can't go to school. We have to go and follow the map."

Josh shook his head. "Haven't you figured out yet that it's dangerous in the wilderness?"

"But we're so close, and with that Loyal Kelton varmint arrested, it'll be safe now."

"You didn't know Kelton was a danger. Who else might cause trouble?"

"Brody told us we could search for the treasure," Lock said, defiance in his tone.

"Well, when he comes back, you can take that up with him."

"We don't need Brody. I know that map better'n anyone, and I'm smart enough to make sense of it all on my own."

"But," Josh snapped, "you need Auntie Michelle here to translate the Spanish. You need Miss Tilda here to research the history of the journal, and you need *me* to figure out anything in those pages of your grandpa's that has to do with sailing. And I've been away from work for days now, Zane longer than that. I can't go treasure hunting with you. Zane can't go. Brody's not here. You're just going to have to wait."

"We don't need to bother anyone," Lock said as he piled more mashed potatoes onto his plate. He then picked up the bowl of stew and scooped some of it over his potatoes. He grabbed two more biscuits. "Now that we have the map, we can go on our own."

Tilda gasped. "You wouldn't, would you? The wilderness is no place for two boys alone."

"I'm sixteen years old," Thayne said. "Almost seventeen. I'm the oldest boy in school. Two of them have left since I got here to find jobs, and more are working here as cowhands. Only a few my age are staying with school much longer, and all three want to be teachers. I'm not a boy. I'm a grown man. And Brody was working when he was Lock's age and helping support our family. So Lock's a man, too."

Tilda looked at Michelle, then at Josh. "Do something. They can't ride off alone."

Zane, from the end of the table, said, "They can't ride off, and they know it. They don't own horses. And we hang horse thieves out here in the West."

Thayne and Lock both whipped their heads around to stare at Zane.

Annie might *not* be the best at managing children, Josh decided. As for Zane, he had a knack for it.

Lock said, "We'd promise to bring the horses back—"

"That's right. We'd *never* steal a horse, uh, Uncle Zane." Sounding solemn and mature, Thayne talked over his brother.

"How far of a ride did you take last weekend?"

"It took us a full day to find Grandpa's cave."

"And how long if you walked it?" Zane sounded like a lawyer questioning a hostile witness.

Thayne lifted his chin. "It would be several days, assuming we don't get lost. Josh led the way, mostly. I think we could find it, but it'd be three days hiking to reach the cave."

"Three days plus camping out at night. You'll need food. And you said you had a lot more of the map to follow after your grandpa's cave, and it was slow figuring it out. So that's several more days to reach the end of your map, with no idea where to go beyond *that* because you only have half of the map. The other half that you hope your brother—who got *shot* on your last treasure hunt—intends to search for, once he can."

"Thayne," Josh interjected, "you say you're a man, but men don't *lie*. Men don't even *consider* stealing a horse."

"We aren't going to steal—"

"Men are *honorable*." Josh cut him off. "They face up to trouble. They help when the family needs help. They don't smirk and boast"—Josh's eyes went to Lock—"about how they fooled honest folks who were taking them across the country, paying for every bit of it, hoping to find them a home. That's stealing money from orphans who'd've *loved* to find a home. You want to claim you're a man, then *be a man*." He jabbed his finger at Lock, then at Thayne. "Show some maturity. And smart isn't the same as wise. You're both smart enough, but neither one of you shows one speck of wisdom with your headlong chase for that treasure—willing to lie, steal, and cheat to get it. You want us to treat you like men, then start *acting* like men. Right now."

Thayne's chin dropped almost to his chest. "You're right."

"No!" Lock as good as howled. "We're so close. We have to—"

"Stop it." Thayne didn't slug his brother this time. Somehow that made this more serious. "We'll wait for Brody."

The brothers' eyes met. Lock the wild adventurer, the explorer. The big believer in the treasure. Thayne, more mature. Plenty of rambunctious nonsense in the kid, but he was growing up. In fact, Josh thought the kid was growing up right in front of his eyes.

Lock finally shrugged one shoulder, then turned away from Thayne and looked around the table. "You're our family now. We never had much of a family before. Ma was always working. Brody was always working too, and then for years he was gone. It's not easy to listen to anyone but myself. Thanks for caring enough to talk to us."

He gave Zane an especially respectful look, then slid his eyes to Josh. "We only got as far as we did because of you and Aunt Ellie . . . no, wait, our *sister* Ellie. We ran off on our own and never made much headway, not until we had your help. Thayne is right. We'll wait for Brody." Lock straightened. Then his eyes flashed. "Unless one of you wants to go now?"

Lock had lasted almost half a minute being reasonable and mature. Now his eyes lit up with hope and just a hint of a wild man.

Josh figured half a minute was the best they were going to get.

"Give us time to look over the journal and study the map." Josh started talking to head off this maverick calf. "Tomorrow, you go back to school. The rest of us all have work to do. Maybe Brody will be back fast with that other map, but he didn't look like he was up to jumping on a train. I'm hoping he rests for a few days before they go. If he takes long enough to get back that we figure out the journal, and we think we know where to go, maybe we can spend another weekend treasure hunting."

"Let's head up to bed now." Annie, always the mother. "We all need sleep."

Michelle asked again for the name and address of Tilda's boss back in New York City.

"Mrs. Worthington. We don't need to go out to the telegraph office tonight, though."

"The telegraph is here in the ranch house. I can send a wire in a couple of minutes and get that handled."

"Thank you, Michelle. Can I look at the journal tonight?" Tilda extended a hand toward Michelle, who still held it.

Michelle's hand tightened on it, and she smiled. "I find myself wanting to keep it, but I'll get my turn. You must be tired, too."

"I am. I just want to hang on to it. It might keep the boys from running off."

Michelle chuckled, and Zane and Josh joined her.

Annie said to Tilda, "There's a key in the door to your room. Use it."

Four

Brody didn't get out of bed for five days.

Sad to say, that had nothing to do with his being a newlywed.

Finally, his body stopped howling in protest every time he moved. Or at least the howling was a little quieter.

His pretty new wife had tended him with loving care.

"This has to be the worst honeymoon a woman ever had." Brody forced himself to sit up and swing his legs over the side of the bed.

"Brody, you lie right back down, now. We are in no hurry."

Since the men who'd tried to kill him and Ellie, and their siblings, were being transported to San Quentin for a life sentence, there probably wasn't any hurry.

"I'm up to moving, honey." Brody reached out for Ellie. "Is that a new dress?"

She smiled sweetly. "It is. I didn't bring a thing along to town. We thought we'd ride in and head right back home. I got you a change of clothes, too."

Brody frowned. "I don't need much."

Ellie kissed him on the cheek. "Good, because I didn't get

you much. But you have almost no clothes, Brody. You showed up to the Two Harts with a single change in your satchel. As a recent graduate from college, you needed a few new things."

"It's all got to be your money. I don't have any. I haven't worked long enough as a doctor to have more than a few pennies to rub together."

Ellie sat down beside him and slid her arm across his back, rested her cheek on his shoulder. "You know I'm a quarter owner of the Two Harts. What I have is yours. We've got plenty of money."

"That's not right, Ellie. A man needs to provide—"

"That's not counting," she said, cutting him off, "the gold you found in your grandpa's cave." She sat up straight and turned to face him. "And that's not counting that you have a profession that'll support us for the rest of our lives."

Brody tried to fight down his pride, which he knew to be a sin.

"But you've been working for over a month now," Ellie continued, "and you haven't been paid a cent. Have your patients not paid you?"

Brody shrugged, which hurt. "I suppose I should charge them something, but the people who come to see me are sick."

Ellie snorted.

Which made Brody smile.

"The people who live on the Two Harts are well compensated. We pay the highest wages of any ranch in California."

"Do you know how much other ranches pay? Is that something ranchers talk about?"

Ellie looked sheepish. "Well, I don't know for sure, but I believe it to be true." She thrust out a hand. "You have those gold coins with you, don't you?"

Brody had them in his pocket. "I don't have a good place to lock them up, so I keep them with my person. Thayne and Lock have the rest."

"Hand one over. I'll take it as payment for your new clothes."

Brody's smile grew. "All right. Um . . . do you want me to carry it for you?"

"That sounds like a great idea. You give me a gold coin, then I'll give it back to you to carry. Do you mind carrying mine, too? I couldn't think of a place to lock mine up either."

Brody watched her pick up her reticule and extract a small leather pouch. "I suppose you're trying to make the point that all we have belongs to both of us."

Ellie leaned forward and kissed him.

"Our first kiss since that parson said 'you may kiss the bride.'" He kissed her this time. But leaning as good as kicked him in the chest.

She was watching him closely enough that she noticed. "We're going to pool together all we have, and we're going to be married for the rest of our long lives. I want you healed up thoroughly before we kiss again. I don't like thinking it causes you pain."

Brody nodded. "I agree. But I am up to riding a train to Sacramento." Or he was determined to do it, which wasn't the same as being up to it. "Is Cord slowly going crazy from the wait?"

"No, he's being very patient. Listen."

Brody couldn't think to what, and then he heard the distant sound of a piano playing. It had been going on since he woke up, but he hadn't paid much attention. "That's Cord?"

"Yes, the hotel owner offered him a job. He's been playing for long hours every day, and the crowds that come in to eat have doubled. He said he just plays for the love of it, and he's not going to sign on to a job that he plans to quit in a day or two. He did play for church on Sunday."

Brody grimaced. "I slept through a Sunday? I don't even know what day it is." He rubbed the bump on the back of his head.

"We got married on Tuesday. You slept most of the week, including through Sunday. Now it's just past the noon meal on Monday."

"I'm ready to move. Thank you for the new shirts and pants. I'll get dressed and join you downstairs. When does the next train leave?"

"The train passes through most every day—in the mid-morning. So it's already gone today." She leaned forward and kissed him again.

When she straightened away from him, he teased, "We agreed not to do that until I'm well." Yet he didn't mind one bit.

"Oops. I forgot. Do you need help getting dressed?"

He was wearing the shirt he'd worn to town almost a week ago. It had to be the same shirt, the gold doubloons in the breast pocket being the biggest clue. He'd been required to unbutton his shirt and show the jury the horrible bruise on his chest. That and his story were all they'd needed to find the criminals guilty.

"I can do it. Thinking about you helping me makes me a little light-headed. You should probably leave the room before I get dizzy and topple over."

Her cheeks pinked up, and she smiled. Then she got his

new clothes out and laid them on the bed and headed for the door.

"We can eat supper downstairs, or I can bring up a plate. You need to get some food in your belly or you won't have the strength to sit up for the trip to Sacramento."

"I'll be right down, but, Ellie?"

She paused as she reached for the doorknob and turned to face him. "Yes, husband?"

That got a smile out of him. "Don't enjoy the music too much."

She laughed and nodded. "I promise."

After she left the room, he got himself dressed to the tune of "Ode to Joy." It suited his feelings perfectly.

"Tilda, your boss says you have to return to New York City immediately." Michelle came into the kitchen while studying a slip of paper. "Something's come up that requires your presence."

Tilda gasped quietly and turned to look at Michelle. The slip of paper she held didn't look like a regular telegraph wire, but they probably had no need for official documents here on the ranch. "Did Mrs. Worthington say why?"

Michelle handed over the slip of paper.

"There's nothing here besides what you said." Tilda looked from Michelle to Josh, who sat across from her at the breakfast table. Thayne and Lock had already left for school, and Josh had come in for breakfast after spending the night as guardian in the boys' dormitory. Annie had asked Tilda to wait an hour before coming to join her and Caroline at the school. It would give Annie a chance to settle the children and get them started in their studies, and then she and Tilda would discuss teaching duties.

Tilda said unsteadily, "I d-don't want to go back. I like it here."

Michelle narrowed her eyes at Tilda. Tilda had no idea what the woman was thinking, but it was clear she was up to something. Tilda decided to give her time and started on her own breakfast of eggs, bacon, and biscuits.

Josh seemed to be willing to let the silence stretch, and so Tilda, after saying little more than "good morning," dug into her steaming eggs.

"I'm going to wire Mrs. Worthington again," Michelle stated. "I'll ask her to either send a lengthier wire to explain herself or else write a letter. And I'll repeat that you're planning to stay here with us on the ranch. Unless . . . could it be you have a family emergency?"

Tilda swallowed her bite of biscuit. "I have no family. I was adopted by an elderly couple who have since passed on. There was a bit of money, but they had three grown daughters, and everything my adoptive parents owned went to them. And those girls never befriended me. No, I just can't imagine what Mrs. Worthington could want. I worked for her, but she threatened to fire me if I didn't find my runaway orphans. She showed no great loyalty to me." Tilda had no idea why Mrs. Worthington would want her to return. She looked at Michelle and shrugged.

"Don't worry, I'll handle this," said Michelle. "I'll ask her for an explanation, and if she doesn't come up with something that makes you want to go back, you won't go. Simple as that."

All Tilda could think was that her life had always been

lived on the edge of disaster. Running the streets from her earliest memory. Always cold, always hungry, always scared. Then a few years in an orphanage where it was crowded and dirty. She was cold, hungry, and scared there, too. She'd had a few peaceful years when the Muirheads had adopted her. But even then, she was more servant than daughter to the elderly couple, and she'd worked hard to care for them as their health declined. They'd both died by the time she was seventeen, leaving Tilda alone in the world again. She'd gone to work at the orphanage and loved it, but then she'd lost the MacKenzie boys, and someone was looking for an excuse to close down the orphan trains. She'd been sent to find her missing charges, and she'd done it.

She'd been eating regular meals since she came to the Two Harts. The work they wanted her to do sounded interesting. No, she wasn't going back. Mrs. Worthington had no need of her, not with so many people in New York City always eager for work.

"Thank you, Michelle. Now, it's been long enough. I'd better get over to the school."

Michelle said, "Josh, will you walk over with her? I want to handle this wire right away. Maybe we can get some answers yet today."

"Sure, are you ready?" Josh rose from his chair.

"Yes, thank you." Tilda should have assured him that she could find her own way. She'd been to the large white building before. But she was nervous about being a teacher and liked the idea of someone coming along with her, even if just to see her to the door.

As they walked toward the school, Josh said, "I'm glad you're staying, Tilda."

Tilda's eyes widened as she looked at him. "You are?"

Josh nodded. "I didn't want to say it in front of Michelle, but, well . . . I know you need to settle in and figure out teaching, but I'm glad."

His cheeks might've had just a bit of pink in them. Not easy to tell on a man, tanned from long hours in the sun, so she might be imagining it.

They were almost to the schoolhouse, so their chance to speak privately was almost over. Words seemed to back up in her throat. All she could do was reply, "I'm glad I'm staying, too."

"Maybe we'll have a chance to speak later." Josh reached the school and opened the door for her.

She couldn't remember a man ever doing such a thing for her before, but then her thoughts were a bit addled by his kind response to her staying.

He let her go in ahead of him before saying, "With the new students yesterday, and a few who've gone on recently to work or college, we've probably got about thirty-five students in all. There are four classrooms, with the students divided among those rooms by age. Annie's in the room with the oldest students."

They stood in a long, narrow corridor with a row of four doors. He gestured to the door farthest to the right, Annie's room. Tilda supposed Thayne and Lock were in that room, unless the scamps had gotten up to some kind of trouble.

Josh knocked on the door, then opened it without waiting for anyone to come. Tilda saw Annie look up and smile from where she sat behind a desk at the front of the room. "Come on in, Tilda," she said. "Thanks for bringing her, Josh."

Tilda stepped into a classroom with around ten students, all boys. Thayne and Lock were indeed there, looking at her and grinning. The door behind her closed, and she walked into her future.

F<small>IVE</small>

"Tilda?" Michelle stood at the door of her classroom just as the children were dismissed. Michelle had struck Tilda as a confident woman. Bold and brilliant, with very little self-doubt. Right now, though, she looked kind of nervous.

Tilda had spent the morning with Annie; in the afternoon, the children had been divided up according to their interests. The four rooms were organized by science, architecture and construction, math, and, for the first time today, history.

She'd been delighted by how many of the children, given the chance, had come into her classroom expressing an interest in history, including Thayne and Lock. She had some ideas about what she wanted to teach, but for today she'd played a few games and given each child a chance to introduce themself, so that Tilda could get to know them a little.

She'd decided, considering where they were, she would start by teaching them about the history of the West, beginning with the Native folks who'd been there first. Then she'd talk to them about the Spanish conquistador Hernando Cortés and his voyage of exploration. She planned to make the students wait a bit before covering the pioneers, the settlers, and the gold rush, which began in 1848—two years before California became a state. And then, after making just one passing mention of gold, she'd noticed the strong enthusiasm of her students.

She knew then she couldn't make them wait too long before teaching about the gold rush, for she didn't want to lose that enthusiasm. She tried to remember why history had always fascinated her and hoped she could transfer that fascination to the students.

"Come in, Michelle," Tilda said.

The last of the students filed out of the room. As Thayne and Lock reached Michelle, she said something quietly to them. They both grinned and nodded, then stepped out into the hall, the door closing behind them.

Tilda smiled. "What was that about?"

"I told them their aunt Michelle hoped they'd stay at the ranch house and eat with us until Brody gets back. They said that suits them fine."

Tilda nodded, knowing she'd be sleeping upstairs in the girls' dormitory tonight.

"I got the wire back from Mrs. Worthington," Michelle began. "We went back and forth a few times because she was insistent that you return. I had to refuse more than once before she finally told me what she wanted." Michelle had a strange, intense look in her eyes. Not quite anger, but she wasn't exactly pleased either.

"What's happened? Is she sick? Does she need me to step in for her? I'm not really the one who—"

"Your brother contacted her. He wants you to come home."

"My . . . my . . ." Tilda stared at Michelle as she thought

of her adoptive parents' three grown daughters. "I-I don't have a brother."

Michelle came the rest of the way into the room and rested one hand on Tilda's shoulder and the other on her rounded belly. How long until her baby was born? Dr. MacKenzie shouldn't have gone traveling right now. At least Michelle moved well, and her belly, though round, didn't seem to slow her down much.

"Apparently you do. And he's coming here to find you."

"What? No." Shaking her head violently, she thought of the adults who sometimes were cruel to orphan children. Could this be such a man? But people like that didn't ride across the country looking for children to prey on. And Tilda was no child. "A man can't just show up here and take me." She grabbed Michelle's hand. "You won't let some stranger take me away from the ranch, will you?"

Tilda felt foolish. She shouldn't be begging for Michelle to stand as a shield between her and whoever this was. She should have the strength to stand on her own. Besides, if she was going to hide behind someone, a very pregnant woman wasn't the best choice. Where was Josh?

Michelle shook her head. "Of course not. This man won't be taking you anywhere. We protect the people who live and work on our ranch. You're safe here, Tilda."

"What does that mean, she's safe?" Josh strode into the room. "Are the boys acting up again?"

"No, no." Michelle waved Josh's worry aside.

Tilda thought that if Josh wanted to worry, she'd give him something *real* to worry about.

Michelle went on. "Some man back in New York City showed up at the orphanage where Tilda worked and is claiming to be her brother. That's why we got that wire telling Tilda to come home. When I told Mrs. Worthington Tilda was staying here, she said the brother would then come here to fetch her back home."

Michelle shrugged one shoulder. "It sounds like we've got company coming."

Josh looked around the room. "I wonder if he's a teacher."

"I don't *have* a brother," insisted Tilda.

Josh flinched. "What, and he's coming all the way here to see you?"

Tilda turned to Michelle, who answered, "That's what Mrs. Worthington says."

The more Tilda thought about it, the worse it sounded. She wrung her hands as she considered all the possible reasons some stranger would claim her as his sister. None of what she imagined was good. "I should run. I'll go out into the mountains and stay there until whoever this is goes away. I'll camp out. Live off the land. I'll—"

"Now, hold up," said Josh, moving closer to Tilda. "You're not going anywhere. Like Michelle said, you're *safe* here."

"Didn't Dr. MacKenzie just get shot?"

"Well, yes, but—"

"And Lock told me he fell over a cliff a few weeks back."

Josh nodded. "That's true. Brody fell over the cliff, too."

"And don't forget," Michelle added, "how that mob overran our mission group and nearly killed all of us and burned down our church."

Josh shrugged as if he conceded the point. "That was before I got home, though."

Tilda wasn't feeling any better.

"Living off the land is hard work, and it's tricky." Michelle's brow furrowed, and yet Tilda saw something in her eyes, something almost . . . amused. "Do you have a gun? Do you know how to bring down a deer, skin it, butcher it, roast it over a fire? Do you know how to start a fire?" Michelle looked at Josh. "We could lend her a blanket and some matches, I suppose."

Josh glared at his sister-in-law. Then, when she grinned, he shook his head and turned back to Tilda. "You're not running off. You're not living off the land. We're not going to let this supposed brother take you anywhere. In fact"—Josh snapped his fingers—"I'll bet this is a case of mistaken identity. You said you're an orphan, right?"

"I was an orphan until I was adopted by the family with three daughters."

"So this so-called brother has you mixed up with someone else. Maybe his parents dropped him and his sister off at an orphanage twenty or so years ago, and now he's searching for you."

"My earliest memory is of living on the streets with a pack of other kids. I got swept up by the police a few times and lived in an orphanage for a while several times. Then when I was about ten, and doing another stint, I got adopted."

"This brother person doesn't know that." Michelle jumped into the guessing game. "He's got you mixed up with his own missing sister. It's a shame he's taking this long trip, but I didn't give Mrs. Worthington one bit of encouragement. We'll wait until he gets here. Give him a good meal. Advise him to go see the ocean while he's close and then send him on his way."

"He's coming from New York City," Josh said. "He's seen an ocean."

Tilda couldn't stop wringing her hands with worry.

Josh patted her on the shoulder. "Now then, I told them in the school dining room that we were both eating at the house tonight. The boys are headed there. I planned to spend time looking at that journal and Graham MacKenzie's papers with everyone, but we can discuss your visitor, too. I've got a few hands eating here to help ride herd on the children. We'll be back by bedtime."

Josh gently steered Tilda out of the room, although she barely noticed she was moving. Her mind was too busy thinking of just exactly what she'd need to know to live off the land. She'd never even *seen* a deer.

Six

There'd been no such thing as a true wedding night yet.

Brody regretted that, but he had to admit he could barely walk. He could barely sit up. He'd only just managed to dress himself. And he was dreading this train ride. In truth, he was just trying not to further injure himself.

Or so he fervently hoped.

Brody lowered himself slowly onto the train seat. His pretty wife sat beside him, and Cord Westbrook followed, carrying all the bags. Enduring was the best Brody could hope to do right now.

He wondered when the longed-for wedding night would happen.

Not until his ribs quit kicking like a feisty, unbroken horse.

"You've picked a poor excuse for a husband, Ellie."

She wound her hand through his arm and hugged his elbow. She'd probably learned it was one of the few places on his body that didn't hurt.

Cord sat down in front of them and twisted to look at them over his left shoulder. Brody envied Cord's agility.

"You look about all in, Brody. We could have waited a few more days." Cord studied his face.

Brody had to wonder what the man was seeing because Brody was doing his best to hide how bad he hurt. The train whistle blasted, and they began rolling with a clacking of the wheels and the chuffing of the steam engine.

"We have to get on. I still hurt, but a train ride shouldn't make it any worse." Unless his broken rib shifted and stabbed through one of his lungs or his heart, that is. He was still seeing double at times, and his head ached like a miner was trying to fight his way out with a pickax. He probably should have stayed in his bed for another week.

"Nor better." Ellie squeezed his arm.

To change the subject, Brody asked, "What does your grandfather remember about mine? You said he talks about my grandpa owing him money."

Cord was a tall man. Dark hair. Serious brown eyes that got a deep, intense look when he played the piano. Brody had never heard such music.

So far, Brody hadn't talked much with Cord. After the trial, he'd gone to his room in the hotel and collapsed. While the worst of the swelling had gone down on his chest, he now had a bruise the size of a dinner plate. Grimly, he admitted it was a miserable excuse for an improvement.

He'd finally come downstairs to eat yesterday and listened to Cord's piano music for a while. They'd hoped to make the train yesterday, but Brody admitted he wasn't up to the trip. He'd returned to his room for another day of lazing around. Today, over Ellie's protests and Cord's misgivings, they'd finally headed for the train.

"Grandpa Westbrook will be thrilled with this. He's not

a man to let a debt go uncollected, and that's how he saw your grandpa. I've tried to get him to just forget it, and he has before, for a time. But I think the word *treasure* eats away at him, and before I know it, he's fretting over it. He knew your pa when he came west, searching for your grandpa and the story of treasure. I think there was trouble."

Brody winced. "Pa was close to out of his mind over that treasure. I suspect if your grandpa tried to lay claim to any part of it, he'd've bulled up and wanted a fight. Pa ran off and abandoned me and my sister and Ma, looking to find that treasure and bring it home. Maybe he would have sent for us. Or maybe he just abandoned us and used treasure hunting as an excuse."

Ellie caressed his arm.

Brody remembered bitterly how his sister, Theresa, died while Brody, then very young, struggled, along with his ma, to keep a roof over their heads. There was never enough food or coal to stay warm. She'd been little more than a toddler, and when she got sick, she was too frail to fight it off.

"When Pa came back, he seemed defeated. Ma forgave him, and he settled back in with us. He stayed a few years and worked, and we were all right then. I got to go to school. Thayne and Lock were born. Things weren't exactly happy, but they were all right. Then he got a fever for that treasure again. He started poring over the journal my grandpa had sent us, the one that had sent Pa off on his treasure hunt before. Reading it as if he could see more than the words printed on the page. Before long, while my brothers were still mighty young, he took off again."

Brody remembered his ma crying in her room at night when she thought everyone was asleep.

"Ma forced me to stay in school . . . well, begged me really." The guilt of that still ate at him. "She talked about how much money I could make and how that could really take care of the family if I had an education. It was the only argument that could have persuaded me to study.

"I worked nights and weekends all through my growing-up years. When it came time for college, Ma said I could work in Boston the same as in New York City. I could send money home. I hadn't seen my family for years because when there might've been a chance to buy a train ticket, I sent the money to Ma instead. I wrote to her, but her letters to me weren't regular. Then her letters quit, right when I was almost done. I finished and rushed home to find Ma had died and Thayne and Lock were gone. Pa was back, a broken man, dying. I stayed to care for him and, in the end, bury him. All the while I was half mad with worry about the boys, searching for them everywhere. I found their names listed on an orphan train and set out to find them, but I knew the journal was gone, and they were as treasure mad as Pa. I suspected they'd have come here hunting. And here I am."

He looked at Ellie. "A married man." He reached out and took her hand. "I wish I could have made my ma's last years comfortable. That's a regret I'm going to have to live with. But I've found my brothers, and they're alive and well, and I've found the love of my life. We'll make a good home for ourselves in Boston."

Ellie leaned close to him, her shoulder brushing against his. He was aware of how gentle she was being with him.

"I suspect Grandpa Westbrook told your pa he owned half of whatever treasure your grandpa had found."

"That would have set him off, no doubt about it. Among the letters and papers we found with Grandpa's remains was a note saying exactly that."

Cord shook his head. "Near as I can tell, my grandpa loaned your grandpa about a hundred dollars. I don't know what this treasure will amount to, but even with interest, you'd repay my grandpa with a few hundred dollars. And Grandpa is a wealthy man. To harass your father, who wasn't wealthy, to try and take half is just pure greedy."

"If Pa wanted money so much, he should have come home and gotten a job. I'll bet your wealthy grandpa worked hard every day of his life. And I'll bet he stayed with his wife and raised up your pa and never shirked."

Brody thought of the gold doubloons he had in his pocket. It wasn't half of the treasure they'd found, but it would be a start. Maybe they could just hand it over to Westbrook and see if that satisfied him.

"It's good that you said that. It reminds me that my grandpa is a good man. A hard, cantankerous man in a lot of ways, but in his heart, I know he loves me, and I love him." Cord's eyes flashed with excitement. "Hey, maybe we can get Grandpa to come to the Two Harts. Maybe he could get involved with looking for the treasure. He needs to get away from that bank. He's in his seventies now and doesn't go in to work much anymore, but he runs a lot of the business from home. It's long past time for him to loosen his grip on the reins."

"There would be a place for him on the Two Harts." Ellie had to wonder if he could teach a class. "I'll be moving out of the ranch house, so we've got space. We could make him very comfortable. I don't know if he'd be up for a long ride in the wilderness, but he could be involved with our hunt in any way he wanted."

"I think all of this is going to make my grandpa very happy."

Brody considered it all. Would finding the treasure have made his pa happy? Nothing much did. He hoped Mayhew Westbrook was a kinder man than Brody's pa.

Seven

"Tilda?" Josh didn't want to interrupt her class, but he had no choice.

"Yes?" She was standing in front of the group of older children, just starting today's history class. A week ago she'd had six students. All boys. Today she had twelve. Most of the older girls and boys now attended her history class. Josh knew she'd been teaching about Cortés and California's interesting past—people and subjects Thayne and Lock were both fascinated by. The rest of the class was as well. Tilda was an excellent teacher. Josh wouldn't've minded attending her class himself.

Harriet Sears came up behind Josh and slipped past him, carrying her baby. "I'm taking over for the afternoon, Tilda. You're needed elsewhere."

Josh thought he heard a few quiet groans. Harriet was a top-notch teacher, but she was a taskmaster, and all the students knew it. Maybe bringing her baby to class would slow her down a little.

Tilda's eyes flickered between Harriet and Josh, but she simply said, "I've got a nice stack of books today about the history of California. My plan was to pass them around and give the students a quiet reading day, with plans to discuss what we read tomorrow."

Harriet smiled. "That sounds excellent."

Tilda gestured toward the books. "I want you to come up and pick out a book. I've got enough for each of you. Don't make Harriet distribute them while she's got a baby in her arms."

Josh recognized the books as having come from the library in the ranch house. Then Tilda came toward Josh. She had a serene look on her face until she was past the last student, and then a furrow of worry wrinkled her smooth brow.

He stepped back and let her precede him. Then he closed the classroom door and remained quiet until they got outside. "Your brother is here."

Tilda tensed up. Her shoulders almost vibrated. "How did he get here this fast?"

"It's been long enough if he jumped on the first train leaving New York City and rode straight through. No stopping to try and get children adopted."

"Josh, what is going on here?"

Stopping before they reached the house, Josh rested one hand on her upper arm. "I don't know. He's dressed very nicely. He seems polite. He's in there getting hit with questions from Michelle. Gretel exchanged a few words with him, and when he heard her German accent, he spoke the language to her. Michelle speaks German too, so I left the three of them chattering and couldn't understand a word of it even though Gretel shouts in German sometimes. Guess I only understand things like 'stop' and 'ouch' and 'get out of my kitchen.'"

He smiled.

Tilda rolled her eyes. Then she forgot about Josh's nonsense because she could do nothing but wonder what the stranger in the main house was up to. She rested her hand on top of his and said, "Promise me you won't let him take me away?"

Josh leaned forward and kissed her on the forehead. "I promise. And my word is good, Tilda."

She studied his eyes for long seconds and read the concern there. "Mistaken identity was your theory, wasn't it? That must be it. In which case, let's go in there and be kind. And then send him down the road to hunt for some other poor, missing girl to kidnap."

Only a few steps away, the back door to the ranch house swung open, and a man stepped out. Tilda's eyes locked on him, stunned—he resembled her very closely. Tight, dark curls, though his hair was very short. Nearly black eyes.

"I'm Ben. I'm your brother." The man's declaration broke Tilda out of her staring, assessing daze. "And you must be Matilda."

The man called Ben, moving with extreme care, reached for her and touched her forehead. "This scar." He shook his head, and his eyes turned all glassy as if on the verge of tears. "This was my fault."

His finger rested right where Josh had kissed her.

"What happened?" Tilda could hardly form the words.

"You were a baby. Just a couple of months old. Ma left me to sit on the bed near you while she ran for a clean diaper. I was five, clearly not old enough to be trusted, but Ma left me in charge anyway."

Ben dropped his hand, and Tilda touched the scar she'd

had for as long as she could remember. It had faded until it was nearly invisible now, yet it would always be part of her.

"You rolled right off the bed," he went on. "There was a small table there with a crossbar of wood at the base. You hit your head on it." The man closed his eyes for a moment. "So much blood. So much crying. Ma came running, then sent for the doctor. You were screaming. Ma was screaming. I was screaming. I felt awful."

"Y-you really are my family, aren't you?" Her voice shook, her hands, her belly, maybe her heart. She felt the wonder of it, yet at the same time she was terrified. Was he really who he said he was? Her brother? If so, why had he only turned up now?

Ben nodded.

"And my name is Matilda? I've never heard that before today. I've been Tilda from my earliest memory."

"That's what we called you. Tilda."

Tilda shook her head slowly. Ten or more questions crowded to get out. They seemed to clog her throat, and she said nothing as she tried to make sense of it all.

Suddenly Ben flung his arms around Tilda's neck.

Tilda felt the impact of his hug and spread her arms wide. She glanced back and saw Josh watching her, only her. He wasn't going to just be bowled over by the supposed brother. He'd promised he wouldn't let the man take her, and right now she had to clamp her mouth shut to keep herself from demanding that he follow through on his promise.

Josh's eyes met hers, and he gave her a short, firm nod as if he'd read her mind.

Slowly, Tilda managed to lower her arms and gingerly

pat Ben on the shoulder. A brother. To have a brother, any family. She ached for it to be true.

Josh pressed one hand to Tilda's back, then another on the man's shoulder. "Let's go inside and sit down."

Ben nodded, then said with a voice so firm it seemed to be built on bedrock, "Yes, let's go inside and talk this out. I'm Ben Cabril, by the way, your big brother." He glanced at Tilda. "And you're Matilda Cabril. Let's get to know each other a bit. Then we need to head back to New York. Father is eager to see you again after all these years."

"M-my father is alive?" Tilda's eyes widened. "And my mother?"

"Father, yes. Mother died a long time ago, I'm afraid. Both of our mothers have been gone a while now."

Both of our mothers? Tilda wasn't sure she'd heard him correctly. And she might have imagined it, but there seemed to be some tone of . . . something in Ben's voice. Censure? Anger? Was he blaming her for their mother's death? And how had she come to be living on the streets of New York City and then in an orphanage when her brother—just the thought that she had a brother shook her deeply—grew up with her father? Oh yes, she had things she needed to talk with him about.

But no matter what he had to say to her, she wasn't going anywhere. She'd lived most of her life on the edge of disaster, often cold and hungry. Then, when the Muirheads had adopted her, she'd had a full belly and a dependable roof over her head. But no affection. Nothing but demands from a couple who treated her like she should never stop working to repay them for the fine act of adopting her.

Being at the Two Harts Ranch was the safest she'd ever

felt. She had an interesting job and kind people surrounding her, with the orphans she'd been called to care for close at hand. After setting out across the country with the bare minimum of money and a daunting task, she was finally in a place where she could fulfill that calling. Over and over in her life, she'd taken risks because she'd had no choice. At last she no longer felt as though she were standing on the edge of a cliff in a high wind. No, she wasn't going anywhere on the say-so of a stranger.

Josh slipped around Tilda without ever taking his supporting hand off her, then opened the door.

Tilda's shoulders squared. Her chin came up, and she marched into the house, ready for some plain speaking.

Josh couldn't remember ever admiring anyone more. Tilda was clearly terrified, but she was facing what was ahead straight on.

He'd worked with a lot of orphans, and many of them had a way about them of trying to dodge trouble, even if it meant not always speaking the plain truth. They knew how to slip past consequences when they could. It was a skill many of them had developed, and no doubt it had helped them survive. A big part of the schooling at the Two Harts included helping the students learn to face trouble head-on.

He thought for a moment of Thayne and Lock and all the lying they'd done to get to their treasure. That was a good example, and those two weren't even orphans.

Now here was Tilda not doing any of that. Her courage was humbling.

Josh held the door and finally let his hand drop from

Tilda's back when she entered the house. He intended to lend her support, but she was handling things well all on her own. He would like just a moment alone with her to reassure her that Ben wouldn't be taking her anywhere. He was her brother almost certainly—the resemblance was unmistakable—but that didn't mean Josh was sending Tilda off with the man. Who knew what Ben was really made of and what his intentions were?

Gretel met them with the coffeepot. There were already mugs on the table and a plate of cinnamon rolls. She looked at Josh, frowning, and then her eyes slid from Tilda to Ben.

Josh couldn't blame her.

Josh went and held a chair for Tilda. He had manners, even if some of the fancier ones had a little rust on them.

Ben sat down across from Tilda.

Gretel poured coffee for all of them, then said, "I've got things to do at home. Rick is with the little ones while they nap. I need to check on them all, but I'll be back in plenty of time to finish supper." She slipped out the back door.

A thoughtful woman, Gretel Steinmeyer. Leaving so they could talk about things that might be very private. Josh should probably leave too, but he intended to stick by Tilda no matter what.

Tilda held her coffee mug in both hands, as if she were desperate for some warmth, and looked at Ben. Wordlessly, Josh came and sat beside Tilda. Rather closer than he probably should have, but he was there to support her, and this felt like the right way.

Quietly, Tilda said, "What did you mean, 'both our mothers'?"

"I'll tell you all about it," said Ben, "but, Tilda, I'm here to take you home. Father is getting up in years. He'd given up on finding you until he saw your picture in our church."

"My picture?" Tilda's brow furrowed.

"There was a picture taken of you surrounded by children, getting ready to board an orphan train."

"Oh, I remember when that was taken. I'd never even seen a camera before that day."

Ben turned to pick up a satchel that sat on the floor at his feet. He unbuckled a leather strap holding down a flap and reached inside. He pulled out a thin sheet of metal a bit smaller than a sheet of paper, then turned it on the table and slid it across.

Tilda looked into her own eyes. Her heart twisted as she remembered the moment. The man with his pushcart. Mrs. Worthington saying the children should have their picture taken since it would maybe garner donations for the orphanage. But Mrs. Worthington, who was also in the picture, looked a bit sad as the children clustered around Tilda.

Tilda had been working for the orphanage for over a year, ever since her adoptive parents had died. She'd traveled with the orphans before. But this was the first trip where she was in charge. Though Mrs. Worthington worried over what life had in store for the children, she believed in finding good homes for them and getting them out of New York City, to where the air was clean and the streets safe.

Josh said, "Thayne and Lock are there, too."

Tilda studied the group, remembering the children. What a wonder it was to be able to take a likeness of someone this way. She looked up, straight at her brother. "And you saw this picture?"

"Yes, accompanied by a small sign asking our church

members to consider supporting the orphanage. A photograph is unusual, and it drew a lot of attention. I looked at it and saw you and knew . . ." Ben rested his hand on Tilda's. "I knew I'd found my sister."

Tilda looked at him, then at the picture again. She didn't know what to say.

"I brought it to Father's attention," Ben continued, "and he went about half mad with excitement. The picture had been taken from church to church to raise donations, so by the time we saw it, you had been gone from the orphanage for weeks on a trip to chase after some runaways. But Mrs. Worthington said she expected you to return, though she couldn't say when, and she wasn't sure where your travels had taken you. Father left our name with her, and we waited anxiously. If I'd known where to go, I would've come tearing out here after you. As soon as I had a location and heard that you might remain here for a time, I headed west. I wired Mrs. Worthington as I traveled to see if you were heading back, thinking to find you along the way. I was halfway here when she told me where you were staying."

Nodding, Tilda said, "Why was I in an orphanage . . . while you seem to have grown up in prosperous surroundings?"

"Our real mother, the woman who gave birth to us, was Father's mistress."

Tilda flinched at that, yet she suspected a good many of the children on the streets of New York City had less than reputable backgrounds, or they wouldn't have ended up being abandoned.

"Father's a typical wealthy man. His version of the story is that he thought there was nothing wrong with keeping a mistress. Our mother was an actress and a beautiful woman. Then Father married a woman who was a Christian." Ben gave a small but genuine smile. "She demanded fidelity. He supported our mother, but they quarreled when he broke off their relationship, and she cut him off from us. When she died, I was old enough that I understood where her money had come from and who my father was, so I contacted him."

"But why wasn't I with you?"

Ben swallowed hard and squared his shoulders as if needing to muster the courage to go on. "Our ma wasn't a fine sort of woman. She got money from Father, yet she didn't spend much of it on us. She . . ." He lapsed into silence and rubbed a hand over his face. "She kept us until the year you turned four. The drink had gotten the better of her by then, and she was given to fits of rage. One day she left. It wasn't uncommon for her to do that and sometimes be gone for days. But this time she took you with her and came back without you."

Tilda shook her head silently for so long, Josh was ready to hold on to her lest she fall apart.

"M-my earliest memories are of living on the streets of New York City." Tilda's eyes seemed to focus inward as she tried to figure out what had been done to her.

"Ma," said Ben. "We called our father's mistress 'Ma.' And we called his wife, who took over and raised us when Ma died, 'Mother.' Ma said she'd left you in an orphanage, that she couldn't handle two children at once. We asked which orphanage because we wanted to bring you home. I was frantic, demanding that we go find you. The things she said, Tilda! It was so awful, and I kicked up such a fuss, she said I'd be next to go. Then she left again and was gone for days, leaving me with no food in the house. I wanted to go to the orphanage to live with you."

We asked... *We* wanted... Josh couldn't help but wonder how many more children Ma had had after Tilda was left there at the orphanage.

Tilda let go of her mug and buried her face in her hands. "I have no memory of you. A four-year-old should remember, shouldn't she? And I've no memory of an orphanage, assuming Ma even brought me to one. My earliest memories are of living on the streets. I went to an orphanage later, after I got swept up with a group of children and sent there. That place was miserable. There wasn't enough food, and the rooms were overcrowded. I ran away and lived on the streets again for a couple of years before getting swept up a second time. I was adopted when I was ten and lived with an older couple whose children were grown. Mr. Muirhead died when I was fifteen. Mrs. Muirhead died two years later when I was seventeen."

Josh didn't hear much affection in her tone for her adoptive parents. He wondered how well she'd been treated as their daughter. It was probably better than the orphanage or the city streets, but it didn't sound as though she'd found a child's dream of home.

Tilda took a long sip of her coffee, then set the tin mug down with a hard click. "Do you think she just dropped me off on a street somewhere and left me? And why don't I remember you?" Her eyes narrowed. "I must have some buried memories."

"A four-year-old should have a few memories," Ben said, "but I was older, so I remember you well. Ma, well, she had a taste for gin. She began drinking more heavily and was gone more and more. Then she died. I was ten and could read by then. Ma had sent us to school mainly to get rid of us. She had no liking for children, but she did like Father's money coming in monthly. Years before she died, I'd found papers in a drawer that told me Father's name. After she died, I found him. Father came and got us and was shocked to see how we lived. He said he'd paid well enough that we could have afforded a decent apartment and plenty of food."

"He'd never come to see you?"

"I remembered him from before you were born, but he quit coming when he got married. When he realized you'd been sent to an orphanage . . ." Ben lapsed into silence. They all looked at each other.

"He took you in?" Tilda asked.

"Yes, and if there was trouble with Mother accepting us, we never heard of it. There had been no children between her and Father, and she treated us as if we were her own. Father spent the rest of his life visiting orphanages in search of you, all over the city. He'd give up, then go back to searching, then he'd give up again. He did this all our lives . . . until I saw that picture of you and the orphans."

Shaking his head, his voice became filled with wonder. "It was overwhelming. We were so excited. One reason Father didn't come here with me was because he thought someone should stay back east in case I missed you." Ben reached across the table and took a firm grip of her wrist. "Let's go home, Tilda. Right now, today. Father will welcome you with open arms. So do I. I love you. I finally have my sister back."

Josh reached behind her, trying to be discreet, and touched

her back. Instead of being comforted, Tilda lurched to her feet. "Well, I don't know you, Ben. I don't love you, and you do *not* have me back."

Tilda was so twisted up inside that it was hard to remember all Ben had told her. She did know one thing clearly, though. She wasn't about to jump on a train and race back to New York City with a stranger. Very likely they were family. Almost certainly they were—the scar story had the ring of truth about it—but it wasn't enough for her to hand her whole life over to a man she knew nothing about.

"I know you've come a long way, but I'm not going back east with you." Tilda's voice was harsh. She hadn't meant it to be, but she heard herself. She'd stay here instead with a bunch of strangers. Yet they were strangers she knew. Honestly, she didn't know them or they wouldn't be strangers, now, would they? Even so, they were a whole lot more familiar to her than her brother, Ben.

Ben's eyes narrowed. "Tilda, you must come with me. I—"

"Stop!" Tilda leaned forward, bracing her hands on the table. She missed Josh's strong hand on her back, but she had to make Ben understand. "You *must* understand that you're a complete stranger to me. I don't have any memories of you, and I will not get on a train and ride away from here with you. The whole idea is frightening. And anyway, I've decided to settle in California. I'm a teacher here at the Two Harts Ranch, and I like it. We can write to each other. Get to know each other that way. And maybe someday I'll come and visit. With the train it's not an impossible distance."

Ben's eyes glinted with steely determination. Tilda was suddenly afraid. Ben didn't look apt to take no for an answer. "But you have to go with me, Tilda."

"Tilda doesn't have to go anywhere." Josh entered the conversation, and it was all Tilda could do not to hide behind him. She refused to show any weakness, so she stood her ground.

Now all three of them stood. Ben glaring. Josh stalwart and ready to protect Tilda. And Tilda sick, scared, confused, hurt beyond measure to hear her mother had as good as thrown her out into the street.

It was a standoff to match any armed meeting at high noon. Silence stretched until it was a cord binding them all, quivering with tension.

Then the door opened, and Michelle stepped inside.

"Tilda, I see you met your brother. Aren't reunions wonderful?"

"My grandpa is going to be thrilled to meet you." Cord knocked on the door of a mansion.

The train trip had taken half the day, with stops at every little town, some of them lengthy. Brody had spent most of it asleep, with Ellie watching over him.

Now here they stood at Mayhew Westbrook's door.

Ellie hoped the man had food available. She and Brody hadn't eaten for hours, and even then, for Brody it wasn't much. In fact, Brody needed to lie down somewhere for a while. Her husband was barely standing upright.

A very starchy man in a black suit opened the door. For just a brief few seconds, he smiled at Cord. This wasn't

Cord's grandpa. Ellie knew enough about how rich people lived to recognize a butler when she saw one.

"Welcome back, Master Cordell, sir. Your grandfather is not expecting you."

"Is he available, Fletcher? He sent me on a mission, and I believe I have information he'll want to hear."

"Of course. He's in his study. Come in. Let me announce you."

"Can my friend sit down somewhere? He's been injured."

"Certainly, sir." Fletcher gestured toward a bench near the front door.

Cord helped Ellie as the two of them eased Brody onto the bench while Fletcher strode down the hall that ran alongside the stairs to the second floor.

Fletcher stopped in front of a door and knocked twice, then opened the door and spoke words Ellie couldn't hear. A few moments passed before Fletcher returned. "Your grandfather will see you now," he stated.

"I should have never sat down," Brody said and regained his feet. Ellie had his arm, as if the two of them were going for a stroll. Only she was mostly holding him upright. Cord stayed a pace behind, probably in case he needed to keep Brody from collapsing.

"Getting shot in the chest really hurts." Brody, voicing the obvious. "I need to be nicer to patients who have this injury."

"Probably all dead, as a rule." Cord stayed close. "You got shot in the heart after all. Not that many people carrying gold coins in their pockets. That's probably why you've never had a real policy for handling it."

An elderly man sat in a chair behind a massive desk, looking like a king allowing an audience to his subjects.

"Brody MacKenzie, sir."

Cord gestured toward them. "Ellie and Brody MacKenzie, this is my grandfather, Mayhew Westbrook."

Mr. Westbrook's eyes shot through with keen excitement. He made no sound. Didn't start demanding information. Didn't kick up his heels and dance a jig, but he was absolutely riveted on Brody.

"Can we sit in front of the fire, Grandpa? Brody was wounded while on a treasure hunt."

Brody sagged a bit, but before he could slump all the way to the floor, Cord slung an arm across his back. With Ellie on Brody's other side, they helped him to the blue-and-white-floral divan that faced a crackling fire. It was a warm day—too warm for a fire in Ellie's opinion—but Brody might appreciate it.

"Wounded by Loyal Kelton, who lied his way into eating a meal with you. He used what he learned from you to track down Brody. This is Brody's wife, Ellie Hart MacKenzie. Loyal threatened Ellie, knocked Ellie's brother unconscious, shot Brody, and tried to steal the map they have."

"Loyal Kelton? I knew he was up to no good," Mr. Westbrook said. "He shot you? Yes, sit. Sit." He rose from his seat behind the desk with more alacrity than Ellie would have expected for such an elderly man. But then talk of treasure no doubt put a spring in his step.

Mr. Westbrook headed for the larger of the two wing-back chairs that sat at ninety-degree angles to the divan. He sank into his chair, big enough it resembled a throne, just as Cord got Brody settled. Ellie sat beside him.

"You're Graham MacKenzie's grandson? Frazier MacKenzie's son?" Mr. Westbrook might be old, but his mind seemed sharp.

Brody nodded and looked to be gathering his strength.

"Dr. MacKenzie and his wife, Ellie, are newly married," Cord said. "Brody came to their ranch searching for MacKenzie's Treasure."

"I'll tell you what I know, Mr. Westbrook," said Ellie, giving Brody a worried look. "We found a partial map concealed in an old journal sent to Brody and his family years ago by his grandfather, Graham MacKenzie."

"The thing is, Grandpa wrote a note saying he promised you half of any treasure he found." Brody must have rested up enough to speak. "We're sure it's his writing, and we intend to honor the debt he owed. He also said you had information."

Mr. Westbrook straightened and blinked. "He did?"

"It would have been thirty years ago, sir." Brody rested his hand on his chest. "And he said . . . well, that part of his treasure was yours, and we'd need to know what you know to . . . to . . . Sorry, but is there somewhere I can lie down for a bit?" Brody asked faintly. Then he sagged sideways on the divan and passed out.

Eight

"I'll go back to the ranch house in time for supper, but not right now. I can't stand it. And your sister-in-law isn't helping." Tilda had stormed out of the house and was halfway to the dormitory when Josh caught up with her.

Josh shrugged one shoulder. "Michelle's been known to step into the middle of things she'd be better to stay out of. No question."

"I'm not going with him." Tilda grabbed Josh's arm. "Where would he take me? To some house I've never been to before? To live with people I've only just met?"

Josh didn't say the obvious. That's what she was doing now. He didn't mention it because he didn't want her to go anywhere. It was shocking how badly he didn't want her to go anywhere.

The doctor's office was just ahead. Inspiration struck. He caught her wrist and brought her along as if he were a tugboat and she a frigate in the United States Navy.

With everyone knowing that Brody was gone, he knew no one was here, barring any unforeseen patients arriving.

He could tell Tilda was addled when she didn't protest. All she said was, "What am I going to do?"

He got them inside and closed the door, then said quietly, "You're going to marry me. And do it fast. I'll arrange for someone to take care of staying with the children for both of us, and we'll slip away to town tonight. Then things are settled. You're a married woman—of course you'd stay with your husband."

The addled look faded, replaced by stunned surprise. "M-marry you?"

Josh had just reacted. All he could think was he had to keep her here. He'd opened his mouth to say just that but instead the most reckless proposal imaginable had popped out. Now, surprised by the words, he decided he really liked the idea. He was determined that she accept him. He tried to be a little calmer and sound less like a headlong fool.

"It's sudden, I know, but we've been . . . um, drawn to each other from the first, haven't we?"

Tilda stared at him. Was she surprised, or was she thinking of how drawn they'd been to each other the few times they were alone together? Truth was, they'd been interested when they weren't alone, too.

"I'll admit I didn't think it was time yet." Josh struggled to be honest. It was a bit much to give a declaration of love. But he'd had . . . hopes in that direction. "We need more time to get to know each other better, but we were going to end up married eventually, don't you think?"

She blinked as if her eyes weren't fully focused. "*Don't you think* is the wrong thing to say to me right now. Thinking is beyond me."

"Then let me do the thinking. In fact, let's have that as a

rule for the rest of our lives. That's how marriages are supposed to be." He was sure of it. His big brother Zane and his overly brainy wife, Michelle, notwithstanding.

Although, now he considered it, Josh had to admit that his ma had done her share of the thinking. Probably. Still, the man being in charge was in the Bible. He couldn't remember the chapter and verse, but he was sure it was in there.

Tilda's hand came up to rub her forehead. Maybe she was coming around, her thoughts clearing. He wasn't sure that was for the best.

"Josh, I—"

"The look on Ben's face, well, he seemed mighty determined." Josh rested his hands on her shoulders. "He thinks he knows what's best for you. Married or not, I won't let him take you from here. But if we were married, he'd never be able to run off with you. Would he?"

"More questions, seriously?"

"If we were married, I could guard you more easily in the night."

She went back to rubbing her forehead as if she had a raging headache.

Then Josh got a notion of what might help. He gently but firmly pulled her hand away from her head and eased her into his arms.

And kissed her.

She froze . . . and then she thawed. Her arms came around his neck. She tilted her head. It was the finest moment of Josh's life.

Josh knew the antics sailors were said to get up to with women in faraway ports, but that had never been for him. He was raised to believe intimacies between men and women belonged within marriage. And there were other sailors on those ships who thought as he did. He'd explored distant lands with good friends who shared his faith, while others tossed away their pay on whiskey and women and gambling.

This moment, right here and now, was the closest he'd ever been to a woman. And he was stunned to realize just how much he'd like to get even closer.

It took every ounce of his will for Josh to lift his head enough to see her. He looked down at her closed eyes. Her slightly swollen lips. No, she wasn't going anywhere.

Resting both hands on her pretty face, he said quietly, "Say you'll marry me, Tilda."

Her eyes fluttered open. She paid rapt attention to him.

"Right now. Let's arrange for someone to tend to the children, and we'll slip away to town. By morning we'll be man and wife, and Ben will have to accept that your home is here. If you want to meet your father, we'll go to New York City together, or he can come out here. But whatever ends up happening, it'll happen with me at your side."

Tilda reached up and placed her fingertips on his lips. "That was my first kiss. I had no idea a kiss could make me feel so much."

"Mine too."

A smile curved her lips. "You know it would be madness to get married on so short an acquaintance. But you're right. I have been interested in you. But, Josh, I'm nobody. I haven't got a penny to my name. Michelle brought so much to Zane. And Ellie is part owner of this ranch. I'm a—"

Josh kissed her again, softly. "You've been interested, huh?"

"Oh yes. But I'd have never dared hope such a fine, successful man would be interested in a penniless orphan. I mean—"

He quick gave her another kiss and made her quit talking since she was making no sense anyway.

Then he pulled back. "Are you saying yes? And not just yes, but yes to tonight, to our running off to town? To marrying me before another day passes? I don't want to lose you, Tilda. I want to do whatever I can think of to keep you here with me."

Tilda's eyes focused. Her head seemed to be clearing. Those eyes then sharpened. "I think I have a better idea than running off."

A wicked pang cut through Josh's heart. She was going to say no.

"How about we tell them? We just announce we intend to marry. That's a very good reason not to go back with Ben. I'd like for my brother to hear my intentions clearly, that I want this ranch . . . and you . . . to be my home. I agree that Ben looked almost furious, even dangerous. I doubt he'd resort to force, but how can we be sure?"

"That's the whole point, isn't it? That you don't know him? Which is why you aren't willing to jump on a train and vanish across the country with him."

"Yes, Josh, I *will* marry you. But not now. Not so suddenly. I wouldn't say yes if I didn't think we could make a good marriage, but we're the next thing to strangers. I want to know you better, let our feelings grow into something deeper than an attraction." She swallowed. "A powerful attraction, I'll admit."

Josh smiled at that.

"I'd be so honored to join my life with yours, Josh. But

let's do it at a time and place of our choosing, not a time and place forced by this shocking appearance of my brother. Instead of getting married, let's go in there and tell him we're engaged, and my home is here and that's final."

"Your brother will kick up a fuss."

Tilda nodded. "He might at that."

"Wouldn't it be better to just present yourself to him as a married woman, with no doubt as to whether you'll leave?"

"Whether or not he likes it, he's going to have to accept it." Tilda sounded sassy.

Josh rewarded her with a kiss. "When the time comes, let's ask the parson to skip that part of the wedding about anyone objecting. Why give him a chance to cause a ruckus?"

"Shall we tell them tonight at supper? Or does that give them too much time to stage a kidnapping?"

Josh drew in a slow breath. "Do you think he might try it? He seemed determined, but how determined?"

Tilda shrugged.

"Let's break the news at breakfast instead. The chances of him running off with you in broad daylight are unlikely." And with that all settled, Josh pulled her close and kissed her some more.

Finally, he turned his head aside. "We need to get out of here. It's not at all proper for us to be alone like this."

"You are absolutely right about that."

"Let's go over to the school and see if anyone needs help with their studies. I'm staying right by your side until I shut your door for the night. And I want you to lock yourself in. The more I think about it, the less I like leaving you alone for the night. I might sleep on the floor outside the door of the girls' side of the dormitory."

"But who will watch those unruly boys?"

Josh laughed. "I'll figure something out. Our foreman, Shad, is usually willing to help. And I've got other cowhands who can step in if needed."

Tilda slipped out of his arms and reached for his hand. He took it firmly and led her out of the doctor's office before someone came to the door and asked him to perform some kind of surgery or deliver their baby.

"Um, what was that you said about the husband doing all the thinking?"

"You're awake!"

Ellie's voice pulled Brody out of a dark place. He felt as if he'd been gone for days.

His eyes focused on Ellie. "We're married."

Ellie rested both her hands on his face and smiled. A rather sad smile. "Yes, we are. And you've been asleep for three days, husband. You scared me to death."

"Three days?"

"Yes, the doctor's been here." Her brows arched. "He suggested we bleed you."

"What? That's not an acceptable form of treatment anymore. They stopped most of that in the 1850s." At least that had fully awakened him.

Ellie patted him on one of his cheeks. "He was old, and Mr. Westbrook is set in his ways. I put a stop to it, though. No leech touched your body, no veins were opened. Or whatever way they bleed someone. I was a bit afraid to ask."

"What happened?"

"We don't know. But that bruise on your chest is a black

circle about six inches in diameter. I suppose something inside you is injured." Her smile shrank, and her voice wobbled. "I'm so glad you're awake."

A single tear rolled down her cheek. She swiped it away with the back of her wrist and sniffled.

Brody laid his hand over his chest. "It's not as swollen as it was. Still tender." He pressed here and there on his chest and flinched. "My ribs still hurt, but not as bad as before. It's settled down to a throbbing ache when before it felt like someone was beating my chest with a club."

"I'm going to send for Cord and his grandfather. They've been very anxious about you." Ellie leaned close. "I think Cord might have genuinely been concerned for your health, but Mr. Westbrook seemed more worried about his missing treasure . . . the old coot."

She rose. Brody caught her wrist and pulled her back. "Don't leave."

She smiled so sweetly it made Brody's chest ache in a way that had nothing to do with bullets.

"There's a footman right outside the door. He's been stationed there day and night."

Dropping his voice to a whisper, Brody asked, "Is he there in case we need help, or is he worried we'll make an escape attempt?"

Ellie shrugged, kissed the hand he had wrapped around her wrist, and slipped free. "I won't even step outside the room. And I'm not going to tell the Westbrooks to come charging in to cross-examine you. That can wait until morning. I'm just going to tell them you're awake." Her voice broke. She sniffled again. "Awake and going to be fine."

"What day is it? What's the time?"

"Um, I've kind of lost track. I think I remember Cord saying he was going to church yesterday? Or maybe that was the day before yesterday. I didn't want to leave you, so I stayed home. And we've had the evening meal, so it's getting late." She gestured to a table beside his bed that had plates and utensils on it. "I've been taking my meals in here with you."

Leaning over him, she kissed him swiftly, then hurried to the door. Brody didn't take his eyes off her. And why would he? She was easily the most interesting thing in the world.

She swung the door open, spoke quietly to someone, then closed the door again and came back to his side and sat. She took one of his hands firmly in hers.

Brody felt the weight of being so sick, so weak. "Impossible as it sounds after sleeping for days, I'm exhausted. Have you been sleeping at my side at night?" He glanced to the side of the bed, away from where she sat, and saw the bed mussed, a tidy little dent in the lone pillow not under his head.

"I have been. I asked the footman to pass on word that we will be ready to talk tomorrow. For tonight, I'm going to insist on quiet and that you rest. Now, you need food and water before you go back to sleep."

And he did need food and water. He couldn't say he was hungry, but the water felt like it barely wet his throat. His dry mouth soaked it in before it could get to his stomach.

The broth was just more to drink, so he swallowed every bit of that.

"Can I have more water, please?"

Ellie smiled as if he'd offered her a bouquet of flowers. He drank another cup of water, then a wave of exhaustion washed over him.

"So you've been sleeping in here with me, in this bed?"

His need to have her close swept over him with more force than the exhaustion.

"Yes." She set the water glass aside.

"I don't want to fall asleep if I can't hold you."

He wanted to be a married man, but right now just holding her was all he had strength for.

Ellie nodded, her eyes brimming with tears. "I'm not going anywhere. Let me get my nightgown on."

Brody had to fight to keep sleep at bay while he waited for his wife to join him. She slipped into bed and rested her hand on his heart and her head on his shoulder. "Go to sleep, Brody. I'll lie awake for a few minutes and thank God that you're going to be fine."

He reveled in the feel of her, close and strong and so sweet. Then a thought niggled into his head to worry him. "You don't think I'll fall asleep and not wake up again for another three days, do you?"

Ellie's hand slid carefully around his waist, below his bruise, and she hugged him, gently but solid as a stone. "No, Brody. I think this time, you're back with me. I have plenty to be thankful for tonight." She hugged him again. "And every night."

Nine

"You are *not* getting married to some *cowboy* from California." Ben slammed both hands on the table and shoved himself to his feet.

Thayne and Lock were eating fast, but they stopped gulping down new bites of food to stare at Ben Cabril as he erupted.

Lock swallowed before he said, "You'll be our aunt now, Tilda, since you're marrying Uncle Josh."

"Really, Josh? You and Tilda are engaged? I'm so happy for you," Annie weighed in.

Josh looked at her and saw an impish smile. He doubted she was all that happy about the speed of this decision. But she likely wanted to balance out Ben's wild protests.

"I like weddings." Caroline continued to eat her eggs, but she gave Josh and Tilda a shy smile.

No one else was around to announce the big news to. Michelle had left early for her invention shed, Zane was out taking the reins into his hands after going off for weeks, and Gretel didn't come over until after breakfast, which Annie usually handled, along with Ellie when she was around.

Josh looked at Tilda, who scowled at her brother.

"I *am* marrying Josh. I don't like the way you act. I'm not a bit sure I'm safe with you; you're so madly determined to take me home. I want to stay here, and I want to be with Josh. Getting married is the best idea I've ever had."

Josh grinned. "Me too."

"As your brother, I have every right to ask you to come home. It's what our father wants."

"I admit we resemble each other, and the story you told about my scar has the ring of truth. But I can't remember getting the scar, and you could have found out my name before you came here."

"Are you calling me a liar?" Ben snapped.

Tilda almost jumped back.

Josh, sitting beside her at the kitchen table, leaned closer to her.

"I am *saying* I have no real idea if I'm the woman you're looking for. And honestly, Ben, neither do you. You saw that picture, and I looked like the sister you haven't seen in, what, fifteen years? But the truth is, we can't know if I'm your sister for certain."

Ben's eyes flashed in a way that frightened Tilda. She was very glad she wasn't alone with him right now.

"You ran out of here last night before I could finish telling you everything," Ben said. His lips tightened as he glared at her. He leaned to grab something from his satchel, and while she couldn't see what he was doing, she remembered that he'd produced that tintype the night before.

He straightened with something in his hand. That same picture again maybe? No, this was larger. And framed.

He turned it, and she saw . . . herself.

Except not herself because in this full-length picture, the dress she wore was spectacular. It was a painted portrait about a foot tall, oval and framed. She wore a pink dress with elaborate embroidery on a neckline much too low-cut to suit Tilda. It had ruffles and draped skirts that looked like silk, and she held an umbrella that dripped with lace. Her hair was intricately pinned up with ringlets on her forehead and by her ears. Bracelets on her wrists and an elegant cameo brooch centered on the neckline completed the ensemble.

This was no outfit she'd ever owned in her life. And she'd certainly never had her portrait painted.

A closer look showed the woman was frail to a frightening degree. Her skin looked ashen. Though she smiled, no happiness reached her eyes. Tilda wouldn't say she looked like that, but beyond those details, this woman was identical to her.

"Who . . . who is that?" She reached an unsteady hand toward the picture. Ben let her take it.

"I regret having to show this to you." Ben frowned until his forehead wrinkled. "I regretted telling you about Ma abandoning you. I hoped I could, um . . . persuade you to trust me and come home with me. I didn't mention Maddie before because it makes what Ma did so much worse." He looked from the painting to Tilda. "Father and I and Maddie—that's who this is in the picture—all of us want to make things right. We want to spend the rest of our lives making things right. They couldn't come with me. Father is elderly and Maddie is delicate or they'd be here.

"I regret it, but now I'll have to tell you who Maddie is and the rest of the story that goes along with it. It breaks my heart, but you would've learned it eventually. I just hoped you'd find a familial connection to me, to Father, and to Maddie before I had to tell you more details of what happened to you."

He looked as if she'd stricken him with grief. For some reason that made her angry. None of this was fair. She didn't want to bear the weight of his grief when she had her own confusion to deal with. And fear? What story broke his heart? She dreaded what he was going to say.

"This is your twin sister, Maddie. Madeline."

"Twin sister?" Tilda gasped so hard she started choking, coughing, and fighting for breath until Josh patted her firmly on the back. When finally she could breathe again like normal, she said, "You're telling me my mother abandoned one twin and kept the other? How could anyone do something so monstrous?"

Ben shook his head. "The drink was on her, as it often was. She wasn't thinking right."

"I'd say that's a fair assessment."

Ben pushed the picture toward her, then dropped his face into his hands and scrubbed as if he were washing, maybe washing the memories of such a cruel truth from his mind.

"You were Madeline and Matilda. Maddie and Mattie. But with your nicknames so similar, neither of you was learning your name, and you were answering to either." Ben shook his head. "I started calling you Tilda. I just think Ma's mind was failing her, and one day she took you and, well, as I said. But she took only you and kept Maddie. The two of us spent the rest of our time with her scared to death we'd be next. I almost contacted Father then, but I had no reason to believe he cared about us. In fact, I doubt he did. Later, when he came for us, after Ma died, he proved to be a decent sort, and we grew into a family. I've done my best to forgive him for thinking money was enough to buy his way to a clear conscience. But it was his neglect that ended in your being . . . lost."

"Not lost." Tilda's voice nearly bit into his hide. "Thrown out. Treated with less care than someone would give a family pet."

Josh's hand was still on her back. He might not realize it, but he was holding her up. Holding her together.

Ben's dark eyes burned with intensity. "You have to come back with me, Tilda. Father is tormented by losing you. And Maddie isn't strong. She didn't come along because neither Father nor I thought she was in good enough health to take such a long trip. While you seem to have forgotten her, she's never forgotten you. She acts as if half of herself is gone, just torn right away from her heart. I want you to come home with me and help me end their suffering."

She had a twin. It was almost more than she could take in, but the picture was undeniable proof.

"Why do you think my coming with you will somehow make everything right for you and your family?"

"Your family too, Tilda."

Shaking her head, she said, "I didn't even know you were out there. It's too soon for me to feel like you are family. Not in my heart anyway." Tilda turned to Josh. "You're my family now."

He smiled and jerked his chin down and up. "That I am, Tilda."

Then she tried very hard to make a serious point to Ben. "And that's why I am not going with you."

He opened his mouth to reply.

"Stop." She raised her hand and shoved the flat of her palm right at his face. "I. Am. Not. Going."

Ben narrowed his eyes and glared. He didn't look like he'd given up, not one bit.

"Instead," she went on, "have Madeline write to me. Have Father write. I promise I'll write back. We can get to know each other. They think they know me because Madeline remembers me and Father's been told about me. But they are strangers to me. What's more, I'm a stranger to them. I'm not able to just miraculously become the missing sister Madeline has longed for and Father has felt such guilt over. Father was able to make up for his years of neglect by taking you both in, but he's made nothing up to me. I have a life I like and will not give it up. Go home. If Madeline ever feels strong enough, maybe she can come and visit. But I am not returning with you. Is that clear?"

Ben shook his head. "Father is trusting me to bring you home."

Tilda stared at him. There was something in his voice. Was it fear? As if he'd never denied his father anything and he wouldn't start now?

"I'm not going home." There was an edge to his voice and a glint in his eye.

Tilda had to wonder how many times the man had been told no.

"However, I will write home and tell my family I found you. In fact, I'm going to write this morning and take the letter to town. I expect I'll be writing daily for a while. But I want to get to know you better. Is it all right for me to stay here on the Two Harts for a while?" His eyes shifted from Tilda to Josh.

Josh leaned closer to Tilda. "You can stay as long as you don't make a nuisance of yourself. I don't like the way you talk to Tilda, but she's doing so well at speaking her own mind that I won't insult her by pretending she's not handling this on her own just fine."

"Thank you." Tilda leaned her head on Josh's strong shoulder for just a few seconds, then straightened.

Josh wasn't finished. "But she's under my protection, and she has the protection of every member of my family and every cowhand on the place. You'll treat her well or you'll be shown the trail. Is that clear?"

"Clear as a mountain stream, Josh." Ben pushed back his chair. "Now, I need to ride to town. I'm going to add a few lines to a letter I wrote my father, then make sure it's on its way. I intend to keep him updated." As he rose, he said to Tilda in a formal, polite tone, "And I wish to know all about you. I understand you're teaching, but I request that we spend time together every day and get to know each other. You're right that I'm a stranger, but I don't have to stay one."

"I'll give your request serious consideration," Tilda answered, yet she couldn't help but doubt her brother's sincerity. She pushed her chair back and looked at Thayne and Lock. "Boys, would you walk over to the school with me?" Then to Annie, "You and Caroline, too." She smiled at Josh. "And you if you've got the time . . . I feel safer knowing my family is all around me."

"I'm your family, Tilda." Ben sounded hurt, and that melted the smile off her face. "I hope, before much longer, you'll feel safe with me around, too."

Ben left the room then. She could even say he *stormed* out. He was sleeping in the housekeeper's apartment because

Gretel didn't use it, having her own home with her family. Tilda heard his feet thudding and the door in the back of the house shut as if his temper was ruling him.

Was he hurt? Was he angry? Possibly both. Mostly, she thought he was driven by a need to deliver what his father wanted. A boy who'd had to hunt down his father and care for his sister. A boy whose mother was gone, who'd lost another sister, might never feel safe. He might do most anything to keep a new home.

Josh rested one of his strong hands on her back and gestured for the door. As they left the house, Josh said to her quietly, "Your brother has a hot temper. I don't think you should ever be alone with him."

A chill of dread raced down Tilda's spine as she nodded and walked with him and the others toward the schoolhouse.

———— ✧ ————

Brody stepped into the study on the first floor under his own power. He was finally up and moving.

Cord was playing the piano somewhere. The rippling, sweet sound he managed to get out of a piano was humbling. It really was more than a simple song. Brody could feel those notes, the emotion behind them, the beauty unleashed.

The butler, Fletcher, had guided him and Ellie to the room and knocked on the door. Brody thought they might have needed someone to lead them through the mansion to find Mayhew Westbrook, but he wasn't sure why he couldn't have knocked on the door and announced himself.

"Send Cordell in, Fletcher." Mayhew rose unsteadily.

Brody, while knowing better than to trust a diagnosis from across the room, wondered if the man had gout or maybe arthritis. The usual joint pain of old age was so often just accepted, but there were things a doctor could do to help. Brody had just come home from medical school and knew all the latest treatments. He wondered if Mayhew took any medicine at all. Brody would recommend willow-bark tea and feverfew, which sometimes offered relief. There were more treatments too, heat and cold packs, some exercises, and changes in diet, all depending on what exactly Mr. Westbrook suffered from.

Brody hesitated to suggest a medical exam. He'd find out more, but not as the very first thing they talked about.

"Please, be seated. I'm glad you're up and around at last, Dr. MacKenzie. I appreciate that you made a heroic and no doubt reckless effort to come here as soon as possible, even with your injuries, all to help me solve the mystery of MacKenzie's Treasure."

He gestured at the chairs in front of him. There were three, all carefully situated to face the man who ruled behind the massive desk.

"Now, because of your injuries, Cord and I haven't turned our attention to the treasure hunt until now. He said you hadn't told him much on the train ride here, probably because you were so badly hurt."

The door behind them opened, and Cord came in and took the empty seat closest to the door.

Smiling like a man who counted his treasure in heaven rather than in gold doubloons, Cord asked, "Are we talking about MacKenzie's Treasure?"

"We are for a fact," Brody said. "I apologize for the delay, but being shot, well, it couldn't be helped. I'm sure you're anxious to learn what I've come to say."

"I find that after all these years of letting that treasure tantalize me, the idea of finding it is almost frightening." Mayhew settled back in his chair and folded his hands across his lean belly. "I've built it up in my head so long that whatever we find can't possibly match what my wildest dreams have conjured."

Brody smiled, then reached into his front breast pocket and pulled out the gold doubloons. Three of them. He stretched forward and laid them in front of Mayhew. "I suppose these are yours, sir. We found"—he turned to Ellie—"how many?"

She shrugged. "A lot happened right after we divided them up." She looked at Cord. "I think there were fourteen of these gold coins. We portioned them out to, let's just say, not put all our eggs in one basket. Then Brody got shot, and his life was saved by those coins."

Mayhew looked more sharply at the coins. He picked one up and ran his thumb over the bullet-sized dent in the coin.

"Half are yours, Mr. Westbrook. We didn't think to count them out and bring a full half along, but rest assured we'll figure out what half is and get the rest of your share to you. I found a note in my grandpa's hand, found alongside his body in a cave, that said that's your due. There was also an old knife with him. That's what we've found so far, but I suspect there's more. You have a claim on half of whatever comes to light."

Mayhew reached an unsteady hand toward the rest of the gold doubloons in front of him.

"We have no idea what they're worth, but we believe they're around three hundred years old. They almost certainly have value as antiquities beyond their weight in gold."

"The size of the coins tells me each has a value of at least one hundred dollars," Cord said. "They're much larger than a twenty-dollar gold piece, and that's not counting whatever historical significance they might have."

"Graham MacKenzie died, then." Mayhew seemed to take that information and let it weigh down his shoulders. "I've been so angry for so long, thinking he took my money, found his treasure, and never paid me back. Even when I met your father, obviously searching for the treasure, which made it plain as day that he'd lost contact with your grandfather, I let myself believe Graham had found the treasure and left his own son with nothing. I clung to my anger, nurtured it, soaked my soul in it." Mayhew frowned at the gold coins, studied them for a moment. Then he looked up at Brody. "You said you found your grandfather's body?"

"Yes, and this is why we needed to come to you. Along with his note saying he'd promised you half was another note saying he sent you something that will help us find the rest of the treasure."

Mayhew's brow furrowed. "I did get a letter from him—thirty years ago."

Brody's breath caught. "Did you keep it?"

The man nodded slowly. "I kept it and have read every bit of what he wrote me dozens of times."

There was a gleam in Mayhew's eyes that made Brody a bit nervous. He glanced at Cord and found ease in the kind expression he saw there.

"Can we see what you have, sir?"

Mayhew pushed back from his desk and opened a drawer on the bottom right. He brought out an old, battered envelope, thick and dirty but intact.

Mayhew opened a flap and tipped the contents of the

envelope onto the desktop. A single object fell out. A leather book, much smaller than Brody's journal, but made of the same old leather. And on the front cover was that same unique cross, cut into the leather, but so worn it was nearly invisible.

Brody looked at Ellie.

She said, barely above a whisper, "The Cross of Burgundy."

Brody reached out and clutched her hand. His heart pounded. They both smiled as they turned back to Mayhew.

He said, "Cross of Burgundy? What is that?"

"It's the insignia on the Spanish flag," said Brody, "what they called the *Cruz de Borgoña*. They've had a few changes to their flag over the centuries, but this one is still used sometimes. Three hundred years ago, Cortés sailed under that flag."

"Cortés?" Mayhew frowned.

"Yes, the Spanish conquistador. He had that flag when he invaded Mexico. It's the flag we found carved into my grandpa's journal."

"And you're saying there's a map hidden in this little book?"

Brody shrugged one shoulder. "There was one in our journal. Grandpa said he sent you the other half of the treasure map so we'd be sure to talk with you if we ever got close enough to find it."

The four of them stared at the little book for long, stretched-out moments.

Then Brody reached for it.

TEN

Tilda almost enjoyed getting to know Ben.

Almost.

Ben had breakfast with her every morning, and she joined them after supper every night. Tilda helped get the children to bed, then went to the main house and joined the family for supper. And, with Josh always at her side, she'd spent the evenings with Ben.

She listened to every word he said about her father, her sister, her mother—the woman who gave birth to her—and her father's wife, the woman who had raised Ben and Maddie.

They traded off asking questions, and she thought Ben was generous in his answers. Though he had an intensity about him that made her nervous still, it seemed he was being honest with her. He loved his father at the same time that he acknowledged the man had ignored his children for too long. He didn't have much good to say about her mother. Though he didn't claim it was as bad as being abandoned on the streets, like Tilda had been, he spoke of experiencing hunger and cold as a child, as well as a woman who was quick with a swat and harsh in her scolding.

He admired without reserve his father's wife, the woman who'd raised him for ten years after the woman who'd given birth to him had died.

Tilda came to think of his mother, Constance Cabril, as Mrs. Cabril, and his ma as Johanna.

She studied Ben as he talked, trying to get an impression. Was his deep intensity honor, or was it ruthlessness? She couldn't quite decide, and it kept her wary.

He definitely resembled her. He had her eyes, as dark as the coffee Gretel poured them. His hair was cut short. He'd have had black curls to match hers if he let his hair grow longer.

He told her he'd ridden to California in his father's private train car. He'd left the train behind at the closest town with facilities for such a thing, and he'd ridden the regular train the last few miles. Now that train awaited his summons. Hopefully to take Tilda home with him, though he seemed to have accepted she wasn't going.

"Father is in shipping, Josh, so you might enjoy talking with him, though he hasn't gone to sea for years. Anyway, you might find things in common. He imports goods, mainly from the Caribbean—he has a special love for that area—and he exports goods to Europe." Ben turned from Tilda's constant companion. "We live in a big, beautiful house with three floors—eight bedrooms on the second floor and servants' quarters on the third."

"I have a hard time imagining a house so big. And servants?" Tilda shook her head as Ben drew pictures with words.

"It's a fine yellow house built with clapboards, not logs like you have out here."

Tilda thought there was a tone to that comment, like he

was criticizing this house as being backwater. She wondered if her father had ever used any of his shipping money to educate orphans.

"Over the years, he spoke often of you, Tilda." Ben turned his black eyes back to her and reached across the table to clasp her hands. "He prayed for you and feared for you. Sometimes he mourned for you. He and Mother truly wanted to welcome you into their home. Now I spend time every day writing long letters to him, telling him everything we've spoken of. He's sent a few telegraphs full of relief and excitement. He wants to see you so badly."

"I appreciate knowing that, but I'm still not going to New York City with you, Ben." Tilda pulled her hands away from his grasp, tugging hard to free herself. The strangely intense way he talked scared her.

Josh must have noticed because he right away took her hand in his.

Ben noticed too. The expression in his eyes was bleak, as if he were trying desperately to think of just what to say to convince her to leave with him. "But mostly he's just happy to hear you're alive and well."

Zane and Michelle tended to linger too, Michelle having a lot of questions for Ben. Tilda was happy to let Michelle ask them. In fact, Tilda was learning more about her brother through Michelle's insightful questions than her own.

The MacKenzie boys, for their part, wandered up to their room. Apparently Ben didn't interest them much. Annie didn't sit around for long either, since she had Caroline to tend, and the little girl went to sleep early. Now that Tilda had moved into the girls' dormitory, Annie had quit spending the night there.

After the long evenings of talking, Josh always walked her home.

She slept near the children. She taught school every day. But instead of helping get the children up and through breakfast, then staying to help cook and serve supper, she ate in the ranch house. With mixed emotions, she spent nearly all her spare time getting acquainted with her brother.

Tilda kept expecting him to bring a letter from her father, but nothing came. It had been long enough for him to write following the first telegraph, and she wondered what was keeping him. Was he more upset at her refusal to come than Ben suggested?

Even though she was getting to know her family from Ben's stories, she still couldn't imagine riding away from here with him. She'd ridden alone all the way west in search of Thayne and Lock, but somehow going with Ben seemed more dangerous than going alone.

Ben urged her to write directly to her father, Carl Cabril.

"I'm not ready to do that yet. I don't even know what to call him." Tilda sat across the breakfast table from Ben. It was a Saturday, so there was no school.

Today she'd been determined to be brave, so on the walk over, she'd told Josh, "I know you don't have a full day to spend talking with my brother. I heard you say you're getting ready for roundup and need to move the cattle to better grass."

"There's always work, Tilda, but it's only right to put you first. Are you safe alone with him?"

She looked at Josh, and their gazes held. "I don't see how he could harm me, not with a ranch full of men just outside. And moreover, I don't see why he'd harm me. He needs me to be alive and well to get me back to New York, doesn't he? And I feel like I'm starting to trust him some."

Josh nodded silently, not looking all that happy about the prospect of letting her and Ben talk alone together.

"I'll let you stay in the house with him, but I'll be within shouting distance across the ranch yard."

Tilda heard the threat in that, and she fully appreciated it. So this morning, there in the house, surrounded by a busy working ranch, she sat alone with Ben for the first time.

"Tilda, I want to tell you again, I love you. I remember you as a child, and I've always longed for you and feared for you."

His eyes flashed when he said this . . . in a way that reminded her there'd been a time she'd been afraid of him.

"I will say one more thing. Our father didn't get to be a wealthy man by accepting failure."

"Everyone has to accept some failure, Ben. He can't succeed at everything he tries. What could be a greater failure than having three children and ignoring them for years? What greater failure is there than leaving his children in the care of a drunkard, who threw one of the youngsters out onto the street?"

"He lets that torment him. Absolutely. But I don't mean *his* failure, I mean *mine*. I mean the failure of those he employs. He's a good man, but you don't get this rich and powerful without being a hard man. I've always wondered how deep his love really goes. I've made it a point to never fail him."

He pulled the painting of her twin out of his satchel again, rose to his feet, and came around the table. She realized she liked having the table between them. As she stood and turned to face him, he held up the picture, drawing her attention to it.

"Please believe me when I say I have no choice."

A hand clamped over her mouth and nose. A heavy, sweet-smelling rag cut off her breathing. As she gasped in shock, the rag made her throat burn and her brain fog.

"It takes a few moments. I measured out a dose that won't harm her, but she'll be sleeping for a while. Keep the bottle handy in case it wears off before we get going . . ."

She heard Ben speak those words as she slid down a long tunnel toward unconsciousness.

Then, just before she disappeared into that tunnel, she heard another voice, one she didn't recognize: "Your private cars should be in town by now, and they aren't gonna like it if they're sitting there when the regular train comes through."

Eleven

"I don't like leaving Tilda in there alone with her brother." Josh should have pushed to marry her right away. As her husband he would have a much stronger place in her life. And it would always be reasonable for him to stay at her side.

Yet it was time for the roundup. They needed to gather the cattle and get themselves ready to drive the herd to San Francisco. And sitting in the kitchen with Tilda, wife or not, probably wasn't necessary. Besides, she'd told him to leave.

As he mounted up to ride to a distant pasture, he decided he'd ask her one more time if she was sure about his not being there with her. He trotted the horse over to the ranch house, swung down, and tied the reins to the hitching post.

"C'mon, Josh," Zane called. "We're already getting a late start."

The rest of the cowhands were riding out of the yard to the far pasture. Roundup took lots of hands but didn't require great cowboy skills. Especially if the inexperienced hands hung back and didn't try to chase after runaway steers on a fast-turning, cutting pony.

Josh said to Zane, "I'm going to check on Tilda before I head out."

Zane nodded and started leading his horse toward the house.

Josh dropped his voice so that no one could hear them. "I shouldn't have left her."

"I thought she told you to go on the roundup."

"She did. And she meant it. But she's been alone in that house with him for too long. Gretel is at her house still. Michelle is in her workshop. Annie has Caroline at the schoolhouse." Josh paused, shook his head. "Between the two of us, I think she had some real rude questions she wanted to ask Ben and thought he'd be a whole lot less embarrassed if she asked them with no one else there."

"I can't say I care for the guy, but he sure knows lots of stories. The things he says, the way he looks . . . I'd say he's her brother all right."

"I'm just going to step into the kitchen for a minute, maybe make a few sandwiches to bring out to the range."

Since they intended to be back at the ranch for the noon meal, no doubt Zane saw right through Josh's excuse.

"Bring her along with us if you don't like her and Ben being alone together. She can ride almost as well now as some of the students."

They glanced at the last of the cowboys riding away. Zane headed out after them.

Josh moved to the back door of the house. He stepped inside to utter silence. Frowning, he called out, "Tilda, are you in here?" Then he saw the mess on the floor—a coffee cup smashed in a hundred pieces.

Tilda wouldn't have gone anywhere with her brother, except maybe to find Josh, yet he hadn't seen them come out the back door.

He charged through the house, shouting her name, looking in every room, until he reached the rarely used front door and saw it was ajar. He was sprinting by the time he got outside.

The tracks of two horses were clear by the hitching post. Josh could tell the horses had stood there for quite a while. How long had they been gone? And to where? The tracks were carefully positioned so they'd ride away with the house between them and anyone in the ranch yard.

He ran back into the house and then out the back door. A quick glance around revealed that the whole crew had ridden away. Looking frantically around, he saw Gretel coming toward the house. "Gretel! Get word to Zane! I'm tracking Ben. Looks like he rode toward Dorada Rio, and he's got Tilda with him. She wouldn't have gone willingly."

Gretel, with a child holding her hand and another in her arms, immediately nodded. "Go, I'll send help."

No questions. No dithering. He sure liked that tough German woman.

Josh swung up into the saddle and was galloping before he left the yard.

He kept a sharp eye on the tracks and saw where they joined the trail to town, just out of sight of the Two Harts. And going by the tracks, they were galloping flat-out.

The train passed through Dorada Rio midmorning. But Ben had mentioned his private train cars, which meant his train could run anytime. Ben had decided to give up on being patient. He was taking Tilda to the train. But how did someone force a person, a captive, onto a train? Surely he'd be stopped by others in town, wouldn't he?

Tilda was dimly aware of motion, but it was as if her arms were limp, her head thick with fog.

Hooves pounded. Someone held her. She tried to open her eyes, but then realized a cloak or blanket had been drawn over her head. She twisted in the grip of something or someone.

Something pressed over her face again. That sickly sweet smell invaded her nose and mouth.

"Careful how much of that you give her." Another voice. One farther away, and one she couldn't place.

"We need her asleep for the train. Once we're in the private car, it won't matter if she wakes up." Ben had her. Ben was doing something with her, but what? Her mind was too cloudy to reason it out.

"You get her on board. I'll load the horses."

Then she was gone again.

Josh charged into town to find no train. He hoped for a single moment he'd beaten the train into town.

Then he saw people milling around the station. They were waiting for the train. He looked around, studying every person, every corner. He didn't see Ben or Tilda anywhere.

Josh thought he heard a distant engine, heading north. The tracks ran straight to Sacramento, which wasn't too far away. He didn't think the train would have to stop for water or coal on its way there. But it would have to reload to head on east, if Ben's plan was to take Tilda all the way to New York City.

He spotted Parson Lewis's wife. He'd had time to think on his mad dash from the ranch.

"Mrs. Lewis!" He rode fast toward her until she looked alarmed. He pulled up just in time. "The new teacher at the Two Harts, Tilda—she's been kidnapped. Zane should be right behind me. Tell him to wire Ellie in Sacramento. She's at Mayhew Westbrook's home. But he'll know that. Tell Ellie to get help and get to the train station, just in case I can't catch the train and stop it."

Her eyes sharp, Mrs. Lewis, a western woman who'd learned to react well in an emergency, nodded. "A very fine private car was on this morning's train, pulled by its own locomotive. I didn't see anyone get on, but someone must have, or why was it here? If he's a kidnapper, she must have been knocked unconscious. Otherwise she'd've struggled. Onlookers would notice a woman being taken against her will. The train left only minutes ago. Go. If Zane isn't along soon, I'll wire this Mr. Westbrook myself. I'm going to the sheriff, too. He can wire the next station down the line and stop the train before Sacramento."

The woman was thinking faster than he was. "God bless you, Mrs. Lewis." Josh wheeled his horse and raced after his kidnapped fiancée.

He asked for everything from his horse. The poor critter had already run at top speed from the Two Harts. Josh should have taken a few minutes and found a fresh horse, yet he couldn't risk the delay. But this was a buckskin stallion Josh favored—a strong horse with great endurance. A road ran alongside the train tracks, and he rushed down it, praying for all he was worth.

He'd ridden half a mile before he heard the sound of a chugging train in the distance.

———◆———

Tilda's head, still feeling fuzzy and oddly detached, cleared enough so she could open her eyes. She was moving, bouncing along. She recognized the motion. She was on a train.

"What am I doing on a train?"

"Good, you're awake." Ben leaned over her. She was stretched out somewhere, lying flat on her back. A chill iced her spine as she looked into his dark eyes.

"I had to take you before you married Josh Hart, you understand that, don't you?" He folded his hands, looking sincere. "We'll meet up with Father. You won't want a western rancher when you see the luxury we live in back east."

She'd known not to trust him. Despite his efforts to be friendly and charming, despite his profession of brotherly love, she'd known. She felt a moment of self-disgust that she hadn't trusted her instincts.

Questions flooded her dazed head, clamoring to get out. In the end, she said, "How did you get me onto a train?"

"I've been planning from the first that you'd likely refuse to come home with me. I don't fail when Father asks something of me. My train was waiting in the nearest town with a rail spur available. I spent last week getting all the details ironed out. It was as simple as taking you out the front door. I noticed how nobody uses that door. And none of the ranch work goes on out front. I've been waiting for my chance to act. Henson has been coming to the ranch daily." He jerked his thumb over his shoulder.

Tilda's eyes shifted to the man standing behind Ben, a

man built sturdy as an oak. Big and tough-looking. Dressed well but with no nonsense in his eyes.

"I've been waiting for a chance to get you away. Last night after supper, when you said we could have a private talk after breakfast, I wired him from the ranch, and he sent for our train in town. I've been using that telegraph any time I like since your family doesn't pay much attention to it unless they need it, which isn't often. Henson got word to Lodi to hitch up my private car and bring it to Dorada Rio. I had the train waiting, but I needed to get moving before the regular train came through. We loaded you onto the train real fast and locked the doors. No one noticed a thing. Or if they noticed, they didn't try and stop us."

"But why? It's reasonable not to want to travel across the country with a strange man. And if you want me to join this long-lost family, it makes no sense to do something so nasty as kidnap me." When Tilda inhaled, she could still smell the sweet scent of the cloth they'd pressed to her face. "And you drugged me."

"Yes. I hoped I could convince you to come with me. But once I accepted that you wouldn't, I made arrangements. Tilda." Ben caught both her hands in his. "Once you're in New York, I know you'll love it. Please give us a chance."

Tilda's eyes narrowed in anger, and she didn't respond.

Ben clearly understood. "I'll drug you again when we get near a town. I've got a double water tank and plenty of coal in the tender car. We can go far and fast and not have to stop for a long time. When we do need to stop, you'll sleep through it."

"Josh won't accept this. He'll be coming for me."

"We got out of town without any sight of him. If he's off

to work for the day, no one should notice you're gone until suppertime."

Ben wouldn't be budged, and his expression was pure determination. The man clearly did not understand western ways. Tilda locked eyes with him. "You're not even my brother, are you?"

"Enough questions. Do you want to continue to sleep on the floor, or do you want to move into the bedroom I have for you?"

Why wouldn't he answer her question? "Are you really taking me to my father?"

"Of course I am. I just want you to give us a chance. Please accept that I know best."

A statement that made Tilda eager for Josh to catch up with them and close Ben's mouth. His words sounded kind, but Tilda decided to trust her instincts this time. "I'll lie down in the bedroom, please."

Ben studied her for a moment, then gave her an almost apologetic smile. "The windows are locked. Just so you don't try and do something foolish, like leap out of a speeding train."

Which was exactly what she'd planned to do. She had to think of something unexpected. And she'd count on Josh's promise to not let them take her away.

But Josh was heading out to herd cattle. And Zane was with him. Michelle was working on her inventions. Tilda had no idea how long she'd spend doing that. Would Gretel think anything of Tilda being gone when she came to the house to cook dinner? On a normal day, Tilda moved back and forth between the ranch house and the dormitory. And Ben spent a lot of time in his room.

He was right—she might not be missed for hours. Dismayed, she thought of how far away she would be by then. If this train carried extra water and coal, who could catch up with them?

Ben slid an arm behind her back. He was gentle for a kidnapper. He helped her to her feet, and she swayed. Whatever drug he'd given her was still affecting her.

He swung open the closest door to reveal an elegant bedroom. This was not how Tilda had traveled across the country before.

He stayed at her side until she lowered herself to sit on the bed. Then he stepped back, all the way out of the room, and said, "It's going to be all right, Tilda. Father is just so desperate to meet you and try to make things right. I'm sure once you meet him—and even more, when you meet Madeline—you'll realize what a dreadful mistake it would have been to stay in a backwater place like California when you can live in luxury in New York City."

"California has much warmer weather. Maybe Father could move out here. All of you could."

"But Father is in the shipping business, working out of the ports of New York, and he owns swaths of property in the wealthiest city in the world. He would never give that up to . . ." He hesitated.

"To what, Ben? To meet his daughter? To try and make up for the neglect we lived with in those early years with a woman who sounds like a drunkard? To show his love now that I've survived without it all my life? He'd never give up his comfortable life to make right what he set in motion all those years ago? That doesn't sound like any kind of love I recognize or want. Not when I have the love of Josh Hart."

But did she have it? While they'd talked of marriage, they'd certainly never spoken of love.

"You'll understand when you see his home, why it's best to bring you to him." Ben slowly swung the door shut, his gaze holding hers as the opening narrowed. "I'll be watching this door, Tilda. There is no escape." With that, the door closed, its lock giving a loud click.

Tilda turned toward the window and watched the countryside sliding past, considering what to do now. Just because she didn't want to prove herself gullible, she went to the window and tugged on the latch. It wouldn't budge. It looked to her as if a line of iron had melted along the edges of the window, sealing it shut.

The train seemed to be picking up speed with every second that passed. She sat and searched her brain for something unexpected.

Then her eyes landed on it, and she had to admit . . . he'd never expect this.

Twelve

Josh saw the caboose up ahead. A slight curve in the tracks showed six cars. Sure enough, he was gaining on them.

He felt the stamina and courage of his horse as he closed the distance between himself and the fancy train. Yet he knew a short train like this, once it reached full speed, would surely outpace him, even if he were riding a fresh horse. And his buckskin was a long way from fresh.

The thundering hooves of his horse, the smell of the coal-fired train, the clacking of the wheels, it all called out to him to hurry. Hurry. *Hurry!*

Bending low over his stallion's neck, he closed the distance even as the train picked up speed. Josh narrowed the gap, his gain slow but steady. His horse was sweating, his coat lathered.

Josh gave all he had to urge the horse forward.

And then the horse's pace faltered, and he realized he was losing ground. He was within ten yards of the train, but he wasn't going to make it. He'd kill his horse trying.

Then the horse stumbled, and Josh stayed in the saddle

only because of experience and his having a firm grip on the reins.

The train pulled away.

"No!"

The horse was pulling up. Maybe lame. Maybe just exhausted. His mind frantic, Josh watched as the train left him behind.

Suddenly a window exploded. A chair flew out onto the ground, and right after that, a body.

A woman's body.

Tilda!

Josh fast-trotted his horse over to her. He swung down and dropped to his knees beside her still form. Then he rolled her onto her back just as the wheels of the train squealed. Thankfully, the train was well away from them.

"Tilda, are you all right?" Josh was afraid to move her, yet he was afraid *not* to.

"Josh?"

"Yes, it's me. Can you move?"

"I'm fine, I think. Just dazed mostly." Her words were slurred but coherent. "I had to get out before we were going full speed. I couldn't let Ben take me away from you."

The words wrenched his heart. She looked battered. The land was soft here, thick with grass, but she could have broken her neck. She was conscious and talking, which was good. He ran his hands quickly down her legs and arms. Slowly, she got up on her hands and knees, and he stood and helped her to her feet. In the distance, the train slowed.

Sweeping her into his arms, he looked around and saw an outcropping of rocks on a nearby hillside. His horse wasn't up to carrying double, nor even single most likely, so he took the horse's reins and hurried with Tilda toward that nearest pile of boulders.

The train, now slowed to a stop, began to back up.

"There's more than just Ben on that train." Tilda sounded more like herself now. "He had a man with him at the ranch house. There must be an engineer and a stoker, probably someone in the caboose."

He studied her as they rushed toward shelter. Her dress was torn, one arm scraped raw. "We'll take shelter behind those boulders"—he pointed up ahead—"and anyone who wants you is going to have to go through my bullets." Josh figured he had a hundred feet or so to cover before the train got back close enough for Ben and his outfit to step off.

He picked up the pace.

"You smashed out a window!" He kissed her on the forehead without slowing one bit.

"I wedged something under the door in case it took me several hard whacks to break the window."

"You could have died from the fall, Tilda." He kissed her again just as the train drew even with him. "Will they shoot? Is Ben a killer?"

"I don't know. Even when I woke up, he—"

"Woke up? He knocked you out? He hit you?"

They ducked behind the nearest boulder just as a shout came from the direction of the trail leading back to town. He looked toward the shout, afraid Ben had more men working for him, riding after him from town.

His heart leapt, and he almost shouted out loud when Zane charged down the road that ran alongside the tracks. His big brother and ten more men! The train's wheels squealed to a stop, and then the engine began chugging forward again. They must've spotted the men coming to the rescue.

"No, he didn't hit me," answered Tilda. "He used something to drug me, to put me to sleep." Tilda shook her head as if to clear it. "My brain feels a bit fuzzy still."

The train had picked up speed and was well away before Zane and his crew got close enough to jump aboard and drag every man off and beat them into the ground.

Josh had never loved his bossy big brother more.

Watching the train as it grew smaller in the distance, he saw Ben poke his head out the broken window. The man looked furious.

"This isn't over, Tilda!" he yelled.

Josh was sure Ben had intended to come after him and Tilda, until he saw Zane. No, this wasn't over.

When Zane drew closer, Josh stepped out from behind the rocks with Tilda in his arms. "Over here, Zane."

Zane's horse was as lathered as Josh's, their critters spent. Zane pulled up along with the cowhands who'd joined him from the Two Harts. Josh had never appreciated the loyal men they had at the ranch more than at that very moment. He walked over to meet his brother, with Tilda held tight against his chest. As he did so, Josh whispered to her, "We need to get married right away."

Not that he was at all sure that would stop Ben from trying to take her again. But it gave Josh more power to defend a wife than a fiancée.

Tilda leaned her face against Josh's chest. "Yes, we do."

She had to feel his heart speed up under her ear.

Zane rode up, then swung down from his black stallion,

Zane's favorite horse. The one he'd ridden out to check the cattle. He rushed to them. "Is she all right?"

Hoofbeats came from the direction of Dorada Rio. Josh looked up, realizing how on edge he was, expecting more trouble. It was Sheriff Stockwood along with five men, all of them riding fast. He glanced toward the train and saw it was too far away to be caught now, even with fresh horses.

Looking more closely at Tilda, he could see fresh scrapes and bruises on her face, her hair tumbled from its pins. He caught a faint whiff of something medicinal and wondered if she might have been drugged just as she'd said. Crouching down, he laid her on the thick grass alongside the road.

"Are you sure you're okay?" he asked.

"Y-yes. I think so." Tilda touched her scratched-up face with her fingertips. Moving her arm made her wince in pain. "I'm battered from the fall, but I don't think it's serious."

"What fall?" Zane said as he approached.

"She smashed out a window on the train and jumped out." Josh dropped to his knees beside her and pressed his lips to her forehead.

"I believe Ben drugged me." Her forehead furrowed, and she hesitated. "That was his family's private train. He said he was sorry, but he was taking me to see my father. He was done waiting. He'd been planning . . ." She stopped and shook her head. "I'm not sure. I think a man snuck into your house, Josh. He was there when I woke up on the ride to Dorada Rio, where Ben drugged me again. I woke up on the train, which was already moving. He stuck me in a private bedroom and locked the door. There was a small table and one chair. I wedged the table under the doorknob.

I grabbed the chair and broke the window he'd had sealed shut. Then I jumped."

Zane gasped quietly. "Gretel told me you'd been taken by Ben."

"You saved yourself, Tilda. You're a strong, brave woman." Only fear she might have injuries kept Josh from hugging her close. He needed to be very gentle with her.

Yet she held him tight, even though her arm hurt. "But when I saved myself, you were there. Thank you, Josh."

He nodded and smiled, then held her closer still.

The sheriff rode up then, and Tilda had to share the whole story again, this time coming up with a few more details under the sheriff's questioning.

"We need to get you to town." Josh rose with Tilda in his arms. "I'll carry you on my horse, but the poor critter is about spent. We'll need to take it slow."

Zane said, "That might be for the best anyway. We don't want to shake her up a bunch."

"Did you send a wire?"

"Yes, I left Shad in town with orders. Mrs. Lewis was shouting and waving us after the train, hollering about sending a wire ahead, all without giving us time to stop. She said she'd already started turning the town upside down looking for the sheriff, and she'd send him after us as soon as he could be found."

"Someone saw a herd of deer west of town. I went out with several men hunting. Sorry I was slow in getting here."

Zane clapped him on the shoulder. "Well, you came fast once they found you, and we appreciate it."

Josh looked down and saw Tilda had closed her eyes. He hoped she was just weary from all the morning's madness. "We need to get her to the doctor. She said she'd been drugged. It might still be affecting her, not to mention the fall from the train. It's a miracle she's even alive."

Josh mounted up, and they started for town. "They'll stop Ben Cabril in Sacramento. We'll teach him you don't put your hands on a woman like he did. Not out west."

But despite taking the time to tend Tilda in town, and a bit more time to go over everything with the sheriff again, no word came from Sacramento that Ben's fancy private train had been stopped. Sheriff Stockwood said he'd wire again and get to the bottom of what happened.

Josh and Zane had been asked to stay out of the examination room while she was with the doctor, which gave the brothers a few minutes to talk.

"I think Tilda and I should get married," Josh said.

"You would have left her alone in the house whether you were married or not. So don't go beating yourself up feeling guilty. But I agree, you ought to marry her now and not wait. She adds a lot to the family."

Josh was sure she'd add a lot to his life, too.

He waited until they were allowed into the doctor's office, then Josh convinced Zane to give him a few moments alone with the woman he wanted to spend the rest of his life with.

"Let's go get this wedding over with." Josh hovered over her as she sat up on the examination table. He took her arm and helped her to her feet.

Tilda wasn't a woman with a lot of fanciful dreams. What's more, she'd never expected to marry. Her mission in life, a calling from God, was to help the orphans. Back when she was an orphan, she'd never been helped—which was why she wanted to be there for these orphans, now, as a grown woman.

She'd expected to dedicate her life to that mission. No husband, no children of her own, just a life of service.

With all that being said, it seemed like Josh's suggestion that they "get the wedding over with" was given by a lunkhead.

On the other hand, she wanted to get this wedding over with, too. She wasn't sure why, but right now, marrying Josh felt like she was rushing toward base in a game of tag.

She'd be safe if she and Josh could just reach a parson.

Because that didn't really stack up to any form of common sense, she didn't examine it too closely. Honestly, a man who'd kidnap a single woman would kidnap a married woman, wouldn't he? Shaking away these fretful thoughts, she went along with her soon-to-be husband with a willingness that she knew was about more than just safety.

She really wanted to marry him, and so, feeling a bit unsteady, with Josh holding on to her, surrounded by Zane and his cowhands and the sheriff—who still wanted to question her further—they made their way to the church.

It wasn't exactly a normal wedding. No white dress and posies, no organ music and bridesmaids. Instead, she had ten or so heavily armed men as her only guests, and her dress was torn, her face barely done bleeding, and her hair a mess. But again, she had no dreams of a proper wedding, so all this was fine with her.

Parson Lewis had heard what was going on from his frantic yet valiant wife. He performed the service with a solemn expression, Mrs. Lewis standing at Tilda's side, so Tilda counted her as a bridesmaid. The second the vows were finished, Mrs. Lewis told everyone she'd sent a telegraph to Sacramento to stop the train. Ben might well be in custody by now.

Moments later, the telegraph operator ran into the church waving a piece of paper. "That private train roared right through the station. The sheriff there was ready to arrest everyone on the train, but it kept going."

"I thought a train could go only fifteen miles or so without having to reload its water supply." Josh stormed straight for the telegraph operator, towing Tilda along. He snatched the paper out of the man's hand and read it.

That's when Tilda remembered something Ben had told her earlier. "His train has two water tanks," she said.

Josh frowned. "How do you know that if you were unconscious when you boarded?"

She patted him on the arm. "Ben boasted about it. He said they were set to go far and fast. I'm not sure how far, though."

The sheriff turned to the telegraph operator. "Let's send another wire farther on down the line. That train has to stop sometime."

As the operator stormed out of the church at a near run, the sheriff turned back to Tilda. "I wonder what else I should be asking?"

"I was groggy, Sheriff. If you ask the right questions, something might come to me." She shrugged apologetically.

The sheriff nodded. "I'll give you a day or so to rest, Mrs. Hart. While you're doing that, we'll round up this sidewinder and the men working for him. I'm even going to arrest that train engineer. They were all in on it."

He spun away and rushed out.

Tilda leaned hard on Josh, and he wrapped his arms around her.

"Let's go home." Josh swept her up in his arms and headed for the door. They were galloping toward the Two Harts within minutes.

This time on Josh's horse, Tilda felt as safe as a babe in his arms, and she fell asleep there in her new husband's embrace.

Thirteen

The sun was dropping low in the sky by the time they reached home. And oh was there ever a fuss.

Gretel nearly collapsed with relief when they returned with Tilda.

They'd known Tilda had been found, thanks to Zane wiring the house, but everyone was almost frantic to see her.

Well, frantic in a very sensible, tough western way.

Michelle led her away to the shower bath in the back room, and an hour later, Tilda emerged in a dress Josh didn't recall seeing before. It wasn't a perfect fit but good enough. Bright red with ruffles and lace. While Josh suspected it might be an old one of Michelle's, who was taller than Tilda, someone had shortened the hem to the right length.

Tilda's damp hair was pulled back and was held only with a ribbon.

Josh went to her side and guided her to the kitchen table, holding her arm as she sat down to a piping hot meal. While he could tell Tilda was on the brink of collapse, not having eaten since breakfast, she did full justice to the chicken noodle soup. He hadn't eaten since then either, but he hadn't been drugged and then later thrown himself out of a moving train.

All the while they ate, the family surrounding them, Zane and Josh talked about the rescue and how Tilda had saved herself, and what a relief it had been when Zane had come before the train's kidnappers got out to fight to get her back.

Finally, Josh escaped with his wife, determined to see that she got plenty of rest. They strolled along in the moonlight. They were being given their own home for the night. The deserted doctor's office.

Gretel had gathered a few people to clean and dust and put new sheets on the bed, even though it was already perfectly clean. She'd whispered to Josh that she'd included a bit of food in the larder in case they wanted to make their own breakfast in the morning.

Michelle had told Tilda she wouldn't be expected to get to school on time. Which Josh took to mean she'd be expected to get to school at some point.

Josh was tempted to kidnap his wife himself and run for the train. They should get a honeymoon. They ought to spend a week in San Francisco.

But that would have to wait. At least for now, he wanted to keep Tilda on the ranch until word reached them that her brother had been arrested.

For a moment, Josh wondered if Tilda's father might show up. Apparently, Ben had suggested such a thing could happen.

"Getting married to you was the best idea I've ever had." Josh smiled down at her. The summer days were long, but they'd worn this one all the way out. "I'm worried, though, that we haven't heard yet about Ben's arrest."

Tilda's hand tightened on Josh's elbow. "C-can we talk about something else? I want to think of being married, not of having a criminal brother somewhere on the loose, or a mysterious father who wants to meet me." She looked sideways at him. "Do you think he really is my brother? Do you think I have a father and a twin sister? Was it all lies? And if it was, then what was Ben here for?"

Josh kissed her under the stars. "I'd like to think about being married, too." Josh opened the door to the doctor's office and guided Tilda through the waiting room, through the examination room, and upstairs. Oh yes. He wanted badly to think about being married to Tilda. But not tonight. Not when she'd had such a hard day.

They reached the sitting room with Brody's kitchen table and cookstove, and he guided her straight though that to the bedroom. His knees were so wobbly, he was afraid that if he stopped, he might not get started again. Two satchels sat on the bed.

Zane had told Josh he'd send over whatever they might need. Zane had packed for Josh, and Michelle had packed for Tilda—which couldn't have been hard, he thought, since Tilda only owned one dress besides the one she'd tore up on her escape from the train, and now this one that Michelle must've given her. Josh went to the nearest satchel, opened it, and pulled out a long, white nightgown. This one had to be for Tilda.

Tilda snatched it out of his hand. He smiled and picked up the other satchel. "I'll let you get ready for bed. I'll do the same in the next room. And, Tilda, we're just going to sleep tonight. You've had a terrible day. You took a beating when you jumped out of that train. It was so brave. I'm honored that you agreed to marry me, but tonight we're going to rest. I want you to be pain-free before we turn our minds to more . . . married things."

Tilda, with a nightgown that had felt to Josh like silk, came to him and reached up to kiss him. "Thank you, Josh. I'm exhausted and feeling battered. But I do want to sleep beside you tonight. I'd prefer a few minutes alone to change, thank you." She looked perfect in the moonlight shining through the window.

He kissed her back and found a fire alive and burning inside him—one he battled down, even though the embers remained. He said, "I won't be long."

He left the room and went across the narrow hallway to the second bedroom, where Thayne and Lock had lived since Brody had found them. They were staying in the ranch house while he was traveling, but this was the MacKenzies' home.

Josh opened his own satchel and froze when he found a nightshirt inside. He usually wore his longhandles, so this seemed wrong to him, but maybe it was what married men wore? He had no idea. He changed into it so fast he hesitated to go back to the other room. Surely Tilda needed more time than he'd given her.

He stood still, though it was quite a fight to make himself do that. He pictured himself being roped and hog-tied to keep from running back to her.

At last he left the second bedroom and knocked gently on the door to where he'd left his wife.

"Come in."

He cracked the door open and saw her standing there, her hair down, the long, dark curls reaching nearly to her waist. She was looking him in the eyes.

His heart, pounding like mad, slowed a bit as he realized she'd changed fast, too. Whether in eagerness to have him return, or terror that he'd come before she was modestly covered, he wasn't sure.

She reached to swing the door wide and smiled, and he decided then it was the former.

———⋄———

Tilda woke up with a husband. So strange that her whole life had changed in the course of a few days.

She'd gone from orphan to sister, daughter, and wife. She was also a sister-in-law, and an aunt now to Caroline. She was such a sweet, quiet little girl, Tilda sometimes forgot she was even there while trying to keep up with the MacKenzie boys and their antics.

Though she'd married quickly, deep in her heart she thanked God for Josh's idea. She couldn't help but be delighted that, after a whole life without much connection to anyone, including her adoptive parents, she finally belonged.

Her head was resting on Josh's strong shoulder, her hand flat on his chest. She felt the steadiness of his heartbeat and lay still, not wanting to wake him up. It was light in the bedroom, but it felt early. While the school didn't get going so early, the ranch did. She heard the faint jingle of a bridle and the quiet clopping of hooves below just outside their window.

Then, with her hand spread wide on Josh's broad chest, she felt the beats speed up, along with his rate of breathing. Fighting a smile, she realized her husband was awake.

She lifted her head and looked at him. Every move hurt.

"Good morning, Mrs. Hart." Then his smile turned gentle. "How bad is it?"

"I'm sore, bruised, and scraped up, but nothing more serious than that."

He ran one of his big, callused hands over her hair. She felt the tangles and wished she'd taken a moment to tidy up. But she saw nothing but admiration in his eyes.

She stretched up to kiss him. "I do like the sound of 'Mrs. Hart.' Thank you for marrying me, Josh. I'm going to be the best wife you've ever imagined."

"Thank you for marrying me, Tilda. You're doing a terrific job of being a wife so far. I have no doubt you'll be excellent." The teasing smile faded, replaced by a look of sincerity. "I will try to make sure you never regret agreeing to marry me. I'm going to treat you like . . . well, like I've found my very own treasure. This is a better treasure than any gold that's been lost in those mountains."

This time he kissed her, and she kissed him right back.

"I looked at the basket that was sent over from the house. Eggs and coffee. Biscuits, butter, and jelly. We'll have a feast."

"That sounds like a wonderful way to start our marriage. I can cook too, you know. We'll make the breakfast together."

Then he kissed her one more time, and she didn't cover a wince.

He pulled away and said, "Let me start the meal. You can lie here a bit longer or at least take your time getting dressed."

"No, I want to be with you. No extra rest is better than working beside you making breakfast."

"Are you really all right?"

"Honestly, that private car was so beautiful. It had to be the most luxurious kidnapping in the history of the world."

Josh managed a smile, but his eyes studied her closely. He

ran a finger down her cheek. "You're scraped here. What else hurts?"

"I've stiffened up overnight. Most everything hurts, but it's just bumps and bruises." She pressed both hands on his chest, and he nodded, then rolled aside and stood. He gave his feet a strange look.

"What is it?"

"I'm wearing a nightshirt. Never before in my life have I worn such a garment."

Tilda chuckled and had to admit that hurt a little.

"Are you going to be all right? I can stay and help you dress."

Tilda felt her face heat up at the very idea. "I'll be fine."

"I'll change in the other bedroom, then."

As soon as he left the room, she threw off the covers and leapt out of the bed. Well, leapt in her mind. In her body, it was more of an aching lurch. But she kept moving because she didn't want to be apart from her new husband.

Josh hated every moment he was separated from his new wife.

He knew there was more to being married than what had passed between him and Tilda . . . a lot more. But it had still been the best night of his life.

He dressed with lightning speed, which was stupid because she was no doubt hurting and moving really slow. But all he could think of was to get her back by his side.

He emerged from the second bedroom and saw her door was still closed. He went to it and knocked.

"Just a few more minutes, please." Her voice squeaked a bit, like she was afraid he'd come barging in.

"I'm going to start breakfast. If you need anything . . . I could help tie your shoes or button up the back of your dress or brush your hair. Just call out."

While he stood there, trying to think of anything else she might need, the door opened so just one eye showed.

"My dress buttoned up the front, so I managed that. But the rest, my shoes and my hair, I would appreciate help with that. The whole left side of my body hurts. I must have landed on it. My shoulder, my hip, my head and feet and everything in between."

"Come out and sit down. I'll get your shoes and a comb."

She swung the door wide and held up shoes, stockings, a comb, and a ribbon. It appeared she was going to ask before he offered. For some reason, as a man who prided himself on never admitting he needed much help, that warmed his heart.

He had her all tidied up before much time had passed. "I don't know how to put up your hair, so I just pulled it back and tied a sailor's half-hitch knot."

"A what?"

"I considered a bowline, then decided this would be better."

She turned and smiled. "I've had my hair done by a man who tied knots for a living. Thank you."

"I've got the coffee brewing, and the pan's heating up for eggs. We'll add biscuits and jelly, and that'll be breakfast. So it's as good as done—you may as well sit still while I finish the meal."

As Josh walked back toward the cookstove, he stopped and bent over. "What's this?" He held up a piece of paper, then chuckled. "It's a note from Michelle. She says arrangements have been made so that you can have the day off. She invited us for the noon meal and supper, but said they'd send food over if we wanted to be alone here."

"I'd be hard-pressed to teach class today. But we could join them for meals later."

Nodding, Josh went to the stove and got to cooking.

Fourteen

A hand slammed against the door to their room.

Josh hollered, "If this is a medical emergency, I can't help."

"Josh, Tilda, come to the ranch house. Ellie and Brody are back." Zane hadn't given them until the noon meal, not even close, though breakfast was done and cleared away. "They've brought Cord and Mayhew Westbrook with them—and a treasure map."

Tilda flinched at the news, then flinched as if from pain. "Come in."

Zane shoved the door open and stuck his head in. His eyes went to Tilda. "How are you this morning? Are you up to coming over? The boys have gone crazy with excitement and are fighting with Brody right now about saddling horses. But Brody still isn't feeling all that well. We've got to calm them down."

Josh gave Tilda a worried frown. "I'd leave you to rest, except I'm not leaving you alone ever again. Not for one minute." Which reminded him. "Have you heard from the sheriff? Did they arrest Ben?"

"I haven't heard from him this morning yet, no."

"They should have caught him by now. I wonder what's going on."

Zane shook his head. "Come over if you're able."

A ruckus downstairs, including begging from Lock and a lot of footsteps, said the party was soon going to be here.

Zane stepped out of the way fast or he'd've been run down.

Josh gave Ellie a hug. Brody, still a little wobbly, got a handshake. "Welcome back."

"You got married, Josh?" Ellie smiled, then turned to hug Tilda.

"Be gentle with her. She jumped out of a moving train yesterday."

Ellie grimaced. "Ouch."

"I hurt, but I'm all right."

Brody sat down, not looking as sturdy as Tilda.

Josh said, "We stayed here last night, but we'll clear out now that you're back."

"We need to study this map." Lock held a paper in his hands that couldn't have been the map. It was white and crisp-looking.

Two other men came in. Josh recognized Cord Westbrook.

"This is my grandfather, Mayhew Westbrook. We found the map under the inside cover of a book Brody's grandpa mailed him years ago."

"I recopied it," Cord said. "Brody suggested it because the original one was crumbling."

Josh studied the map. "It has the same strange writing as your grandfather had, with the little pictures. And right here, at the edge of the paper, that must be where your map ended."

Tilda knew what they were after. "You think this map will lead you to the lost treasure of a group of Spanish conquistadors?"

Her voice trembled, and her eyes took on a look that some might call "gold fever." Josh sure hoped not.

"Can you imagine the history contained in this?"

At Tilda's obvious interest, Brody slid the old journal across the table to her. She stared at the Cross of Burgundy insignia. Then Cord slid the smaller notebook Graham MacKenzie had mailed so long ago to his grandfather. She lifted it, focusing on the same insignia.

While they were handing things to her, Ellie produced a single gold doubloon.

Tilda gasped. "This coin is over three hundred years old. It's worth a fortune. Far more than its weight in gold."

Zane said, "Michelle knows someone deeply involved in studying California's history with an eye toward creating a museum. He has to see the doubloons, of course, but he said they'd be very valuable and there are collectors of such things who will pay dearly for them."

"We've got to go." Lock pulled a matching coin out of his pocket and held it in front of his eyes, transfixed. "We have fourteen of these coins. Who knows how many more there might be."

Brody said, "We'll go soon, boys, but my ribs are still so sore, every move hurts."

"Can I go?" Tilda asked fervently. "I make no claim on any of it, but I would love to see what else is there, I mean beyond the coins. Are there more notebooks?"

"When we found Grandpa's remains, he had an old knife

on him. I suspect he brought everything with him, at least all he could carry. I don't expect to find more gold, though."

Lock howled in protest. "No, Brody, don't say that. You'll bring us bad luck. We think there's an entire pirate's chest of gold."

"Captain Cabrillo wasn't a pirate, Lock. He was a sailor. The captain of a ship that sailed north from Mexico, exploring the coast of California. Any men who sailed with him would have been sailors like your uncle Josh, not pirates. I see no reason they'd have pirate booty with them, but they might well have *artifacts*."

"Are those like treasure? Are artifacts made of gold?"

His wife didn't have gold fever; she had artifact fever. Which might be its own kind of trouble. But Lock for sure had a bad case of this madness.

"Lock, my saying something about treasure will *not* bring us bad luck." Brody sounded both exhausted and perturbed. "For heaven's sake, brother, where's the logic in that? Saying the wrong word now won't affect what happened three hundred years ago or change what was left there. Or go back thirty years; nothing now can change what Grandpa found back then. You can't believe that."

Lock clamped his mouth shut, but he looked mutinous.

Thayne said, "Brody, we want to follow that map. It's been two weeks since you got hurt. You're walking around. You must be well enough by now."

Had it been that long? Josh had lost track. He'd been busy finding a wife, fending off her mysterious visitor, and getting married.

Brody sighed and looked at Ellie as if he were actually considering it.

She shook her head at him. "Absolutely not, Brody, not until your ribs heal." She turned to direct her gaze at Lock. "Two weeks may be enough for cracked ribs, but your brother's ribs were broken. And his head still aches terribly."

Josh's head still hurt as well, and Brody had been slammed into a rock wall by the force of a bullet. Of course, Josh had been cracked over the head with a gun butt . . . twice. Josh watched Ellie move until she stood behind Brody, where she gently wrapped her arms around his neck.

"I didn't know you were hurt that bad, Brody." Josh knew he was battered, but this seemed more serious. "Did you go to a doctor in Sacramento?"

"I had my own personal physician look at him." Mayhew Westbrook spoke up for the first time. He shook his head, scowling at Brody and Ellie. "But these two didn't take his advice."

The frown lines in Westbrook's aged face fell right into place with that scowl. Josh suspected the man had spent most of his life with that exact expression.

"He wanted to *bleed me*. The old man still believes in the four humors theory of medicine!"

Cord had been quiet most of the time. Now he lowered his head and seemed to be coughing into his hand . . . or covering a laugh.

"Oh, good heavens." Tilda brought a hand to her throat. "That dates back to ancient Greece."

"Remember how I told you about having to swear the Hippocratic oath?" Brody glanced over his shoulder at Ellie.

"That's bad, Brody," Thayne said. "I'm thinking of becoming a doctor, but I'm not gonna start swearing. And it's best not to be a hypocrite either."

"Hippocrates," Tilda the historian said, forging onward, "who lived four hundred years *before* Jesus was born, was one of the fathers of medicine. But much has been learned since he applied the theory of the four humors to medicine. And one of the things we've learned is that bleeding people is—" she shrugged—"well, bad."

"My doctor is the finest in California," Mayhew sniffed.

"Oh, he is not." Brody rolled his eyes. "The old coot would have used leeches on me if I'd've let him. *I'm* better than him. *Michelle* is better than him, and I've never seen Michelle do one second of doctoring. Even Josh's *horse* is a better doctor than him. The four humors fell out of favor before the Civil War. You're lucky to be alive, Mayhew."

"Can we please get back to the map?" Lock was practically bouncing.

Josh had to give the kid credit. He kept the ship sailing dead ahead. Josh had a plan spring to life right then. "Brody, would you be okay with being left behind?" he asked.

"The boys shouldn't go out there alone."

"I'm not a boy." Thayne crossed his arms defiantly. "I had friends in New York City who were married already."

Brody gave Thayne a startled look, then shook his head. "I do want to help bring Grandpa home from that cave we found him in. But I'm not up to it right now. Of course, we could do that later. I suppose I could sit out this part of the treasure hunt."

Josh nodded. "I think it'd be a good idea to get Tilda out of here for a while."

Tilda leaned her head on her husband, who stood right beside where she sat. "Where do you want to go?"

"I have been wrangling around in my head that we need

to post a guard or do something to protect you, even if we stay here. Even if Ben has been arrested, someone was with him when he was here. And he was writing someone all the time . . . or at least he said he was. I'm not sure about your safety. If Brody isn't up to a treasure hunt right now, maybe you and I could go with Thayne and Lock." Josh looked around. "Cord too." He looked down at Tilda. "Would you be interested in coming along?"

She gave a brief nod. "I'm up for it as long as you're there."

"I'd hoped to come." Mayhew had that scowl again.

"It's rugged, sir. It's all horseback riding. And we'd be on the trail, sleeping on the ground, eating over a campfire for days. If you think you're up to it—"

Mayhew waved Josh's words away. "I haven't done much horseback riding for years. And I've got a touch of gout in my left knee."

"I suspect you have arthritis, Mayhew." Brody sounded kinder, more his usual doctor demeanor.

"You really think you could help me?" asked Mayhew.

"Yes, I can probably help you feel some better. There's treatment for gout, too."

Mayhew met Brody's eyes. Somewhat sheepishly, Mayhew said, "Before the Civil War? Really?"

Brody nodded. "Don't ever let anyone bleed you. And encourage your doctor to retire or take on a younger partner." Brody clamped his mouth shut, and Josh remembered that Brody had a partnership of his own to return to in Boston.

Josh was going to miss his sister terribly. But Brody said he'd given his word he'd honor the partnership agreement he'd made. He'd borrowed money on that promise. The man could be paid back, of course. But the doctor didn't need money; he needed help. And Brody refused to go back on his word.

Brody looked back at Ellie again. "What do you say? The search for that treasure is . . . well, it's been interesting, fun at times. Gunshots notwithstanding. I guess you could go. I'd miss you, but—"

"Brody, we'd bring everything we find back here." Lock saw his opportunity and jumped on it. "It'll probably take more than one trip. We've searched twice already. If you miss this hunt, you could go on the next one."

Josh could almost see the frantic thinking going on in Lock's head.

"We're wearing down the summer," said Josh. "It can get chilly at the higher elevations. Bone-chilling cold in the wintertime. Remember how cold it was the time we chased after you, right after Brody got here? And the next time, we ended up not going straight for Big Windy Mountain with our half of the map, so we weren't up as high. But who can be sure where the next half of the map will lead? And who can be sure we'll find it on the next trip? I think we'd better go now—before winter closes in on us."

Brody was looking at Ellie, who said, "I'm not going anywhere without you, Brody." She leaned down and kissed his cheek. "Instead, let's have Josh and Tilda go with Cord and the boys."

"You should stay, Doc," Zane interjected. He'd pretty much hung back listening until now. "Michelle's time is close. I'd like to have a doctor near to hand."

Brody nodded. "If you wait for me, it'll be at least another week. Maybe two or three before I can ride a horse any distance. The ride out here from town about killed me."

Ellie's arms tightened around his neck, and she whispered something into his ear. He patted her arm.

"We'll stay behind, then." Brody turned to Josh. "You and Tilda lead this crew. Find that treasure and bring it back for all of us to see. But don't bring Grandpa's remains back just yet. I'd like to be there when we move him."

Nodding, Josh said to Tilda, "I'm glad you're up for it. I'm dead serious about not letting you out of my sight, not even if you're surrounded by people. Let's pack some things, then start saddling the horses." Josh looked at the man he'd just met. "Cord, did you bring your own horse or rent one from town?"

"We rented them."

"I had one of the men take those horses back to town," Zane said. "And I asked him to check with the sheriff about arresting Ben the kidnapper. I wonder if he is Tilda's brother, or if that's even his real name. And I wonder if your father is really alive and if that picture is of your twin sister, or if he hired someone to use that tintype of you to paint up a fancy 'twin' picture."

Josh hadn't thought of half of that. But the portrait had Tilda's hair and eye colors exactly right. They couldn't have known that from a black-and-white tintype.

Mayhew Westbrook said, "We also need to look for information concerning Graham MacKenzie's land . . . or maybe it's a mining claim. We could search at the land offices around here, find the exact location of that claim. He must've registered a claim on the spot where he found the treasure."

Josh jerked his head up. "Why didn't you say that before? We don't need to go haring off after this map if we've got the exact location of his claim."

"Josh, we have to go." Lock looked as if Josh were trying to pry the gold right out of his hands. "We already found where Grandpa died. Who knows what else we'll find following the map. He may have left gold at every landmark along the way."

Zane nodded. "Lock's right. You need to follow the map."

Mayhew said, "Brody, after you rest up, maybe you and I and Mrs. Hart can go searching for paperwork."

Brody quietly groaned. "We'll see."

"Boys," Josh said, "come and help Tilda and me saddle up."

"I'm not a boy anymore," Thayne insisted again.

Which Josh had to admit was true. He'd left for the sea when he was seventeen, and Thayne was sixteen now.

"Fair enough, *men*," Josh laughed. "And you know how to pack a bedroll and saddle a horse. So let's get moving. We've been waiting for that map, and now we've got it."

Lock shouted with joy and went thundering down the stairs and out of the building. Thayne wasn't far behind him.

Adults in some ways, but not in others.

Josh took Tilda's hand. "Are you sure you're up to this?"

"I think getting away from the ranch right now is a good idea. I can ride."

Josh nodded and led her out of the room. Cord came along.

Brody was right. The treasure hunt so far had been fun, despite the beating they'd taken.

Zane came along. "When I sent those rented horses back to town, I asked the men to hunt up Sheriff Stockwood. By the time we've packed food and saddled up, they'll be back."

Fifteen

Tilda had been moving as fast as her aching muscles would allow, Josh right by her side as they packed up food from the ranch house kitchen. Cord was with them, following orders.

Shad Donovan, the foreman of the Two Harts and a grizzled old-timer, brought back a report that made Tilda pack with double speed.

"They must've cut the telegraph wires, Josh. That train went through Sacramento without stopping, and by the time they wired on ahead, the whole line was down. The sheriff thinks they cut them. The lawmen in Sacramento rode out to see why no telegraphs were coming in and found the wire down. They rode on to the next town thinking they could get past the break and send the wire on, but it was down again."

Shaking his head, Shad said, "Folks in the next town said the train had come in and refilled its water tanks and loaded coal into the tender car, then it had gone on. Someone even noticed a broken window. It's an unusually short and real fine-looking train, so it stood out to folks as noteworthy."

Josh dragged his hat off his head and whacked his leg. "Those coyotes might do that all along the rail line, or at least until they're out of California. Once California is behind them, no one will take the word of a small-town sheriff over a rich man like Ben. And they use that telegraph wire to warn towns down the line that a train's heading toward them; they use that information to get trains off the rails in the towns with sidetracks. His selfish run for New York City could get people killed. He could get himself killed, too."

Tilda grabbed his hat from out of his hands. "Stop beating on your hat."

Josh had nearly battered it to death.

"Well, at least this means he's headed back east."

"Unless someone got off that train and is coming back here. If they had more men than just Ben and the one varmint you saw . . . there could be trouble."

Shad tugged on his own Stetson. "I'm going to recommend we be suspicious of strangers for a time."

"Some guard dogs around this place would be a good idea, too," said Josh.

"I'll ask Annie about that, Boss," Shad offered. "She talks to more folks than the rest of us, it seems."

Tilda saw Josh straighten a bit when Shad called him Boss. Josh seemed to like being called that. Tilda had heard several of the men call Zane their boss. She wondered if her husband had more of a fight on his hands than she realized in finding his place here on the family ranch.

"Will you be needing backup on this trail ride you're going on?" Shad asked.

Josh gave Tilda a long, considering look before turning back to Shad. "You're busy moving the herds to get ready for the fall cattle drive. We'll be all right."

"I'll pass the word on about the telegraph wires being

down. The damage is all north of Sacramento, so we should still be connected to Dorada Rio and on south. I'm sure they're working on repairs, but that private train will likely stay ahead of them." With that, Shad tipped his hat and left.

Once Tilda finished packing the saddlebags with hardtack and beef jerky, she handed them to Cord and said, "I'm ready."

Annie came into the kitchen with Caroline. "I asked Jessica to take my class. She's becoming so dependable, I . . ." Annie stopped talking, her eyes landing on Cord. "Um, who are you?"

Tilda thought that sounded rude, and she'd never heard Annie be other than perfectly mannered.

"Cord Westbrook. I came back with Brody and Ellie, along with my grandfather. I guess he'll be staying here with you while I ride off with Josh and Tilda. But if someone would lend my grandpa a horse, he could ride to town and stay in the hotel. Zane returned the horses we rented."

Annie looked from him to Josh and Tilda. "I suppose he can have the housekeeper's room with you two and the boys gone. Brody and Ellie will stay in the rooms at the doctor's office. We'll figure it out. Your grandfather can stay."

Josh said to Tilda, "I think we should ask Jilly to build us our own house, Tilda."

"We don't need our own house. If this one keeps us warm in the winter and keeps the rain off our heads, I'll be more than satisfied—I'll be downright grateful."

"Something we can talk about on the long ride. We're going after the treasure," he told Annie, quickly filling her in on the telegraph wires and Ben's escape, which meant Tilda was still in danger.

Tilda watched Annie as he talked. She seemed strange, not her usual calm self.

"Are you all right, Tilda?" Annie asked.

"Parts of me ache something fierce, but I think it's just bruises and stiffness. I'm fine."

Annie sounded wistful as she said, "How come I never get to go on a treasure hunt?"

Tilda felt immediately guilty. "Do you want to go? You can get Jessica to cover the younger grades, and Lila to teach the older girls. Randal has shown some talent for teaching. He could handle the older boys, I suppose. And Caroline rides better than I do. If you really—"

"Not this time," Annie said, cutting her off. "But it does seem like you're having all the fun."

Based on what Tilda had heard so far of Brody being shot and Josh being bashed over the head twice, Tilda wasn't sure a treasure hunt was all that fun. It didn't sound much better than her own narrow escape from Ben.

"Next time, then," Josh said. "You were always good on the trail and handy with a gun."

Tilda gave Annie a surprised glance. She seemed quiet and steady, not an outdoors woman really.

Josh went on, "Maybe Michelle can babysit Caroline."

"She can't watch Caroline." Annie shuddered, then gave Cord an apologetic smile. "Don't get me wrong. Michelle is wonderful. It's just that she tends to have small explosions happen in her invention shed. It's no place for a child."

"We'll figure that all out later." Josh loaded up their third saddlebag.

Tilda wondered how long they'd be in the wilderness. Maybe she'd see a deer. Although she probably didn't have to worry about living off the land anymore.

Annie's eyes shifted, and she looked nervous. Tilda had to wonder what was going on in her head. She didn't think they had time to ask.

Josh touched Tilda gently on the back. "We're all set to go."

Nodding, Tilda followed Josh out the door with Cord following, carrying two of the saddlebags. Tilda realized she hadn't heard the man talk for a while. She didn't know him, of course. Maybe he was always this quiet. She didn't have time to ask that either. Everything was happening so fast.

No matter what, she felt surrounded, Josh beside her and Cord a pace behind. She had a husband to guard her. The thought almost startled her, and she wasn't the type to startle. She had a husband. That was an unusually pleasant thing. Josh kept especially close to her as they walked toward the corral. Five horses stood there already saddled.

"Can your buckskin stallion handle another long ride?" Tilda had seen how worn-out the horse had been just yesterday.

"I wouldn't take him if we were doing any hard riding. But he's tough, and he's had some time to rest a bit. He's a good horse, one I bought in San Francisco when I left my ship to come home. I like having him along. And the boys . . . I mean, the young men . . ."

Tilda looked sideways at him, and they grinned.

"They *are* young men now. We need to remember that. I'm just afraid I'm going to slow you down."

"They're determined to go," Josh went on, "and we need

to get you away from here. They need me with them because Brody's not up to it, and he couldn't find the trail we followed last time even if he was." He slid his hand between her shoulder blades, maybe to give her support and encouragement. Maybe to block any escape attempt. "I think those boys will give us all we can handle if we refuse to go, and I'm not leaving you here alone."

"Don't worry. This trail sounds so remote, Ben shouldn't know a thing about it." She remembered again that Brody had ended up shot on their last treasure hunt and felt a chill race up and down her spine. She wasn't a superstitious person, which probably meant being afraid was completely reasonable. That made her chill turn into a shudder.

This was Josh's fourth time going off on a treasure hunt. Each time he'd gone farther along the trail left by the map, and it had been a painstaking search because the map was so difficult to decipher. On this ride he'd gone straight to where he'd ended before, then started slowly picking his way forward.

The first time he, Ellie, and Brody had gone searching for the runaway Thayne and Lock. They'd caught up with them climbing a mountain, about half frozen, and brought them home to thaw out.

The second time, Thayne and Lock had ridden along with Ellie, Brody, and Josh. Lock and Brody had fallen over a cliff, but they had found the green pond Graham MacKenzie called "Loch Uaine"—the name of a beautiful green lake in the Scottish Highlands. Not much genius was involved in finding that lake. Josh would have avoided falling over the cliff if he'd've been in charge, and never found it.

Of course, Lock almost died, but they'd found the landmark and knew they were on the right track. Since then, they'd read the map differently and were fortunate they were able to stick to lower elevations, but no one knew where they'd end up.

The third trip they'd ridden straight to Graham's green pond and proceeded on at a snail's pace, following their half of the map. Of course, they hadn't known it was only half at the time. That's when they found the cave where Grandpa MacKenzie had died. They'd intended to spend another day hunting because they hadn't reached the end of their map. Then Loyal Kelton, Ellie's miserably *dis*loyal former fiancé, had tried to steal the map and kill Brody. This trip, Josh felt a strong need to keep up the hunt until they reached the end point of the MacKenzie map, then on through to the end point of the Westbrook map.

Today they'd ride straight to Grandpa MacKenzie's final resting place and ride on from there. Josh, once he knew where he was going, found a much easier trail to ride directly there. They'd press on to the end of their map and the beginning of the map Grandpa MacKenzie had sent to Mayhew Westbrook.

Josh looked at Tilda riding beside him and reached for her. "You let me know when you need a rest."

"I will, but so far I'm fine." She caught his hand and smiled.

He studied her face for signs of pain or exhaustion. She still had scrapes on her cheek, but she looked sturdy and interested in the treasure hunt.

Josh had never ridden a horse and held someone's hand before.

"The first day on a trail ride can put a lot of aches and pains in your body. And you've already taken a beating."

"I'll let you know. So far I think moving and the fresh air are making me feel better."

He suspected she'd feel different by the end of the day. He planned to watch over his brand-new wife.

The MacKenzie brothers were paired up behind him, Cord bringing up the rear. He rode as if he'd spent time regularly in a saddle, so beyond glancing back every so often, Josh didn't worry about him overly.

Later, as the trail widened, Cord came up beside the MacKenzies. Josh heard them talking quietly, Thayne and Loch no doubt filling Cord in on all that had happened.

Josh hoped their love of the treasure didn't make the stories too fanciful. Yet he heard enough to know Brody and Ellie had told Cord a lot, so the man was getting a fair version. Josh even filled in gaps in the story, with Tilda occasionally adding tidbits of historical background.

They reached Grandpa MacKenzie's cave within half a day. But since it had taken them about three days over two trips to get this far before, Josh felt encouraged by that.

Josh looked at Tilda, then at Cord. "Graham MacKenzie died in that cave. That's where we found Mayhew's name and the gold coins. There was writing left by Graham with a few notes that must've been part of what he'd found because they were much older and in Spanish. Michelle is still translating them, but we decided, their historical value aside, they don't explain where they're located. Graham's notes tell us that. So we didn't wait for her to finish. Do you boys want to go in and pay respects to your grandpa again?"

"I think we should keep moving, Uncle Josh." Thayne sounded mature and reasonable. But the kid wanted to hunt treasure, not spend a moment of silence over the grandpa he'd never met.

"Tilda? Cord? I don't think we missed anything important last time." Josh looked between the two.

"We heard Brody ask to visit his grandpa here." Tilda looked solemnly at the cave. "We can leave our visit for another day, for when Brody can join us."

"Okay then, let's keep moving." Cord seemed deep in thought. "So much of my grandpa's life was wasted being angry at a man dead now for thirty years. I think I'll have a word with him about laying up treasures in heaven. Again. And forgiveness. And thinking on things that are true and honest and just and pure and lovely and so on."

Josh knew that verse, for it had been one of Ma's favorites. He quoted it solemnly: "'Finally, brethren, whatsoever things are true, whatsoever things are honest, whatsoever things are just, whatsoever things are pure, whatsoever things are lovely, whatsoever things are of good report; if there be any virtue, and if there be any praise, think on these things.'"

He considered it good advice.

Tilda said quietly, "Why does that make me think of Ben?"

"Probably because he was thinking on things that are false and dishonest, unjust and impure. Oh, all sorts of reasons it made you think of him."

She gave Josh a wry smile. "I wonder if he really believes I'm his sister. Or was it all a lie? And if it was, what's the point of it? I wonder about so much." She touched the faint scar on her forehead. "If he made up that story about this scar, he's a very talented liar."

"The sheriff is looking into it. And the railroad will get the telegraph lines up and running. He can't walk away from that fancy train of his. I mean, he can, but wherever he finally parks it, folks are gonna know who owns it and be able to track him down."

Tilda met Josh's eyes. "Let's ride on."

He nodded. "What are we looking for now, Lock?" Josh dug into his saddlebags and handed out jerky and biscuits he'd packed for the journey, several days' worth.

"That arch of rocks, or some kind of arch." Lock pointed west. "It's said to be on west of here, but 'on west' is mighty vague."

"We thought it was on a . . . what did Ellie call it?" Thayne grabbed the food Josh handed back, then passed it on to Lock, who handed some to Cord. "She thought a river might've once run past this cave." Thayne studied the copy of the map.

None of them had the originals since the paper Graham had drawn them on was too brittle. But they'd replicated them. Brody had worked on the map he'd found at Mayhew's house, glued beneath the inside front cover of an old leather book Graham had mailed the man who'd loaned him money thirty years ago. Graham's map was thirty years old, but if that journal was left by someone who sailed with Captain Cabrillo, it was closer to three hundred years old. Mayhew's book was a match for the journal Graham had mailed home to New York City before he'd died.

"A dry riverbed?" Josh asked, looking around. "Over hundreds of years a river can change course. I've heard their routes can be changed by floods, earthquakes, and landslides. The ground is low here. I can imagine a river once running through here. I think we should follow this westward for a while."

As they rode on, Tilda said, "If sailors found a river that led them inland, and they sailed along it, they may have come along this very path."

"As a sailor, if I came upon a bay or got blown by a storm into one no one had ever heard of, and a river led inland . . . I might've been tempted to follow the river. I'd figure to turn around at some point, even if I had to sail alone all the way back to Mexico. I'd see myself as a great explorer. That's what Cabrillo and his men were, right? Explorers? I'd imagine being named a hero even. Especially if the land was as beautiful as California. Yep, I can see letting my sails take me onward."

"Think of the history we might find. That's where my imagination takes flight."

"Think of the gold," Lock said from behind. "Mountains of it."

Josh glanced back. The trail had narrowed, and the boys now rode two abreast with Cord following behind.

"My grandpa Westbrook has spent his life daydreaming about a mountain of gold. It seems to me dreaming of it, thinking of it being kept from him, has soured him about most of what is a wonderful life. You boys see this as an adventure, one that's fun and real interesting. But don't let it take over your life. Remember what's important. Faith and the people who love you and taking every opportunity to do good for others."

Josh looked back and saw Thayne nodding, and he noticed Lock roll his eyes.

Josh said a prayer for the boy with his wild desire to find treasure. Finding it might well ruin him. Not finding it, if he couldn't put it aside and get on with his life, that might ruin him as well. It'd ruined Lock's father, and it sounded like it had grated on Mayhew Westbrook too, with all his years of anger toward Graham MacKenzie.

As Josh followed a riverbed that took every ounce of his imagination to see, he wondered what the right thing was to say to Lock. And then he saw the arch. "Will you look at that."

He felt everyone around him buzz with tension. Lock gasped.

A stone arch. A pretty thing about twice as high as Josh's head as he sat on horseback.

"I've never seen such a thing," Cord said. All three of the men riding behind Josh and Tilda caught up and stared at the arch.

"There are arches down the coast of California. I've seen a few of them with my own eyes. But I thought they needed water to erode a hole in the rock. Does this prove a river ran through here? Or was it just wind and rain and soft rock that made it look this way? That's red sandstone, which would wear away over time if the conditions are right. Look, we can ride right through it."

They all paused to marvel at the beautiful formation. Josh could imagine it long ago as a narrow wing of a rock wall. The west edge of it was solid rock, then the narrow stone arch curved down.

Finally, Josh said, "What next, Lock?"

Josh had studied the map too, but none of them knew it as well as Lock. Josh figured he'd defer to the expert.

"It looks like we ride through it, then on west." Lock looked forward doubtfully. "Along this dry riverbed, if that's what it is. And the next landmark is right by the X. Then we'll reach the end of our map and, Cord, we'll need to pick up with yours."

Cord nodded in silence, his attention still on the pretty red arch.

"What's the next landmark?"

"It's never made much sense to me. It looks to be just a flat circle. So maybe a flat, round rock? It appears to block the trail." Lock studied the map, then shook his head in frustration. "I hope it makes sense when we see it."

"You said your grandpa was a sailor?" Josh asked.

"When he was young," Lock said. "When he was a boy really, he sailed the oceans out of Scotland. I heard tales of it from my ma and Brody mainly. Pa once in a while. Now I wish I knew more."

"So do I," Thayne said, then added, "Maybe Brody can tell us stories. Let's get on with our search. It doesn't look like it goes on much farther."

Josh led the way single file through the arch, ducking his head even though he thought he would have made it through without doing so. Yet it was narrow enough he could have brushed the sides if he'd held his arms out straight on both sides. He had to ride about ten steps in shadow before he came out the other side into the sunlight. Once he was through, he looked back. Tilda didn't duck. Instead, she looked over her head and then side to side, as if to see every bit of the inner part of the arch.

As she emerged, Josh realized the day was wearing on, the sun getting low in the sky.

This time he was determined to stay with the search until they reached the end of both maps. He'd abandoned his ranch. Tilda had abandoned her teaching. The boys had abandoned their education, and Cord had abandoned his grandfather.

Not one of them felt any regret, except Josh suddenly had a twinge. He'd wanted to get away from the ranch to ensure Tilda's safety, but now he felt guilty for not waiting for Brody to heal up. He was a part of this search for his family's treasure, too.

He was honestly starting to believe in all of this. Of course, he'd believed for a while now that Graham MacKenzie had found *something*. The maps and the old journals and those fourteen gold doubloons were proof of that. But Josh had decided Graham had found all the gold there was and brought it out. Josh had decided they might find some old trace of the remnants of an ancient expedition. But now . . . that arch was such a marvel, it stirred a strange hope deep inside Josh. He had to wonder what it was the old man had found.

Sixteen

Brody sat in the sunlight on the boardwalk outside his doctor's office.

He'd been married for a while now. He paused, trying to count the days. He'd spent a few of them unconscious, so he wasn't sure. And he had felt terrible the whole time. But this morning he'd awakened to feel not quite so battered. He could inhale now without it feeling as if a horse had kicked him in the chest.

He wasn't seeing double anymore, at least not today. He was a married man with a doting wife who'd spent all the days of their marriage so far being more nurse than wife. And his little brothers had gone on their treasure hunt without him.

Now, after a quiet day of being available to do doctoring work but having no one stop in, Ellie had gone to the ranch house to rustle up some food. Or that's what she'd said. He had the distinct feeling she'd just decided he wouldn't collapse if she stepped away from him and ran off, just to do anything besides hover over him.

He hadn't managed a wedding night yet. That might have bothered him if he hadn't been feeling so wretched.

And he had to go back to Boston. All morning as he'd sat here alone, he'd been wrestling with the fact that his brothers might well not go with him.

Thayne had told him "I'm not a boy," not once but twice. And his birthday was coming up in November. He'd be seventeen. Lock, fourteen, was still a gangly youth, but that wouldn't be true for long.

When Lock's age, Brody had worked every night and every weekend to help their ma support the family. But his brothers weren't so dependent on him now, and they didn't want to go with him. They liked it here.

He couldn't quite tell if he had a broken heart, or if his ribs were just aching.

Right about then, a very pregnant woman came walking toward him. Michelle Hart. Brody hadn't been around her much, but he'd sure heard talk of her. Smart as a whip. Liked to run things to suit herself, and mostly everyone let her because she had a gift for making things run right.

He wondered how she'd handle the often-disorganized business of being a mother.

She came up the steps and tilted her head sideways to study him.

"You really think I'm a better doctor than the one who takes care of Mayhew Westbrook?" she asked.

Michelle hadn't come to the doctor's office yesterday to find Brody. Most everyone else in the family had, including Zane. He must've told her.

"Did Zane mention I told Mayhew that Josh's horse was a better doctor than Mayhew's?"

There was an empty rocking chair near Brody. Ellie had produced them from somewhere. Brody didn't want to know who she'd stolen them from. She'd declared he needed to sit, and he might as well sit outside in the sunlight. She'd obviously intended to sit beside him, but then she ran off and didn't come back.

"He did mention that," said Michelle. "The four humors, huh?"

"Mayhew is the luckiest man alive to have survived that man and his leeches all these years."

Michelle laughed, then settled into the second chair.

"How far along are you with that baby?"

"I'd say I've got two weeks left."

"So it could come anytime." They sat looking forward, rocking. "Two weeks early, two weeks late—those fall within the range of a full-term pregnancy."

Michelle nodded. "I'm hoping you'll stay to deliver it. I know Harriet very well, and she said you're a good doctor. A *great* doctor, in fact."

Brody said quietly, hoping to put an end to this conversation, "I'm planning to stay that long. But I'm not planning to stay forever. I gave my word to a doctor, who treated me well out in Boston. My word of honor that I'd come back." He turned to face her. "You wouldn't expect me to break my word, would you, Michelle?"

She rocked in silence for a moment. Thinking maybe? Finally, she answered, "I don't expect you to stay, no. But I wish you would anyway. We need more men of honor in this world, and I'd like to have one giving medical care here at the Two Harts. Maybe you should consider if your promise to the Boston doctor is a lifetime promise. Or if you might work with him for a year and call that honoring your word. We're going to miss our Beth Ellen, who insists on being called Ellie. She and her very honorable husband will always be welcome here."

She reached across from her rocking chair and patted him on the back of his hand, then rose with fair agility for a very pregnant woman.

As she walked away, Brody saw Ellie coming. The two women stopped and visited for a minute or two, and then Ellie came toward him, carrying a tray. When she got close, he smelled chicken and maybe apple strudel.

He got up quickly, realized he hardly hurt at all, and got the door for her. Then he followed her through the doctor's office and up the stairs to their living quarters.

She set the tray down on the counter next to the dry sink. He came up behind her and whispered, "I'm feeling better."

She turned, her expression joyful. "I have noticed you haven't had to move quite so carefully today. I'm so glad."

He leaned forward and kissed her. "I'm glad too." He kissed her again and pulled her against him. "And it's much too early for supper."

She eased back enough to meet his eyes, her smile widening. She took his hand and led him away from the food.

The afternoon turned into evening. No patients came looking for help.

And together, at last, they became fully and beautifully married.

Seventeen

The sun was setting on a long, tedious day of fighting their way west along land that Tilda, using her most vivid imagination possible, might be able to see as a riverbed that had dried up hundreds of years ago. She was exhausted and hungry and demoralized, about ready to demand they stop.

And then she saw something that didn't seem entirely natural.

"What in the world is that?" Tilda pointed at a . . . a circle.

A circle just like on the map. It wasn't a natural formation, for it was hanging from a tree, lashed there about ten feet up. Reddish in a way that . . .

"Is that thing rusty?" She rode up to it, staying well back but close enough to study it. She'd seen pictures in paintings and books that told her . . . "Yep, that's a shield! The kind the conquistadors wielded."

She tore her eyes away from the shield and looked at Josh, who was riveted on the circle that as good as barred their path. They could have gone around it, of course. They weren't on a trail, but rather following the bed of a long-gone river. There was a circle drawn on Graham MacKenzie's map close enough that they had to be in the place he'd marked. After the circle, the map ended, and the other map, Cord's map, began.

Then Tilda looked at Lock, whose eyes grew wide, while Thayne studied the landmark through narrow eyes. Cord, who was shaking his head and leaning forward to rest his forearm on the saddle horn, said, "It's real then. There's a treasure." Cord closed his eyes and bowed his head.

Tilda wondered if he was praying.

Josh swung down from the saddle and tied his mount well away from the shield, if that's really what it was.

Tilda followed suit and only then realized that every muscle in her body ached. Including some she didn't know she had. She added it to the renewed aches from jumping out of a train, almost sinking to her knees. Yet she forced herself to remain standing because she wanted to get a closer look at the shield.

She walked forward, Josh at her side, along with Lock and Thayne, who moved as one toward the iron circle. She studied a mass of rust. It was badly damaged, but looked like something that was ancient. In addition to that, it had been hanging between two trees for thirty years... or maybe three hundred years.

"I know something about iron," Josh said. "It doesn't rust through easily. My guess is, this was buried, or partly buried, around here somewhere. And your grandpa Mackenzie found it and hung it up there to mark this spot. I'd say he found this shield right here. Or maybe he found something here he wanted to make sure and find again."

"That's a lot of guessing," Cord said. "I want it to be true, but we need to keep our minds open."

Lock said, "It's late. Let's camp here for the night, then search some more in the morning. Spend a day trying to figure out why that shield is hanging there. Why Grandpa might have wanted us to stop here."

Josh nodded. "You're right—let's set up camp. Maybe we'll have the energy to hunt more after a meal."

Tilda turned to her husband, who had been leading them in their painstaking search all day. She knew he said this about hunting with more energy for her benefit. It swept through her mind that she loved him.

It was too soon for her to feel such a thing. And she knew she'd been lonely all of her life. Even after she'd been adopted. Maybe especially after. She wondered at the strength of her feelings, yet she didn't doubt them.

For now, though, she wouldn't tell him. It felt pathetic somehow. Desperate. Something a terribly lonely woman would do. Fall in love over the course of a few days with a man just because he'd showed her simple kindness.

Even knowing that, the feeling became like a low-burning fire in her chest. She knew, whatever the future held, she'd cling to that feeling. Cherish it. And know that she'd loved someone. Loved Josh. And what's more, she knew she'd love him for the rest of her life.

Dismounting, leading her horse after Josh's, she tied the gentle mare to a tree branch.

"I'll get our horses settled," offered Josh. "Strip the leather, make sure they graze for a bit. You should lie down, Tilda. I know you're hurting and exhausted. Anyone would be after what you endured yesterday. You rode for hours today—go rest now. It would give me great pleasure as your husband to care for you tonight."

As the others got busy setting up camp, he walked toward her to remove her mare's reins from the branch. He then stepped closer, and she didn't think that was an accident. Shielded from the others by the big bodies of their horses, she kissed him.

Drawing back, she saw the delight in his eyes.

There was no way to tell him of her love. Not now. Not in front of the MacKenzies and Cord. But she met his eyes with her own. This time he bent down and kissed her back. Kissed her deeply.

She loved him and, if God was merciful, would have the rest of a long life to show him just how much.

He drew back and pointed. "Rest there for a bit while I build us a fire. I've got the makings of a stew. We've got plenty of water, too." He nodded to his left, and her gaze was drawn to a small spate of water gushing from a stone. She hadn't noticed it. She was sadly lacking in the knowledge a body needed to survive in the wilderness. But she had Josh. He'd take care of them both.

But right now, his eyes were on her. His words were for her. She closed her eyes as if she could capture the kindness in his gaze and keep it inside her. Nodding, she said, "Thank you, Josh. I feel near collapse."

"Sitting in the saddle for hours is different from sitting on a soft blanket in front of a warm fire. Trust me on that."

She did trust him. She laid her hand against his cheek for just a moment. "Thank you," she said again.

Tilda then moved to the place he'd indicated to rest for a while. And that was the last thing she remembered before Josh woke her up, holding a bowl of hot stew in the twilight.

Once Josh and the others had finished setting up camp, he gathered wood for the fire. He was careful to clean out an area where the woods wouldn't catch fire. Soon he had a blaze going, and he'd done it all quietly while his sweet wife slept.

Lock brought a bucket of water from the nearby spring, Thayne just behind him with a coffeepot.

Josh started dicing up strips of jerky, then added an onion and potatoes he'd hauled along. Minutes later, the stew was steaming over the fire, though the vegetables needed a little more time to get tender as the jerky released its flavor into the stew.

The boys were walking around the campsite, studying the ground, talking quietly to each other.

Then everyone gathered to eat, all of them famished. They ate quickly, then went right back to their searching.

Cord studied the shield, if that's what it was. It was hanging rather high, at eye level, yet Cord was a tall man. "Tilda, come and look at this." Cord reached for the shield, but then stopped before touching it, his finger moving back and forth an inch away as if tracing something.

Josh couldn't resist going to see what Cord was looking at.

Tilda had been helping them search the area. Josh saw lines of fatigue etched on her face, and he had to clamp his mouth shut to keep himself from fussing over her and urging her to lie down again. In truth, she'd been walking more to stretch her legs than to do any searching.

Josh focused on the circular shield, and when Tilda came close, it was high enough she couldn't get much of a look at whatever Cord wanted her to see.

Josh eyed a good-sized rock, but not so big he couldn't move it, off to one side of the shield. He went and pushed it over so that Tilda could step on it and get high enough to look at the shield.

He knelt on another stone. When he sat back on his heels to ease his weight off the rock, he saw something that was *not* a stone. "Everyone, over here." His tone snapped their attention to him. He wasn't watching the MacKenzies, but he heard them coming.

Tilda rounded the shield and gasped. "That's a helmet. Again, the kind the conquistadors wore." Tilda knelt beside Josh. Cord was only a second behind her, dropping to look at the object, which was metal and curved and blackened with age. It was definitely iron.

"A Spanish helmet from that time had a unique crest on top that went from side to side." Tilda bent low and brushed at the dirt on its front. "Some of them had a face mask with openings for the eyes and mouth. Some had a T between the eyes to cover the nose and mouth." She leaned back and pointed. "This has that T shape."

Josh felt his heart speed up. "This is the place, then?"

Cord said, "Not for the treasure. We haven't even begun traveling the stretch of trail on my half of the map. But it does look like a promising find."

Josh looked at Cord, then at Thayne, then Lock. "We've got it, or a good part of it. Your grandpa called this a treasure. He sent us right to it."

Tilda nodded. "No doubt he's the one who hung the shield here. He found that and the helmet, and almost certainly something else or he wouldn't have drawn two maps. He hung the shield to mark the spot, then dragged that stone over at least part of what he'd found."

As she reached for the helmet, Josh saw her hands trembling. He laid a hand on her wrist. "Is it too delicate to move?"

She pulled back her hand, then looked around their tight little group. "I think it's strong enough to be moved. It doesn't look as worn and rusted as the shield, which has been hanging in the open air for at least thirty years. Yes, I think we can move it. Thayne, Lock, you do it. This is your treasure hunt."

Thayne and Lock exchanged looks, then the two of them reached forward.

"Be very gentle, Lock," Tilda cautioned. "Old iron can become thin enough to break if not handled with care."

Lock nodded gravely. He traced one finger along the curving crest. That part was thin and stuck straight up. It was what Josh had knelt on, thinking it was a rock.

The boys, across from each other, tugged on the helmet. They'd pause every few seconds and brush dirt aside, then tug some more. They were going slow so they wouldn't damage the helmet.

Tilda watched as it finally emerged, the T on the front becoming visible.

"This helmet hasn't been here for three hundred years," Josh said. "Your grandpa found it, and he found the shield. What else is down there?"

"Did he get the gold coins from here?" Lock asked, his voice vibrating with excitement as they kept working on the helmet.

A few moments later, the entire helmet had been freed with most of the dirt cleaned off.

"We've got it!" Lock said. "Let's lay it gently aside and see—" Lock screamed and fell over backward as a skull rolled out of the helmet right toward him. It splintered as it rolled, breaking apart.

They all leapt backward.

Lock scrambled back as if the skull were chasing him. Then he was on his feet, still backing away as Thayne fell over to sit on his backside. Josh quickly stood, then helped Tilda to her feet.

When Cord jumped up, he cracked his head on the shield, a chunk of which broke off and landed on the ground, crumbling nearly to dust. Cord slapped a hand to the back of his head and pulled it away, blood-soaked.

They all stopped and stared, the skull momentarily forgotten.

Josh, the first to regain his senses, rushed over to Cord. "Let me look at that."

He thought of how a man could die by being scratched with a rusty nail or wire. This had to be dangerous. A look at the wound showed nothing serious, though the blood flowed freely as head wounds tended to do.

"Move your hand, Cord. It's best to let a wound like this one bleed for a bit because that washes away whatever poison might be in that iron." Josh parted Cord's hair, hoping and praying the wound wasn't serious.

"Let's build up the fire and talk." Tilda stepped well away from the skull. Everyone followed her.

Josh figured himself to be the toughest of them, but he had to admit he wanted no part of a skeleton. He thought of Grandpa MacKenzie's body they'd found in that cave. There'd been some yelling when they'd found that, too. This seemed different somehow. Not knowing who this dead man was made it feel like they were grave-robbing.

Josh swallowed hard. "We definitely need to talk." He was glad now that camp was set up and he'd sent the MacKenzies to find more firewood before Cord had drawn Tilda's attention to the shield.

He urged Cord to sit down.

"That's bled long enough. I'm going to pour water over it in case there's anything left to wash away, then wrap it."

Tilda stepped away from the camp behind a tree.

Josh heard fabric ripping. Living in the West had taken a toll on Tilda's clothing. Now she was tearing strips off another of her garments.

He positioned Cord on his side on the ground. Josh had the cut washed clean by the time Tilda, her dress still intact, came back to help with the doctoring.

She wrapped a strip of what looked like cloth from a petticoat around Cord's head and knotted the ends so that it stayed.

As Josh settled himself by the fire next to Tilda, Cord leaned against a tree, looking ashen. The boys stared at the helmet, which was lying where they'd dropped it when the skull had rolled free.

Josh and Tilda and Cord all looked at each other and laughed.

Josh said, "It's time to talk."

"No." Lock gave Josh the most mature look Josh had ever seen on the kid. "It's time to dig. We came out here searching for a treasure, and we've found one. That skull about scared me to death, but I've settled down now. We need to dig up what else is buried around here."

Thayne sat forward, his forearms resting on knees he'd drawn up to his chest. "Grandpa must've hung that shield. He put that rock over the helmet. He wanted us to find it. I have to wonder whether another look at all those notes Grandpa left might reveal some reference to a shield hanging over a rock to mark the spot."

Thayne shook his head. "Probably much of what Grandpa wrote in the journal was written in the hope we'd come out here, and he'd guide us to the treasure. He didn't expect to die in that cave with a broken leg. We've thought his notes were strange and hard to understand, but he was probably writing them for himself so he could find this spot again and whatever Cord's map leads us to. He mailed things off. Maybe he hadn't found the gold yet, or maybe he had and didn't want to trust it to the mail. Back then, before the railroad, getting a letter back east would be a slow business. Grandpa sent it, likely thinking we'd come west to find him. Pa did after all. Grandpa went back to explore and was hiking back out when he broke his leg."

Thayne looked at Lock, who nodded and said, "That sounds right to me. He went back to his treasure hunt and expected we'd join him here. I wasn't born yet, but he was hoping Pa and Ma and Brody would be here with him to keep searching."

"And then, his leg broken, he crawled into that cave, wrote what messages he could, and died," Josh said. "It makes sense." He glanced at Tilda. "You know enough about conquistador history to recognize the shield and helmet as armor they once wore. What else are we likely to find?"

Quietly, Tilda spoke on something different, not answering Josh's question. "We were all shaken by that skull. And for a moment I couldn't think of this find as anything other than a man whose grave we were robbing. But now that I've quit jumping around, I think Lock is right. It's time to dig."

They all turned to stare at the skull and the helmet.

Josh said, "That's what we came here for, to search for treasure." He exchanged a look with Cord. "You haven't said anything yet."

Cord looked pale where he sat, his head wound bandaged snugly now. "It's dusk, my head aches, and we're all exhausted. It's time for bed now, but first thing tomorrow morning, we start digging."

Eighteen

"We have to stop." Tilda gently laid a curved metal chest plate beside their growing pile of iron. They'd found four bodies already, all of them men who'd been buried in their full armor. They'd found spearheads, too. Some of the pieces of iron were rusted, which seemed to depend on how well they'd been buried and the type of soil. Whether these four had been warriors or soldiers or sailors, Tilda wasn't sure.

She wanted more time to study the artifacts. She'd need a good library with history books she could compare with all that they'd found. And she wanted to go back to the Two Harts. They'd dug up more things than they could hope to carry. What was the point of digging further?

"I've found another grave!" Lock shouted.

Tilda had started calling them graves, but even that she wasn't sure of. Could they have died here in an earthquake, a flood, or maybe a landslide? And the years covered them, making this a burial ground. She wished a true archeologist were there to study everything with her.

"Josh, Lock, we have to stop now. How will we get home

what we've already found? What's the point of unearthing more?"

Josh's eyes were bright with the excitement of discovery. "You're right. It's almost full dark anyway. Let's finish up and get some sleep."

Tilda gazed up at the stars, twinkling through the treetops.

"Tomorrow," Josh went on, "we'll figure out a way to take home what we've found. We need to decide if we should take everything with us, even the skeletons, or rebury some of it."

"No, we can't quit!" Lock as good as howled.

Thayne straightened from the grave he was working on and leaned on the long handle of his shovel. "We can't carry it all, Lock. It's best to leave what we can't carry underground. It's safer there out of the wind and rain. And we need to go through that packet of papers we found with the first skeleton. It looks like more notes from Grandpa. Maybe it will help us find the way to the end of Cord's map."

Fascinated, Tilda brushed a bit of dirt away from one of the helmets. It felt odd, almost a wonder, to touch something so old, something that had survived for over three hundred years.

Thayne brought over a strangely shaped metal object. A type of ax maybe. Tilda wasn't familiar with it.

"I'll help Lock finish up, then we'll turn in for the night." Thayne studied the ax-like thing for a moment. "Do you know what this is?"

Shaking her head, Tilda said, "We should get an archeologist involved with this."

"A what?" Josh and Lock said in unison.

Cord straightened from where he was digging. He lifted a

curved piece of iron Tilda thought might be for girding the loins. It was about the right shape, yet she couldn't think of the name for it.

"An archeologist. Sometimes they're called antiquarians. They study ancient artifacts like these. A college may know who to ask. There's information to be learned from this burial site, although I can't think what all that might be. But an archeologist would recognize these pieces of iron and be able to set this burial ground properly in history. They'd know if something killed these men and left them buried here, like a landslide, or if this was the burial ground for some kind of settlement."

"But wouldn't they try and take our things?" Lock sounded as if he was ready to fight for their artifacts.

Tilda smiled at him. "They might, and we should do our best to prevent that. Maybe Michelle would know who we could talk to about identifying the armor and these men and what happened here. I'm inclined to believe they were individually buried because of the way they were laid out. It seems neat and planned, not like they died in an avalanche or from floodwater sweeping them to their death."

"Archeology." Josh said the word slowly as he approached the campfire. "Does that have something to do with Noah's ark?"

Tilda smiled. "No, but I suppose if someone dug that up, it'd be quite a find."

"I've got everything out of this grave, and we're just taking the armor, right? Not the bones?" Josh leaned the shovel against a rock wall and went to build up the fire.

"Leaving the bones is the right thing to do. I don't know for sure, but I think we've found something extraordinary here." Tilda noticed Josh was using beef jerky to make stew again. They were all hungry. She got to work cutting up an onion.

"No gold, though," Lock grumbled.

Cord came over and plucked a potato out of a saddlebag and used the knife he carried in his boot to peel it. "I wonder just what went on here with Graham MacKenzie. Did he find all these graves, or even some of them, and carefully rebury these men? They don't seem to have been disturbed. And where did he find those gold coins?"

"All good questions," Tilda said. She looked over at Josh, who set the coffeepot on the fire, then picked up his stewpot. "Why are we so alone out here?" she asked. "We haven't seen any sign of civilization. Do you know where the nearest town is? Why are there no settlers around here? This area isn't good for farmland, but a person could fell enough trees for a garden. They could hunt, raise a few cattle maybe."

"We're not far from the town of Cornerstone. That's where I'd start looking for a land office to see if Graham bought any land or staked a claim. There's never been any gold found around here to my knowledge. We did once find a pocket of gold on the Two Harts, but it was a small deposit, and we were quiet enough about it that it didn't start another gold rush. Could be others have kept quiet, too."

Thayne came up carrying a shield. "The graves all had a shield laid on top of the body, except that first one. But that's because Grandpa found the shield and then hung it to mark his find."

Lock came next with a helmet. Each one of them had a skull in it. They had returned the bones to their graves, treating these long-dead men with some respect.

Tilda had carefully laid the armor out as the different pieces were being unearthed. Now the beginning of the fifth suit of armor lay beside them.

Josh shook his head. "Lock, we've got to head back to the ranch tomorrow."

Lock's eyes flashed, but he remained silent. Tilda thought that for the first time, he was showing some restraint. Maybe he *was* turning into a man.

Josh, scanning the armor and weapons, said, "We can't take even this much back, can we? What would be the point of digging up more, and we'd have to leave all this lying here. It would probably be all right, but if someone did come along..."

Thayne nodded, bringing over what looked to Tilda to be a breastplate. "Or a wolf pack or bear might come by, scatter everything and damage the armor."

"But how do we take all this with us?"

Tilda imagined herself riding along with a fully assembled suit of armor riding behind her. "Yes, how?"

"We could build a travois."

"What?" Cord reached for the coffeepot that sat over the fire.

"It's an Indian word, I reckon. It's a kind of sled, dragged behind a horse. I used one to transport an injured calf home from the range; another time it was an injured cowpoke. A travois is just two long poles attached to the back of the saddle, with strips of cloth holding them together to make a sort of bed between the poles. The Native folks, usually when following a buffalo herd, use the travois to transport whatever they need to bring along. If they have enough horses, they can tear down a whole village and drag it along with them. I know how to rig one, too. We'll get to work on moving these suits of armor home, get them stored away somewhere safe, and talk about what to do next."

Cord said, "I'm ready to head back with what we've got and follow my half of the treasure map another time. Just because Grandpa had a map doesn't mean he owns what we find by following his half. Honestly, I'd be real surprised if my grandpa demanded half of what you find here. He's let this treasure Graham MacKenzie found become an obsession, but for him it's not about the money—he's got plenty of it. It's the feeling he was cheated. And as he's aged and doesn't work much anymore, he's let it burrow inside his head and burn there. I think he'll be delighted to see all these things and will want to be involved in studying them and figuring out what to do with them."

"There's a big museum in New York City that keeps artifacts like these," Tilda said. "My adoptive father took me there a few times, and that gave me a love for history. Does California have a such a museum? If not, maybe we could start one."

"My grandpa is friends with Edwin Crocker," Cord said. "He passed away recently. He and his wife have an extensive art and artifact collection in Sacramento. I heard she turned a wing of her house into a museum."

"A wing of her house?" Thayne looked confused. "How big is it?"

"Big," Cord said. "Real big."

Tilda thought of how Thayne and Lock had talked of sharing a bedroom over the doctor's office. Brody had his own. Thayne had said he'd never had such a nice place to live. She'd never lived anywhere big enough to have a spare room, let alone "a wing."

Josh checked the stew, stirring it slowly. "We will head home tomorrow, then. We'll show everyone what we've found and plan to come back here soon." Crouched beside the fire in the starry night, he added, "Stew's ready. Let's everyone eat."

Tilda smelled the stew and realized how hungry she was. The boys looked doubly so. Josh knew about feeding growing boys, and maybe he was hungry himself because there was plenty.

They were soon fed and rolled up in blankets beside the fire. The crackling of the blaze eased the chill of the cool night. Josh pulled her into his arms. After a long, hard day of work, they were both asleep before long.

Once settled in bed, Josh closed his eyes on the night and then opened them and it was morning. It seemed as though the night had passed just that fast. He had Tilda in his arms, her head resting on his chest. He lay there marveling at how nice it felt to have her so close. And she'd always be close for the rest of his life.

He pushed away the blanket before he did something stupid, like kiss his very own wife right in front of three sleeping men who'd never notice.

Tilda stirred as he stood. She smiled up at him, the sweetest smile he'd ever seen. The thought of waking up to that smile every day made something warm surround his heart.

"How are you feeling this morning?" He ran one finger across her silky-smooth skin where it wasn't scraped raw, gently brushing one of her dark curls back.

He should have probably whispered, but it was full daylight, and they had a long day ahead of them. They might as well get moving.

She sat up, groaned, and pressed a hand against her back. "Like I jumped off a moving train, then rode a horse for hours, then spent more hours digging and moving armor."

Josh winced. "That bad, huh?"

"I'm battered and stiff, but no real damage has been done. The best thing I can do is get moving."

He nodded, and at the same time he regretted she couldn't just take one day to try and heal up. Instead, they had to pack up all the armor and artifacts, then mount up for the long ride ahead.

"Maybe you can have an easy day tomorrow. Ben's probably long gone by now, but it might be wise to get away. We came out here so fast for that reason. We need a honeymoon, and Michelle's family has a beautiful home in San Francisco. We could ride a train you don't have to jump out of and stay there for a week. Ben would never think to look for you there."

But Ben had at least one man with him. Might he send that man back and make another attempt at kidnapping Tilda?

She smiled again. "Let's talk more about that when we get back to the Two Harts."

Cord rolled out of his blankets. "I've never made such a thing as a travois and can't quite picture it, but if you'll boss the job, I can take orders."

Tilda stifled another groan as she stood. "I'll get breakfast going."

Josh turned to her, frowning. "You don't have to do that. I'll get coffee going, and we can eat jerky and hardtack."

She shook her head. "You get the fire going and bring in water—I'll do the rest."

Josh really liked being married. He grabbed the coffeepot while Cord and the MacKenzies gathered wood. By the time he was back, they had a small blaze going.

"The coffee will take a while to brew," said Josh. "Let's get to work. You can all help with the first sled we build. Then if you think you've got it, we can each make one of our own." He turned to his wife. "You mind the coffee."

"I'm supposed to watch water boil?"

He nodded, then a grin broke out on his face. "There'll be plenty to do once we're ready to load up the armor."

He led the men to the woods and talked while he chopped down saplings. He had ten of the slender trees cut before Tilda called out that the coffee was ready, the jerky and hardtack laid out.

After they finished eating, Josh showed them how to weave rope between the splayed poles.

They were fast learners, and by the time Tilda had stowed away the cooking supplies and doused the fire, Josh had one travois finished and three men sure they could do one on their own. He'd make a second one for Tilda, so they'd each have one to haul behind their horses. He talked with Tilda about how best to load their treasure, then left her to stack one complete suit of armor on the first travois he'd built while he put together a second one.

It went faster than he'd thought with everyone working, so they were ready to ride by midmorning. He'd hoped to leave before noon.

Taking a narrow trail that wound through heavy woodland, they started for home. It was sure to be a much faster trip than the slow, searching one that led them here along the dry riverbed as they followed Graham MacKenzie's map to where they'd found the hanging shield.

Yet even after they'd come upon a game trail where they could move more surely, they still had to be careful. Though tied down, the armor was slippery. Every so often, someone would holler because they saw something shifting on the travois ahead of them.

When they reached the cave where Graham's remains had lain undisturbed for thirty years, they paused so their horses could have a breather.

Josh twisted in the saddle to face the others. "We're not going to stop, if that suits you. I'd like to press on. We'll eat as we ride. We won't get home in time for supper, but we can beat nightfall." Everyone was handed more beef jerky, and after a few minutes for the horses to drink from a spring, they moved on.

Soon they rode past the green pond Graham had written about in his journal. They then carefully rode up a steep slope to a decent trail at last, the final leg home. They'd been riding along it for about an hour when Zane came riding fast up the trail with Shad and Bo Sears, their foreman and their ramrod. Josh was on edge the minute he saw them. His brother wouldn't ride out here searching for them, especially with no idea where they might've gotten to in their search—not unless something bad had happened.

"What's wrong?" Because the trail was wider now, Tilda came up beside him, her horse pulling its travois.

"I've come hunting Tilda. We need you back at the Two Harts."

"Is it Ben? Did they finally catch up to him?"

Zane shook his head. "Nope, it's more than that."

Josh didn't ask what. He figured Zane had a story to tell.

Zane leaned to look around Josh's horse, eyeing what they were carrying with them. "What is all this?"

Josh wanted to shake his brother to get him to talk. Instead, Josh quickly explained, "We found a burial ground and all these pieces of iron—old armor—at the final spot Graham marked on the MacKenzies' half of the map. There wasn't any gold, but we dug up so much that we figured we'd better haul it home before we hunted any further."

Josh glared pointedly at Zane, and Zane got the hint.

He opened his mouth, closed it, then gave Tilda a look so full of worry, Josh set aside the idea of laying a hand on his brother.

Finally, Zane said directly to Tilda, "Your father showed up."

A faint gasp had Josh turning in case she fainted and fell off her horse. Her face had gone pale, and she gripped the saddle horn until her knuckles went white. "A man claiming to be my father is at the ranch?"

Zane nodded. "And I think he's telling the truth, too."

"Is . . . is Ben with him? Has he been arrested?"

"No sign of Ben. I haven't heard a thing about any arrest. Sheriff Stockwood would have told us if Ben had been caught. And I didn't stay to ask your pa many questions. I just came a-runnin' to bring you back. I brought Shad and Bo along so they could stay and help with the hunt if you needed them to. Instead, Tilda, you and Josh switch horses with them. Let the menfolk drag the iron back to the ranch while the three of us run for home."

"I'm not going with him." She gripped her reins tight enough that the horse threw its head back.

Before the fidgety horse could toss everything off the travois, Josh reached across from his horse and steadied it. Once her horse was calm again, he said, "No, you're not going with him. You're a married woman now. I'm your husband, and you're staying with me."

She gave her chin a firm nod.

Josh swung down, rounded his horse to where Tilda was on his left, and helped her down. He had to tug her hands free of the pommel and nearly untie her fingers from where they'd twisted up the reins. Finally, he got her down and on her feet.

Shad and Bo took over with the travois. Josh boosted Tilda onto Shad's horse, the steadiest critter on the property, but still a strong, lively stallion. He made sure she was fully settled before mounting up on Bo's horse. They said their goodbyes to the others, then headed out, riding side by side with Zane in the lead.

Minutes later, after glancing back at Tilda as if to judge her steadiness, Zane asked, "Can you gallop, Tilda?"

Josh doubted if she'd ridden a horse at a gallop before. But he knew she'd gotten much better in the saddle than she was that day when he ended up carrying her home.

Tilda nodded. "I think I can . . . I hope."

Why was Zane in such a hurry? Maybe he was still fretting about Michelle and his coming child. Good chance he didn't want to be separated from her for long.

"I'll stay a pace behind so I can catch you if you start to fall," Josh said to reassure her.

Zane nodded. "And I'll stay ahead so I can grab the horse if he gets the bit in his teeth."

They took off running. Zane set his horse to a gallop from the first step, which was better than trotting. Josh was worried about that. He'd shown Tilda how to trot, but she was still a beginner. But Shad's stallion took off right after Zane and Tilda, who clung to her saddle horn, not even trying to direct the horse.

Now all Josh had to worry about was stopping her and that horse . . . and keeping his wife in California.

And not letting her get kidnapped again.

He had so much to worry about that he should probably find paper and a pencil and make himself a list.

Nineteen

Josh led both his and Tilda's horses into the barn, Tilda glued to his side. "You stay close to me, all right?"

She gave her head a frantic little nod. "I didn't need to be reminded, but thank you." She squeezed his hand. One of his cowpokes came and took both of their horses, while another took Zane's.

"Thanks, Pete," Josh said. "I usually tend my own horse, but just this once, well, we've got trouble in the house."

The cowhand nodded and led the horses away.

Zane came then to stand beside Tilda. She was surrounded by strong Hart men.

Just as they reached the back door of the ranch house, it flew open and an older man stepped out, his eyes wide with excitement. Silver hair, tall and thin, dark brown eyes. "Matilda, I saw you ride in. My girl. My darling girl."

He reached for her, and in that second all she saw was broad shoulders. Josh had stepped between her and whoever this was. She heard a low grunt and felt Josh's body shake a bit from an impact.

"You say you're my father?" She peeked around Josh to see her father's shock turning to anger.

"My daughter doesn't have to be protected from me," her father said, his fists clenched.

Zane closed the space beside Josh, so she had two men blocking the stranger from her.

Josh snapped, "You come here, a complete stranger, all excited about a reunion with the daughter you abandoned and then have the nerve to act angry when she's afraid?"

"I didn't abandon her."

Tilda stood on her tiptoes to see between Josh's and Zane's shoulders. "The only thing I really know about you is you sent Ben to find me, and he kidnapped me. In my efforts to escape, I threw myself out the window of a moving train—your train, in fact. Am I to believe you approved of his actions and even demanded he do it?"

"I did not!" He shoved at Josh, who didn't so much as move back an inch. "And I didn't abandon you. Your mother was a madwoman who soaked herself in gin. She's the one who sent you to an orphanage and wouldn't tell anyone where you were."

"How many years had Tilda been gone when you were forced into taking Ben in?" Josh crossed his arms and spread his feet apart, a human shield. "Maybe Ben did such a drastic thing as kidnap Tilda because he doesn't trust you and is afraid you'll abandon him again."

The man gasped. "He knows better than that."

But Tilda didn't think her father sounded absolutely sure. Suddenly she realized she had never felt so safe in her life.

"Had you ever even *met* Tilda? How is that not abandonment? Did you bring Ben to live with you only because you were forced to? Do you even know Ben, or is everything he said a lie? You're going to have a hard time proving to me, and more importantly to Tilda, that you're her father."

The door at this stranger's back swung open, and a new stranger stepped outside. Except how could a person be a stranger . . . when she had Tilda's face?

Tilda staggered back, and Josh caught her and kept her on her feet.

"Y-you . . ."

"Tilda is having trouble getting any words out," Josh said.

Finally, she tore her gaze from the mirror image in front of her and looked at Josh. All she said was, "Somehow they're going to try and take me away."

Zane, standing at Josh's side, said quietly, "Tilda, this is your twin sister, Madeline."

Tilda's attention was drawn away from her husband to focus on whoever this was—almost certainly her twin sister—charging for her, arms open wide. She ran right into Tilda and clung to her like the ivy Tilda had seen on one of the oak trees.

Madeline burst into tears, Josh holding them both up. Tilda would've managed on her own if Madeline hadn't nearly tackled her.

Zane added dryly over the sobs, "She's happy to see you."

"So it would seem." Tilda stood with her arms raised slightly, not unlike a bird getting ready to take flight. "I remember that kidnapping fool Ben saying you were too delicate to make the trip here, but here you are." Tilda closed her arms around Madeline. "I really do have a twin sister." She looked past her weeping sister to see Carl Cabril. "So I have a father, a sister, and a brother?"

Mr. Cabril smiled. "That's right. Come on now, Maddie. Let's go inside. Pull yourself together. You've longed for your sister all your life. Let's give her room to breathe while she takes all this in. Let's get to know each other a little."

It took some doing, but without being too forceful, Mr. Cabril pried Madeline loose from her twin.

Tilda glimpsed through the doorway and saw Michelle watching the whole show as if it were the most interesting thing she'd ever witnessed. And to hear tell of it, Michelle had traveled and studied and invented. She'd gone to mountaintops and had brilliant tutors. She'd found and mined gold and had beaten up a man with a copy of *War and Peace*. She'd witnessed a lot. Which didn't speak well of the spectacle they were making.

She turned to Josh and said, "I'm *not* going with them. I don't care how many trains I have to jump off." She felt as if she were repeating the same thing over and over. And Josh had promised—

"You're here to stay, Mrs. Hart." Josh's eyes were kind, but then he looked up, and the kindness faded to ice. "Let's go on inside now."

"Mrs. Hart?" Carl gasped and spun around to stare at his daughter. "Ben never said anything about your being married."

———◆———

They all settled around the table. Gretel poured everyone coffee, with Tilda and Michelle helping.

"Ben should not have harmed you," Cabril began. "I'm afraid the way he grew up, first without me, then having to hunt me down when his ma died, well, he's become a man who doesn't allow himself to fail. You must have finally convinced him he couldn't talk you into coming home with him."

"She *is* home, Carl." Josh took some satisfaction in pointing that out.

Carl Cabril seemed kind, but Josh couldn't forget the sight of that private luxury train, something he had never imagined existed, and how Ben had used it to take Tilda away.

The man's white hair was elegantly trimmed. His clothes, well, Josh didn't know much about fashion outside of denim pants, a Stetson hat, and a good pair of boots. He also had a mighty fancy string tie with a chunk of turquoise to fasten it.

Josh knew it when he saw money dripping off a man.

Tilda's father was slender with sharp eyes that Josh would never be so foolish as to not take very seriously. This man claimed Tilda was his daughter, and apparently he intended to make up for all the years he'd failed her.

Michelle settled in at the head of the table. Zane leaned against the wall near the back door, looking as if he was prepared to block another kidnapping. Old Carl here was in for a disappointment if he thought Tilda was going home with him.

Madeline, sniffling beside him, her father's arm wrapped around her shoulders, was wearing a silk dress, and her hair was so fancy, Josh figured they'd brought a lady's maid along on the trip west.

He thought of Tilda and her two dresses—one of them ruined when she'd jumped from a train, and another Michelle had managed to make fit her. Tilda had one pair of worn-out half boots, with no bonnet to call her own. Josh much preferred this version of the identical women. The one he'd married, the one with the strong spine and a willingness to work for her supper.

Josh locked eyes with the older man. "Before you say anything more, Cabril, you need to get the notion out of your head that Tilda is going home with you. She is not. She is my wife. Her home is right here with me on the Two Harts Ranch."

Cabril's eyes flashed with determination. Ignoring Josh, he turned to his daughter. "Give me a chance, Tilda, please. I want to make everything up to you. I want to get to know you."

Josh kept right on with what he wanted to say. "Furthermore, we let Ben stay here for the same reason—he told us he wanted to get to know Tilda. Well, Tilda had no interest in heading out on a cross-country ride with a complete stranger. But we trusted him enough to leave her alone with him in this house, and we should have run him off. Now you're going to pay for his mistake."

"I never told him to do anything as foolhardy as take Tilda by force. You can see we got here fast. We headed out as soon as Ben's telegraph reached us, saying he'd found her and where she was, and that she was resisting coming home."

Josh didn't repeat that Tilda was already home. He figured Cabril for a smart man. He understood what was what. "You're welcome to come daily and share an evening meal with us, but you're not invited to stay here. You're not going to spend time with Tilda all day, every day. And I am never going to leave her alone with you. We have the law after Ben, and it's not gonna be enough for him to say, 'Sorry about that little assault and kidnapping. Sorry my actions caused a woman to *throw herself off a moving train*.' I don't rightly know if the sheriff has a long enough reach to arrest him in New York City, but if he's seen around these parts again, he's going straight to jail."

Cabril lowered his head into his hands. He looked the very picture of demoralized defeat. Josh wasn't about to trust any of it.

"So you're Madeline?" Tilda raised her coffee cup, took a sip, and waited.

Madeline nodded, her eyes filled with longing as she looked at Tilda. "Yes, although my friends and family call me Maddie. You probably know your full name is Matilda. Mother called us Maddie and Matty, even into the second year of our lives. She thought it was cute to have our names be so similar. Ben was around five when we were born. He referred to us as 'the girls' or 'the sisters,' since it was too hard for him to keep our names straight. But because our names sounded almost the same, Mother started calling you Tilda, which helped a lot."

"Did it help Tilda to have her name changed when she was just two years old?" Josh asked.

Cabril's brow furrowed. Josh couldn't guess if it was anger at Josh for his question, or anger at himself for being such a wreck of a father.

"I-I don't know. I mean, we were so young. I only know what Ben told me."

"I wonder if changing Tilda's name made it easier when it came time to pick one of her children to throw away." Josh knew none of this was Maddie's fault, so he tried to temper his words. They were mainly meant for Cabril, though Maddie was getting hit with them too, and he could tell she was fascinated by her twin sister.

Then he had a stray thought. Michelle was sitting here absorbing every word, and Josh liked that Zane and Michelle were also present. Yet he didn't want either of these Cabrils to know about the treasure. They'd never mentioned it to Ben, and they weren't about to bring it up to Carl and Maddie. But the men would be riding in any minute with the iron armor and whatnot, and someone had to figure out where to put it all.

Josh had given Zane the rundown on what they'd found, but only a very brief one. He rested one hand on Tilda's arm before she could ask her next question.

"I need a private moment with Zane, and I don't want to miss a word of this. I promise, I'll not step out of this room."

Tilda nodded.

Josh stood and went to Zane. It only took a few words to tell his brother what he wanted.

"Michelle, can you come here?" Zane watched the Cabrils as Michelle rose and rounded the table. She and Zane stepped closer to the back door, out of earshot of those at the table.

Josh couldn't hear a word as the two whispered back and forth, but he saw Michelle's eyes widen with surprise. Louder, she said, "I'll handle it. You're better with a gun, so you stay here."

Josh wondered where Brody and Ellie were. He wouldn't mind more witnesses. Then he remembered they'd planned to search for a mining claim or a land purchase. For a ranch with a lot of people living on it, it seemed they were mighty short on folks to guard Tilda. Where was Annie? She'd always been a tough woman and a crack shot. At least Gretel was here, hard at work on getting supper ready. She was a tough western woman, too.

And he'd just sent Michelle away to keep the treasure hunters from showing themselves, busting into the house talking about Spanish artifacts. Michelle was especially quick on her feet when it came to thinking.

The Cabrils could stay for the evening meal, but then they'd have to head to town to rent rooms for the night.

Michelle rushed out of the kitchen. Zane took a seat at the table between Tilda and her father. Josh, returning to his chair next to Tilda, sat across from the fragile, delicate Maddie.

Tilda went back to peppering these two with questions. Josh heard some interesting details, but nothing that made much difference. It all amounted to the fact that Tilda was probably this man's daughter. When just a toddler, she'd been abandoned by everyone in the world who was supposed to take care of her. And she wasn't going anywhere.

Twenty

"You know, it's the strangest thing that you've come in here searching." The lanky older man sat behind a solid-oak desk in the land office in Cornerstone, California. He had on a threadbare black suit and wore gold, wire-rimmed glasses. His bushy mustache was as gray as his perfectly trimmed hair.

"Why is it strange?" Brody and Ellie, along with Mayhew, had come to this land office first in their search. Knowing where Grandpa's cave was, they decided if Grandpa MacKenzie's property was near the cave, or the area west on the map, then Cornerstone would be the nearest town.

"I had a couple of men in here not long ago, one of 'em dressed all fancy. Like you, sir." He tipped his bald head at Mayhew.

Mayhew looked down at his clothes. Brody glanced at him, then looked back at the land agent.

"When was this?" Brody asked.

The man shrugged and seemed to look back into the past. "This month, I reckon. Like I said, not long ago."

That was around the time Loyal Kelton and his partner

Sonny Dykes, two men now in prison, had attacked and shot Brody. And Loyal had indeed been dressed fancy.

"Do you remember what they were looking for?" Brody very carefully didn't look at Ellie or Mayhew, trying to act calm. "We may know these men. If they found what we're looking for, we can maybe go talk to them about it."

"They didn't tell me nuthin', but I didn't like the way they acted, and we don't get many folks buying land out here. So I remember 'em. And I didn't trust the one in the fancy suit. I do think they found what they were lookin' for. It was in one of them far drawers, toward the bottom."

Brody glanced at the chest of drawers and sighed as he thought of all the work it'd take to rifle through them.

"What order are they in?" Ellie asked, the very picture of good manners and pretty, fluttery eyes.

Good luck to her.

"First claimed is first filed," the man answered.

"Not alphabetical?" Mayhew the orderly banker sounded affronted.

"Nope."

"Are they all land purchases?" Brody asked. Maybe they could cut the job down if claims and purchases were separated. Of course, they didn't know if Grandpa's land was a mining claim or a land purchase. Homesteading had come much later.

He shook his head. "Mining claims and land purchases are mixed together. First claimed, first filed," he repeated.

"We don't know the year your grandpa filed." Ellie shrugged. "But it was thirty years ago or more. Let's start with the bottom drawer and work our way up."

Mayhew, very wise and polite for an old curmudgeon, said, "Thank you, sir."

The three of them moved to the chest of drawers, pulled out the bottom one, and dug in.

"Are you certain you don't remember me? You were almost five when you . . . uh, left." Maddie seemed utterly shocked that Tilda hadn't remembered her.

"I'm sorry, I really am. But I think Ben kept memories of me alive for you. There was no one to do that for me, but somehow having a twin sister feels . . ." Tilda shrugged. "Well, it feels right to me. I'm glad you're here, Maddie."

Once again, Maddie burst into tears.

Josh looked at Tilda and shook his head.

"So, Mr. Cabril," Tilda began, shifting her attention to the other interloper at the supper table.

"Please, can't you call me 'Father'?"

The table wasn't full tonight. Michelle never returned. Rick, Gretel's husband, had come to the back door and whispered something to Zane, then left. And the MacKenzie boys, who'd been eating their meals here in the house, hadn't come in after their arrival. Tilda knew good and well that everyone was back and that they were all looking at those artifacts.

After the meal was served, Gretel left.

It was Josh, Zane, Tilda, and the family she didn't even know she'd had.

Zane hadn't told anyone what Rick had said. Tilda thought that was wise, but Michelle not coming back told its own story. She was studying what they'd found. Even

Annie and Caroline weren't here, and neither was Cord. They were having all the fun. Tilda would prefer to spend her time looking at old armor, too.

Besides that, she was almost rabid with curiosity about what Cord's map might lead to and how soon they could go treasure hunting again.

"Mr. Cabril," Tilda said more firmly. "With my identical twin sitting here, claiming you as her father, I feel almost certain that you are in fact my father, too. But I'm finding it difficult to think of you as such. No, I can't call you Father. Not yet. Maybe never."

Her father's shoulders slumped, but he didn't protest.

"It's been a long day for us, Carl." Josh wasn't calling him Father either. "And it's getting late. We have a couple of hired hands who'll ride with you into town. We can send them in tomorrow to escort you back to the ranch if you wish."

"I'm not done talking to Tilda yet." Carl's hands fisted on the table.

The meal was long done. They'd even cleaned up the kitchen while Carl talked and Maddie sat, with neither of them offering to so much as wipe off the table.

"We've been talking for about three hours now . . ." Tilda tried to force the word *Father* past her lips and just couldn't do it. She was angry about the way she'd been "lost" and wasn't able to get over it. She thought of her childish longing for a family and how her adoptive parents, the Muirheads, had worked her so hard and treated her so coldly. She had dreamed of a family finding her and taking her home. Now it was too late for those childish dreams. But it didn't mean, if she could ever trust them, she couldn't come to care about them. Eventually.

"It's late. You don't want to be riding after dark, and I'm ready to . . . to . . ." Tilda hesitated, thinking of going to bed for the night with Josh. "You need to head out now. And I'm a teacher here. I have work tomorrow. If you come back about three o'clock in the afternoon, we can talk again for a few hours. It's been interesting, even fascinating to spend this time with you, but for now, please go on to town."

She could've tacked on *Father* at the end of her statement, but instead she gave her head a mental shake, wondering if she'd ever be able to jar that word loose.

"Are the boys sleeping upstairs tonight, Zane?" Josh asked as he rose from the table.

"Yep. They're staying with us until Brody gets back."

"Do you mind seeing our guests out? Tilda and I are exhausted, and she's still a little battered from jumping off a train."

Father flinched. Maddie looked stricken.

Tilda took her own turn, giving Josh a dry look.

He took her hand. "We'll take the housekeeper's apartment. We might move in there permanently. I wonder if we should have Jilly build us our own house."

Zane said, "Jilly likes to build. She may get the idea herself, and we might not be able to stop her."

Josh tugged on Tilda's hand, and they headed for the back rooms.

Tilda stopped and looked back. Her father and sister both appeared dismayed as they watched her go. She said, "I'll see both of you tomorrow at three."

They left the kitchen to the sound of scraping chairs and Zane saying, "This way out, folks."

They reached the housekeeper's apartment. Once inside,

Josh closed and locked the door. "Well, that was mighty strange," he said.

Tilda turned to look at him. "I suppose that sums it up nicely. A twin sister. Yep, strange for sure."

"It sounds like he's a rich man. I wonder if you should be nicer to him. Maybe he'd divide his vast wealth with you."

She swatted him on the chest. "Hush now. I don't want his money." Then she caught the front of his shirt in a tight grip. "I don't mind getting to know them, but you'd better keep your promise and not let him take me."

Josh leaned down and kissed her right smack on the lips. He straightened and smiled. "I wouldn't let him take you for a Spanish ship full of doubloons, Mrs. Hart. You're my wife, and you're not going anywhere. You can say I'm doing it for you and how I'm a hero and such, but the truth is, I want to keep you so badly, you're never gonna escape me."

She stood on her tiptoes and kissed him back. "That sounds just fine. Thank you."

"You know, Wife, we've been married for some time now, and we haven't yet acted like married folks."

"We've slept in each other's arms every night since the wedding. That's a very married way to act. Or so I'm told." Tilda gave him a little grin.

"The first night, you were so battered I was afraid to touch you."

"Fair enough. And I hurt too much to let you touch me."

"Then we went on a treasure hunt and slept on the ground, with two mostly grown boys and Cord sleeping across the campfire from us."

"And yet we shared a bed. Again, very married."

Josh pulled her into his arms. "How are you feeling now?"

"Much improved, thank you. But, Josh, don't you think we should talk for a while about what we're going to do about my father and sister . . . my brother, too?"

"I don't want to talk anymore tonight about my brand-new in-laws."

"Then what are we going to talk about?"

"How about we do a lot less talking." He kissed her and guided her toward the bedroom. "And a lot more being married."

She came along willingly.

Twenty-One

Tilda went to bed a bride and woke up a wife.

It was early yet. She could see the dawn had just broken by the slant of the sun coming in through their window. She lay so close to Josh, they were almost one person.

He had his arm around her shoulders while she rested her head on his chest. His hand slid up and down her arm.

"Good morning, Mrs. Hart. It's a pure joy to wake up next to you this morning. I'm going to see to it that we spend every night for the rest of our lives sleeping in each other's arms."

Tilda sat up slowly, looking down at his kind blue eyes and his tousled, dark blond hair. "I want that, Josh. Being a married woman, finding a good man, it's more than I'd ever hoped for. I've spent most of my life just aiming for enough food and a warm room. And I wanted honest work that was a service to the Lord."

"I'd say you've found all of that." He reached up to kiss her even as he tugged her down to meet his lips.

Pulling away just a bit to smile at him, she said, "I most certainly did, but I found so much more. I found *you*."

She wanted to tell him she loved him. It seemed impossible

when they'd gotten married in such haste. How could a woman say such a thing, one who'd never known love? Certainly not from her parents. She should call them the couple who'd adopted her, for they could hardly be called *parents*. And not from a boyfriend since she'd never had one. Not even from the folks she worked with, though Mrs. Worthington had been kind in her own brusque way. How could she recognize this warm, sweet feeling as love?

He ran his hand over her forehead and into her hair, watching every blink of her eyes, every slight expression. No one had ever paid this much attention to her.

He said, "Michelle told me that the three students interested in teaching are doing well, and they can keep on filling in for you. I've seen you teach, Tilda. You've a rare gift for bringing history to life, and you should continue with it. It would be a service to your students. But I want us to take another day to just be married."

She wanted that, too. "But you have been gone now more than at home for days. Rescuing me, then marrying me, then searching for treasure. I don't want to make demands on your time."

For some reason that made him smile. "It's almost time to gather the cattle for our drive. We run a thousand head to San Francisco every fall. But right now, we've got the cattle grazing our best land to fatten them up. And watching cows eat grass isn't demanding work. Things are a bit slow. I'd like to ride to town with you, with a few bodyguards included, and buy you a new dress. And a few other things. Taking a woman along would make for a more fun shopping day for you. But we probably can't. Michelle shouldn't be out riding when she's so close to the time the baby arrives, and Annie is still teaching. But a couple of men can ride shotgun. We'll head into town, eat the noon meal at Fatty's Diner with your pa and sister, then spend a bit more time with them before bringing them here for supper."

Tilda frowned at him.

"If you don't want to eat with your pa, that's fine. I just thought it'd be rude to be right there in town and not say howdy." He shrugged and tried his best to look sheepish, but she could tell he felt not one speck of worry over being rude to her father. "Or we can slip into town and do our shopping quick and hide from him."

"That would be nice, Josh. I think there are yard goods out here, though. I can sew myself a dress in the next few days. I don't want to start right in costing you money."

Josh snapped his fingers. "That reminds me, you'll get paid for teaching school."

"Does Annie get paid?"

Josh froze, then said, "You know, I don't think she does. And she should. But no. I'll have to fix that."

"We'll see what Annie says about getting paid, and I'll think about whether I care to accept any money. As it is, we can think of my work as a donation to the orphanage."

"Fair enough. I just don't want you to think you're costing me a bunch of money when you should be getting paid. Maybe we can say a dress or two is your payment. Though it'd give me great pleasure to buy my new wife a few pretty dresses anyway."

"Let's go eat breakfast. While my New York family isn't here, I'd like to see what Michelle has to say about the artifacts we brought home."

"Do we have to go to town?" asked Josh. "That armor is really interesting. I'd like to spend more time with it."

In truth, he wanted to spend a quiet morning with his wife. This wasn't exactly how he'd planned it, with Shad and Bo riding along with them and a lunch shared with Cabril and Maddie. But he supposed it'd been his idea, and this was as "alone" as they were going to get.

Josh went on, "Michelle already wired a man at the University of the Pacific to ask him if he wants to inspect what we found. He said he'll come here soon. Maybe it would be more interesting to study it after he arrives. For now, they moved the armor into her invention shed."

"She calls it a 'laboratory.' That's a pretty word. We should use it."

"We can do whatever you want, Tilda." He leaned down and kissed her. "I learned the word *archeologist*, so I reckon I can wrangle *laboratory*."

Tilda had such a contented smile on her face, he couldn't help but believe she was happy with him no matter what she said.

"Anyway, she moved the armor in there and wants to spend the morning working on a new quick-attaching hitch for the undercarriage of a train. She said she's almost done with it and wants it finished and sent off for a patent before the baby comes. She'll keep the armor locked up while she does her work. We'll be back this afternoon, and you can look over the armor with her. I want to see it again, too."

They rode along, Josh just as contented as Tilda, though he kept finagling around in his head about how they could keep from attracting Carl and Maddie's notice. Not that easy in a town as small as Dorada Rio, which had only one restaurant. They were bound to run into them unless they worked hard to avoid them.

The seamstress in town had a few ready-made dresses, and two were a decent fit for Tilda. One was a dark blue broadcloth that looked beautiful with her dark hair and eyes. It had ruffles and lace at the wrists and the collar. The other was a bright yellow calico sprinkled with blue flowers that made her look like a sunbeam. There was also a black riding skirt that needed to be hemmed and taken in a bit. She said she could do that in the time it took Josh and Tilda to eat lunch. There were two shirtwaists in a dark green and a bright blue that'd fit.

He overrode Tilda's protests and bought all the clothes that would fit her. He wanted more for her. He remembered Maddie's elaborately draped silk dress adorned with ruffles and lace and wished Tilda had something so fine. But neither did he want to get into some foolish contest between the twin sisters, so he settled for the two dresses there were.

As a final touch, he added a white cotton nightgown and let the seamstress select what she thought was necessary for Tilda's underpinnings. He bought her two bonnets, one for everyday and one for Sunday. And then he took her to the mercantile, where they found a pair of kid half boots made of shiny black leather. It made him smile just to think of them on her feet.

Then they went to the hotel to rustle up her family. Josh had found out from the hotel owner that Carl had rented the whole second floor and left four rooms empty besides having one for himself and one for Maddie and a lady's maid.

When he knocked on Carl's door, Tilda's pa opened it, and he saw Ben stepping out of sight at the far side of the room.

———◇———

Tilda, standing off to the side, saw only Josh as he stormed into the room. Before she could do more than gasp, Shad and Bo, who'd waited at the bottom of the stairs, thundered up and headed straight for the door. The fierce expressions she saw made her step back.

Once the men rushed into the room, she quickly followed. She entered just as a fist thudded. Ben staggered back and slammed into the wall only inches from her.

"Don't you touch Tilda, or I'll—"

Before Josh could quit roaring, Bo caught Tilda around the waist, pulled her farther into the room, and tucked her behind him.

Josh lunged at Ben, grabbed him by the shirtfront with one hand, and punched him right in the jaw.

"No! Josh, stop!" Maddie cried out. She grabbed Josh's arm, nearly hanging from it.

"Josh, let me explain!" Mr. Cabril tried to hold back Josh's other arm.

Shad caught Mr. Cabril by the back of his suit coat and tossed him across the room, where he fell onto the bed.

Josh shook Maddie off and then shoved Ben against the wall so hard dust filtered down from the ceiling. He roared, "Bo, take Tilda with you and get the sheriff."

From the bottom of the stairs, the hotel owner yelled, "I sent for the law, Josh. The sheriff is coming."

"No, no, please, let me explain." Old Man Cabril was blocked from reaching Josh by Shad simply standing in his way.

Maddie jumped on Josh's back, wrapping her arms around his neck as if to strangle him.

"I'm fine, Bo," Tilda insisted.

Bo glanced over his shoulder and surprised her by grinning.

Nothing about any of this was funny. Tilda jammed her fists onto her waist and shouted, "Get that woman off my husband!"

Bo looked at Josh, then at Shad. He must have decided Tilda was secure because he stepped forward, hesitating briefly as though trying to figure out where to grab hold, then caught both of Maddie's arms and pulled them off Josh as he dragged her away. Bo was again standing guard with his back to Tilda while Maddie kicked up a ruckus while he held her around the waist, her arms pinned to her sides.

"Maddie Cabril, you hush up right this minute and settle down! Josh isn't hurting your brother, despite what Ben did to me." Tilda turned to Ben, who was up against the wall, the front of his shirt in Josh's grasp. "Did you really think you could kidnap me and not get into trouble?"

The whole room fell silent.

Ben glared at her. "I did *not* kidnap you. I was taking you home. I was scared to death you'd hurt yourself when you threw yourself out of the train. I tried to come back to get you and saw a bunch of armed men coming fast. I had no idea what they had in mind, but I recognized at least one of them from the ranch."

"Shut up." Josh gave him a hard shake. "None of that is true. You drugged her."

"I did not."

Instantly, Carl's expression changed from indignation to one of shock. "You drugged her, Ben?"

"I just said I didn't."

"But you did," Tilda insisted. "And you hauled me unconscious into town."

Ben shook his head furiously. "You said you were ready to go home."

"I assure you, I said no such thing. And when I started to wake up, you drugged me again."

"You wanted to meet Father and Maddie."

Tilda swiped an arm at his lies. "When I came around on the moving train, you locked me in a bedroom."

"I *put* you in a bedroom. I did not *lock* you in."

"I heard the lock click, although I wouldn't have tried to escape out that door anyway. You were right there, and you wouldn't have let me leave."

"But you said you wanted the life you could have in New York, a life with your real family."

"You're a liar, and a poor one at that. Cornered in that room, I knew every second I waited, jumping would be more dangerous as the train picked up speed. So I smashed the window and jumped out."

"I had no idea you thought I'd kidnapped you. I'll talk to the sheriff. I welcome the chance to clear this up."

"We'll clear it up by seeing that you're locked up in jail," said Josh. "You don't put your hands on a woman in this state and expect to walk around a free man."

Sheriff Stockwood stormed up the steps. "What's going on here, Josh?"

However important a man, Carl was from New York City. This was Josh's town, and the sheriff had heard the whole story on the day it happened. He'd been trying to find Ben to arrest him for days.

Ben raised his hands. Josh had never let up his hold. Now he released Ben with a hard shove.

"Let's go, Sheriff." Ben straightened his coat, his eyes glinting with determination.

"He's the one who vandalized the telegraph wires," Josh said. "If he was so sure he'd done nothing wrong, then why did he do that?"

"Father," Ben said, turning to Carl, "get me a lawyer. You know the governor, don't you? Ask him for the name of someone who can get a little respect in this town."

"I'm right behind you, Ben."

"You lied to us, Carl. You knew we were looking for Ben. You knew he was wanted."

"He wasn't with me yesterday when I was talking to you. He showed up late last night. He told me he got off the train, unloaded his horse, and rode back to town."

Ben nodded. "Once I saw that gunmen weren't chasing me, I hoped you'd all calmed down and I could find Tilda, make sure she was all right."

"I only knew he was coming when he knocked on my door in the middle of the night. I didn't lie to you," Carl said. He began to exit the room, following his son. Then he halted to glare at Bo. "Let her go."

Bo opened his arms wide and let Maddie leave the room.

Josh said, "Bo, send someone out to the ranch. I don't want either of you to leave Tilda's side. I want reinforcements, and let's get Michelle involved. Carl claims to know the governor, and I know Michelle does. She called the former governor 'Uncle Newt,' so maybe she knows Governor Pacheco, too.

She shouldn't be riding anywhere in her condition, but she could send a wire." Josh snapped his fingers. "What about the Westbrooks? They live in Sacramento—we'll ask them about it. Mayhew is gone, but maybe Cord will come to town to help us get some justice. In the meantime, let's go make sure the sheriff doesn't fall for Ben's pack of lies."

"T-thank you, Josh," Tilda said.

He leaned down and kissed her soundly, then held her arm as they made their way down the stairs. Which was a good thing because her knees were still shaky, mostly from fear. But add in a little shakiness from that wonderful kiss.

"I've got it!" Ellie waved a slip of paper. It was dated over thirty years ago.

Brody was at her side instantly, Mayhew Westbrook only a pace behind.

Brody scanned it quickly. "I recognize Grandpa's signature."

"Let's go find where this is on the map." Ellie carried it to the land agent, who pointed to a large map on the wall.

Very casually, Mayhew asked, "Did the other men who were searching the files search for the claim location?" He shrugged. "It doesn't matter. We can just ask them when we see them."

"They didn't," the land agent replied. "I'm not sure why they wanted to find the claim if they weren't going to look it up on the map. I didn't pay it much mind at the time, them not studying the map. Your friends behaved rudely, that's why I remember them. Of course, I don't get many folks in here. Cornerstone is becoming a ghost town, I'm afraid. When the train didn't even come near us, I figured that would finish off the quiet little town."

Ellie nodded encouragement and just in general did a fine job of pretending to care about anything the man said that wasn't about the claim and Loyal Kelton, as the searcher was almost certainly him and his partner, Sonny Dykes. Mayhew might be a wealthy, cranky old man, but he was smart at how he handled people. Ellie should be taking notes.

"But I'd've remembered them anyway because they whispered as if they were hiding something. Then one of them yelled. I thought he must've found what he wanted, but it was loud enough it got my attention. One of them, the one not dressed so fancy, glanced back at me in a way that told me he regretted the outburst. I wondered then if they were up to something, maybe thinking they'd steal the land claim. But I saw them put it back where it belonged and shut the drawer. The fancy-dressed one thanked me, tipped his hat real gentlemanly, and they left. Mighty odd, though, that they wanted the land claim but didn't check it on the map. I suppose if they wrote down the particulars, there are other maps around to look at."

"We'd like to study your map, sir," Mayhew said, "and we'd appreciate your help in finding exactly where this claim is. We're fortunate to have found someone so knowledgeable about land claims. I'm sure you don't get thanked enough for the service you provide." Mayhew reached out to shake the man's hand, and Ellie saw a coin slip from Mayhew's hand to the land agent's.

The agent fisted the coin and smiled. He gestured to the

wall map, took the claim and compared the two, and before long they'd found just what they were looking for.

Ellie fought the urge to shout with excitement and run for her horse.

Brody shook the agent's hand. Mayhew patted the man on the shoulder. And Ellie, as part of her new life of holding Loyal Kelton in absolute contempt, thanked the agent and gave him her best smile, resisting the urge to invite him to Thanksgiving dinner before walking sedately to her horse.

Twenty-Two

"He won't say another word, Josh." Sheriff Stockwood had left his prisoner firmly locked up. "He first wants to talk to the lawyer his pa is bringing in from Sacramento. I can't force the man to talk. He can sit silently straight through his trial if he wants. His pa told me they're waiting for the lawyer even if his son has to stay in jail for a couple of days."

Josh's mouth twisted with disgust. "I'd hoped we'd have him on his way to San Quentin before too long."

"I heard some of what he said to you in the hotel. He tells a good story."

Josh's face flushed with anger. "If you—"

Sheriff Stockwood held his hands up in surrender. "Don't worry. I take Mrs. Hart's word for everything. A woman don't cast herself out of a train without good reason. But like I said, he tells a good story. His lawyer will believe him, as he's being paid to. Then they'll talk to the judge, who knows only what he's told. Maybe you should get a lawyer too, someone who'll help you tell your side of the story."

"Do victims of a crime or witnesses to a crime need lawyers?" Tilda came close to Josh and leaned against him. "I thought that was just for the person charged with a crime."

Josh wrapped his arm around her.

The sheriff shrugged. "First time I ever heard tell of such a thing."

"If we can trust you to keep him locked up, Sheriff, we're going home." Josh raised his voice for the benefit of Carl Cabril and his family. "To think we came to your door to invite you to share the noon meal with us."

Carl turned, his face flushed with anger.

It was all Josh could do not to roll his eyes. Instead, he jabbed a finger straight at Carl. "That makes two times we were wrong to trust your family. The Cabrils who aren't headed to prison should head on back to New York City." Josh looked down to see Tilda nodding with a fierce look in her eyes.

"Whether you're my blood relations or not," Tilda said, looking at Maddie, and Josh saw a trace of longing in her eyes, "you're *not* my family. I don't see how I could trust any of you ever again." She turned back to Josh, and the fierceness in her expression had faded, replaced by pure happiness. "Yes, let's go home."

"Sheriff, whenever the kidnapper is done talking to his flashy lawyer, send us a wire out to the ranch, would you? We'll ride into town to testify at the trial. Let us know the lawyer's name, too. Zane's got connections in Sacramento. He can get the measure of the man they hire as fast as Michelle telegraphs the former governor to ask what kind of sidewinder we're facing."

With that, Josh and his wife left the jailhouse.

Josh saw Ellie near the back door of the ranch house, swinging off her horse, a piece of paper in hand. Josh got close enough to hear her say the words "mining claim in the name of Graham MacKenzie."

Cord held his grandpa's horse while Mayhew dismounted, looking mighty tired.

It was only a moment before Thayne and Lock came running toward Ellie and Brody. School must be out because the children were milling around outside the school.

Annie came from the school, holding Caroline's hand.

Zane and Michelle were there. Zane was questioning Ellie.

Michelle hung back, listening, which caught Josh's attention because she usually took charge of family conversations—that is, if someone needed to take charge. When it came to ranch talk, she didn't pretend she knew more than the rest of them. Going by the excitement on Lock's face, there was a good chance they weren't talking about moving cattle to better grass.

Still, Michelle, for all her inclinations to be a leader, just stayed back and watched.

"I need to talk to Michelle about the governor," Josh said, "but first I want to see what Ellie found. We can't go back out looking for treasure until after the trial, but next time we'll head into the wilderness and finally reach the end of Graham MacKenzie's map."

"They sure seem excited. You'd think they'd found a bucket of gold," Tilda remarked as she tethered her horse to the hitching post.

He realized she was all healed up from her kidnapping.

Brody looked well from being shot. Everyone was healthy again. Maybe all the wild goings-on around here were finally over.

Ellie saw them and squealed. She ran over and flung her arms around Tilda. "Welcome to the family."

Tilda grinned and hugged Ellie tight. It was a big old contrast to the way she'd acted around Maddie.

Brody strode over next and shook Josh's hand. "The Hart family is growing."

For some reason that drew Josh's attention to Michelle again. She caught him looking at her and gave him a rather faint version of her usual smile. She said, "I think it's going to grow a bit more very, very soon."

In all the ruckus, her quiet words exploded like a stick of dynamite in the middle of a pile of rocks.

Zane whipped around so fast his hat fell off. He rushed to her side.

Annie sent Caroline into the house and went straight to Michelle and placed an arm across her back.

Brody, the doctor in their midst, said, "How far apart are the contractions?"

"Less than every ten minutes. I've been in labor since before the noon meal."

"You *what*?" Zane's voice cracked like a whip.

Everyone jumped except Michelle, who simply patted Zane on the arm.

"Are you having a contraction now?" Brody asked.

"It just finished."

"It's around three o'clock. If you've been laboring for three hours . . ."

"More like six."

"What?" Zane said again, this time much louder. Sweeping Michelle into his arms, he said, "Lead the way, Brody."

Michelle slapped him gently on the chest, smiling up at him. "I can walk."

"Yep, I reckon you can. But for right now, you don't have to."

Brody, taking charge, snapped, "Lock, go fetch my doctor bag."

He nodded and took off at a run.

"Annie, the boys can watch Caroline if you want to come and help, but a birthing is no place for a child."

Michelle said wryly, "Unless they're really young."

Brody kept on issuing orders. "Gretel, boil water and bring plenty of clean towels. Thayne will give you scissors and a cord to boil. Ellie, you and I need to wash thoroughly. Zane, we'll be with you as soon as we can."

Josh said to Tilda, "You want to watch a baby be born?"

She shook her head and very definitely said, "No. Maybe I can help get a meal on."

Gretel came to the back door. "Zane will be kicked out pretty soon. He'll need company. Tilda, I'd appreciate some help, though I suppose half our number will miss supper. We'll leave something warming for them, even if it has to wait all night. Beef stew keeps well, so we'll make that."

"All night?" Tilda's voice was just barely shy of a scream. "Having a baby takes all night?"

Josh had sat in the house a few nights while Brody delivered babies. Michelle had delivered a few before Brody came. So Josh had an idea of how long it took for a baby to be born. Apparently, no one had ever informed Tilda of such things. He wondered what else she didn't know.

"For now," said Gretel, "there's coffee and strudel. Come on in, everyone. The main thing with babies is to be patient." As a mother of two little ones, Gretel likely knew more than all the rest of them combined, including maybe the ones upstairs with Michelle. "We might as well get on with being patient right now."

Lock and Thayne came sprinting back from the doctor's office. Gretel stopped them long enough to get the things Brody had ordered to be boiled. Then she leapt out of the way because they weren't exhibiting one speck of the patience Gretel had just called for.

As they were thundering up the stairs, Gretel said, "I'd offer them strudel too, but I was afraid I'd turn them aside from their mission if I had."

Brody and Ellie came rushing down the stairs and into the washroom at the back of the house. Thanks to Michelle and her sister, they had an indoor shower bath with hot and cold running water. It was a modern house in all respects.

Mayhew said, "I could stand to wash up, too. I was on that trip with Brody and Ellie."

Josh said to Tilda, "I wonder if there's room in this house for all of us to sleep."

Mayhew cleared his throat. "Cord and I could ride to town and stay in the hotel."

"Nonsense. There's plenty of room," Gretel said, "when you consider Michelle, Zane, Brody, and Ellie probably won't sleep tonight. And if they do, they'll go to the doctor's office for the night. I'll make sure they take the MacKenzie boys with them."

Josh clapped Mayhew on the shoulder, and a puff of dust rose up from the old man's coat. He could stand to clean up for a fact. "We've got plenty of room for everyone. No need to go to town. Anyhow, Dorada Rio is lousy with those low-down Cabrils, so they might try and kidnap you."

Cord turned to stare at Josh for a second. "Did you say their name is Cabrillo?"

That struck them all to silence.

"No . . ." Tilda sounded hesitant. "It's Cabril." Then she and Josh exchanged a long look.

"Those names are just *close*, right?" Josh said. "They're not the same name."

Mayhew rubbed the back of his neck. "Lots of immigrants coming to this country changed their names, either to fit in better or to simplify the spelling."

"Seems farfetched that the name could possibly be connected to this mess." Josh closed his eyes and inhaled long and slow because he knew what he needed to do. "We have to talk to your troublesome father again."

Cord said, "You know a lot about Captain Cabrillo, Tilda. Not a name most folks usually know, even those that study history. Why is that?"

Shaking her head, Tilda said, "My adoptive father loved history. He had a collection of history books at the house, and I read when I had a spare moment, which wasn't often. I had a lot of chores. I loved reading about history, especially about the Spanish sailors. They interested me far more than Cortés in Mexico or the explorers who followed Lewis and Clark's expedition to Oregon. Cabril, Cabrillo . . . is it possible? I never knew my last name as a child, not that I can remember. But I was young when I was left on the streets to fend for myself, or so my brother told me. It's very likely I knew my full name at one point. Cabril . . ."

She said the name as if wishing she could summon her long-ago memories. "Maybe Cabrillo touched a chord in me. Maybe it was familiar."

"You got turned out on the streets of New York City as a four-year-old?" Cord's voice squeaked as he said the words.

"That's what I've been told. My mother was a mistress to Carl Cabril. He rejected her when he married. He sent her money for the three children she bore him, and my mother had a taste for gin and thought twins were too much trouble."

"If your father did change his name from Cabrillo to Cabril, might he have done it recently?" Mayhew asked. "Or maybe he used an old family name with a mistress to hide his true name? His hair and eyes are dark, so he could be of Spanish heritage."

Tilda had those same dark features. So did her twin sister and her big oaf of a brother.

Silence stretched as they all tried to put the puzzle together with a few of the bigger pieces missing.

Thayne poked his head out the back door. "Gretel's poured coffee. Are you coming in?"

He didn't wait for an answer. The strudel was too strong a lure.

"We need to ask your pa about this," said Josh, "but I'm not going to town while Michelle's bringing my second-ever little family member into the world. It's been a long time since Caroline was born. Maybe we can get a cavalry unit to back us and go into town tomorrow."

"We weren't going to tell them about our treasure hunt, remember?" Tilda said.

"If it is his name, he might know the family history." Josh

could smell the strudel now. He decided to forget about all this until tomorrow.

"Or at least be really interested in it." Tilda took his hand and held on as if he were her anchor.

He liked that. He squeezed her hand tight and started with her for the back door, ready for some coffee and strudel.

Twenty-Three

Zane prowled the office like a caged cougar. Restless, prone to snarling, and dangerous for anyone who might try and stop him or even draw his attention.

"I can't believe I'm not allowed to stay with my wife while she brings our child into the world."

Tilda closed her eyes, hardly able to listen to the man say the same thing over and over. "There was some mention of you . . . um, fainting. I believe Ellie's words were that she didn't have time to tend to you and your wife at the same time. They dragged you, unconscious, into the hall. Brody called down for us to fetch you, then slammed the door on you. I heard him propping a chair under the doorknob so you couldn't get back in."

"I didn't faint, for heaven's sake. Men don't faint."

"Swooned?" Josh suggested.

"Vapors is what I'd call it." Cord snickered quietly.

"I passed out for a few seconds. It was a little upsetting is all."

"They shoved you into the hall, laid out like a corpse."

Lock had joined them and now sat on the floor with a sleeping Caroline in his arms.

Cord had come to sit beside him and offered to take a turn holding her.

Lock handed the little girl over. "We should probably carry her up to bed soon."

Thayne shook his head. "Aunt Annie said there might be some hollering before the baby comes."

Zane, who was pacing, stopped, then sat down suddenly. Everyone watched him.

"I say if he gets another fit of the vapors, we let him drop to the floor and leave him there to sleep," Josh said as he eyed Zane, whose face had gone white. Yet the word *vapors* seemed to get his gumption up.

The telegraph started tapping. No one bothered to check it. They'd sent a wire to Michelle's family, who stayed in a mansion on top of their own mountain through the logging season. It was a short telegraph since none of them were much on Morse code. Mayhew had used the written-out code Michelle left by the telegraph machine and had taken forever to tap out the message: MICHELLE IN LABOR.

A storm of writing had come back.

Michelle did the most work with the telegraph machine. The rest of them could neither read the incoming messages nor respond with their own. Mayhew did manage to write the message a second time.

Michelle came from a family of genius women, or so Tilda had been told. Everyone claimed they were rational women who knew how to think things through. Tilda hoped they figured out Michelle wasn't available to respond and didn't panic.

Josh said quietly, "Michelle's ma and her two married sisters are all up on the mountaintop, where their small army of lumberjacks are working. They've got a mansion there, another one in San Francisco where they live during the winter. They often come for a visit in cold weather. Or we go into town to see them. They'll probably come and stay here for a time when logging shuts down for the season. Laura, Michelle's younger sister, had a baby girl two months ago while Michelle and Zane were up there. Jilly, the middle sister, is expecting."

A door opened upstairs, followed by the sound of footsteps, giving Zane enough energy to get to his feet. Annie came down with a bundle in her arms. She looked at Zane, who rushed over to her. "It's a girl."

He pulled the blanket aside to look at the little one, who squalled and waved her arms wildly. A smile that was pure glory broke out on Zane's face. He looked up at Annie. "How's Michelle?"

Annie smiled back, and a single tear ran down her face. "She's absolutely perfect. Brody said to give him just a few more minutes with her before you come upstairs."

"Was it like this for you when Caroline was born, the miracle of it all?"

A second tear rolled down Annie's face as she nodded. "It's wonderful beyond belief, Zane. A baby is a miracle right up there with the parting of the Red Sea."

The others quickly moved to see the baby for the first time.

"C-can I hold her?" Zane touched one of the little waving hands with one of his work-roughened fingers.

"You know how to hold a newborn. You were around often enough when Caroline was born." Annie glanced at her own daughter. Her eyes widened in surprise to see her sleeping in Cord's arms. "Thank you for watching over her."

"My pleasure, Annie." Their gazes met for a second too long before Cord looked down at Caroline, and Annie looked back at her bundle.

She eased the newborn into Zane's arms. She was vigilant until she was sure Zane had a good hold. Then she stepped back.

"Zane, come on up. Michelle's ready to have company now," Ellie called from the top of the stairs. "Bring the baby."

"Have you named her yet?" Annie asked. She rested one hand on Zane's back, the other on his arm as she leaned in and smiled at the baby.

"Not yet. We decided we wanted to meet her first."

"This reminds me so much of when Caroline was born. There is no more precious, sacred moment than when you welcome your child into the world." She gave Zane a kiss on the cheek, then patted his back. "Go on up."

Zane smiled and headed up the stairs with the baby.

"We can risk putting Caroline to bed now." Annie went to Cord and reached for her daughter.

Cord seemed reluctant to let the little girl go. "She's an armful. I'll carry her upstairs for you."

Annie stepped back but with some hesitation, as if she didn't know whether to go forward or back. "Thank you," she finally said.

Cord followed her upstairs to the room where Caroline slept with Annie.

Tilda watched them ascend.

Annie adjusted the bandage left from Cord banging his head on that shield. "I should check this for you."

Tilda couldn't hear Cord's response.

Ellie had gone into the room with Zane, but moments after Cord and Annie had gone past the door, Ellie came out and Brody followed, rolling his sleeves down.

When they reached the bottom of the steps, Brody studied the group crowded around him. "Michelle is fine."

"We sent a telegram to her family." Josh clapped Brody on the back. "They wrote back, but none of us know Morse code. We didn't think we should pester Michelle."

Ellie, her eyes shining from what she'd just witnessed, said, "Good because she'd've probably come right on down here and spent time conversing with her family. She handled having a baby well and could probably have managed it."

Brody looked at Thayne and Lock. "Ellie and I are going home to the doctor's office. You boys want to come and sleep there?"

His brothers nodded.

"Holler if there's anything you need help with." The MacKenzie family left.

Cord, from the top of the steps, said, "I'm going to get a few hours' sleep. You ready to come up, Grandpa?"

Mayhew nodded, tired but with a smile on his face. Even an old curmudgeon like him could get his heart softened by a new baby.

Annie had stayed in her room with Caroline.

That left Tilda and Josh alone. He took her hand. "Let's go to bed."

A shiver of pleasure raced down Tilda's backbone. She'd watched everyone else enjoy the sight of a new baby, but just now she realized she had a dreamy smile on her own face. "You know, Josh. We could have our own baby before long."

Josh slid an arm around her waist and tugged her toward the housekeeper's apartment. "That's an idea that warms me all the way to my soul, Mrs. Hart."

As they headed back, Tilda set aside thoughts of the baby and of her Cabril family and their possible connection to Captain Cabrillo.

Her thoughts just now were only of Josh and the surprising realization that having a baby would be pure wonder, something she wanted even though she'd never considered having a family of her own.

The day had started out so lovely, awakening in her husband's arms.

Then the new clothes, then finding Ben and the fight and having him arrested. For all that bedlam, they'd finished the day with a tiny miracle.

Twenty-Four

Josh saddled up two horses, and four of his men added four more.

"We have Brody back now, Josh. We should probably go on one last treasure hunt and get to the end of the Westbrook half of the map."

"You've said that five times, Tilda."

She flinched. "Do you think I'm turning into a nag?"

She didn't say it like she was mad about it. More like she feared it might happen, and she didn't want that.

Josh suppressed a smile to think of his sweet Tilda being a nag. The woman just didn't have it in her.

"We'll go to the telegraph office in town and wire the Stiles, give them details of the new baby. We'll ask if your pa's name used to be Cabrillo and if he knows of any connection to the conquistador. Cortés and his crew didn't get called 'conquistador' because they were friendly, so you might not want to count them as kin."

"Should we tell Carl there might be a lost treasure out there?"

"We could tell him we found a map that led us to that

armor without mentioning gold and see if it taps into old family lore. Now, in the full light of day, I'm thinking it's likely a waste of time. Still, we'll ask the man if he knows anything."

Josh boosted her into the saddle, then swung up onto the chestnut mare he sometimes favored. Just as they headed out of the yard, Lock came dashing out of the doctor's office, waving his arms. "Where are you going? We need to follow that map the rest of the way."

"You know we can't go quite yet, Lock. Right now we need to settle the trouble with Tilda's family, and Zane has to stick close to the house for a while until Michelle is up and around."

Thayne came running right behind Lock. "Last night was so busy with us all thinking of Aunt Michelle, we didn't tell you that she went over the armor half the day, then sent a wire to a man she knows at a college back east who studies old artifacts. He was all excited and said he's bringing a team out here to study the armor."

"They're gonna want to search for the rest of the treasure, Josh," said Lock. "We've got to find it before they get here. If they find it, they may decide it's theirs to own."

Brody came out next. He was holding a slip of paper. "If this title to a piece of land is what I think it is, Grandpa MacKenzie owned that land. I have a map I think will lead us straight to the same piece of land Mayhew's map leads to. Surely no one can come here and lay claim to any artifacts if they're on MacKenzie land. And Michelle thinks we should start our own museum. Maybe here at the ranch."

Josh dragged a hand over his face. "Does she want tourists to come to our museum? In addition to the orphanage and the fruit trees and her houses for the cowhands and the doctor and what all else? At this rate, we won't have any room for cows."

Brody nodded and said, "Maybe we could convince her to set up the museum in Dorada Rio or maybe Sacramento."

Josh chuckled. "More likely she'll end up convincing us. After all, she's a real convincing woman."

"She also said," Brody added, "that each one of those gold doubloons is worth at least a thousand dollars. The armor is valuable, too. And after talking over the buried conquistadors you found, she thinks Grandpa probably dug them up. And whatever gold coins he found there, he kept them. Who knows if there's anything more to be found at the end of Mayhew's map. Grandpa was coming back to send for us when he died in that cave. Michelle doubts there's any more gold, but there might be more artifacts."

Lock groaned as if he'd just had all his dreams shattered. The boy wanted gold. A natural enough inclination, though it appeared the MacKenzies had found all they were going to find.

"We found a total of fourteen coins, Lock," Brody pointed out. "That's fourteen thousand dollars. Which is enough money to live on for the rest of our lives if we're frugal. Those coins will give us a mighty comfortable cushion. So there's nothing to groan about. We could build a bigger orphanage, hire more teachers, and help more children."

Lock's eyes narrowed. "Don't start giving our treasure away before we've even found it all."

Josh said, "If there ain't any more gold, and the MacKenzies' land lies under the end of Mayhew's map, then it doesn't matter if that team of artifact teachers shows up and helps us hunt."

"Gold coins may be small enough to steal, but they can't sneak past us carrying a suit of armor. Right now, though, we need to head to town and see if Tilda is related to a conquistador."

"What?" Brody, Thayne, and Lock all shouted as one.

Ellie was coming toward them. Looked like the menfolk had made an escape, and she was only now catching them. She smiled at Tilda and said, "You're related to a conquistador?"

Tilda shrugged. "Maybe. It's just something Cord suggested last night, seeing as the names Cabril and Cabrillo are similar. He thought we oughta go ask Carl about it."

"When we get back," Josh said, "we'll ride out for the treasure hunt. We shouldn't be gone long, unless Ben's lawyer has turned up and the trial is today. Treasure hunting sounds a lot more interesting than getting to know Tilda's surprise family."

Tilda's expression told him she wholeheartedly agreed.

Lock seemed to accept the idea, leastways he quit nagging.

Josh and Tilda turned their horses toward the trail leading to town, the four cowhands right behind them.

Yep, Josh would much rather be going on another treasure hunt.

Tilda was riding straight to the jail. At this point it seemed as if she'd gone to the jailhouse every time she'd been in Dorada Rio. She was wearing a blue shirtwaist and the new black riding skirt Josh had bought for her yesterday, so at least she was well dressed.

They found the Cabril family with the sheriff. Carl and Maddie sat in chairs on one side of the bars, with Ben on a cot on the other side.

"Has your lawyer shown up yet?" Josh asked.

"He'll be on the morning train into town," Carl answered. He rose and started toward Tilda, but Josh stepped in front of her.

Carl stopped.

Peeking around Josh's shoulder, Tilda said, "I've come here this morning to ask you one question."

Josh glanced back at her. Right now it was all she could do to be in the same room with the Cabril family.

Carl raised a staying hand. "First let me tell you something."

"Go ahead."

"I hope we'll be able to clear up all this unfortunate business about Ben's treatment of you."

"Is that what you wanted to tell me?"

Shaking his head, Carl continued, "I'm staying in California, Maddie too. We're hopeful Ben will soon be freed from jail. If so, he'll return to New York City and manage the Cabril holdings there."

Tilda was struck by that. Carl was placing a lot of trust in Ben. Was the kidnapping out of character for him, then? One desperate act in a lifetime of honor? Her father certainly seemed to trust him.

Carl went on. "Eventually, he may sell everything and move here, too. But, Tilda, I was serious about my wanting to get to know you. Maddie wants that as well. Ben too, but he handled things so badly that you're hostile to him, as well you should be."

"Father." Ben surged to his feet. "You demanded I bring her home. I do as I'm told. I did not—"

"Enough, Ben," Carl's voice thundered.

Tilda frowned as Ben's face distorted in the wake of his father's anger. She was surprised to feel a pang of sympathy for Ben. He'd been around ten when he found his father. A boy who had his father for the first five years of his life before being abandoned by him, then suddenly lost his mother only to be restored to his father—moving from one life to another so fast had to be hard, a shock for him. What would that boy do, even as a man, to win his father's approval and love?

Carl went on storming at his son. "You're going to be very fortunate to not end up in prison over this catastrophe. You need to stay out of this and hope you get to go back east. Now hush."

Ben sank back on the cot, rested his forearms on his knees, and let his head sink low. Tilda studied Ben. He didn't seem angry, more like the chastisement of his father had cowed him. That didn't seem quite right. He didn't look to be the kind of man to back down easily. Of course, he was a liar and a kidnapper, so maybe he was being wise or even sneaky. Had Carl demanded Ben bring her home? Was the kidnapping Ben's idea, or was it in fact Carl's?

"I've already begun the search for a house in Dorada Rio," Carl announced. "If we can't find one that's appropriate, we'll stay in the hotel until one can be built. We intend to spend our lives out here, getting to know you, Tilda, and trying to make up for all the wrong I did as a foolish, arrogant young man."

Carl leaned sideways to look around Josh at his daughter.

Josh finally stepped aside so that Tilda could see her father face-to-face.

"When I was young, an up-and-coming businessman in a huge city, well, it seemed all the men in my station of life had mistresses. In my arrogance I saw nothing wrong with that. And nothing wrong with letting her bear my children, and nothing wrong with being a worthless father who thought sending some money every month made up for my sinful choices. Then I got married, right about the time you and your sister were born."

Shaking his head, Carl said, "My wife, Constance, was a strong woman of faith. She demanded nothing less from me than fidelity, and that I sit at her side weekly at church. She was adamant about wanting a Christian marriage. I fell madly in love with her. I promised her all that she asked for, and that included cutting ties with my mistress and you children, though I never admitted to Constance that I had children. I simply broke things off with your mother just weeks after you girls were born. I saw the two of you once, but even then, even while trying to present myself as a Christian to Constance, all I could think of was to shove my past out of sight. I sent money and turned my back on all of you. It's the greatest sin of my life. One I have begged forgiveness for every day since Ben contacted me to tell me his mother had vanished and left him and Maddie alone for days.

"I confessed then to Constance because by this time I'd turned my heart over fully to God and knew this last hidden sin had found me out. And if it cost me my beloved wife, it was no more than I deserved."

Carl swallowed hard and went on. "She said to go see what had happened. When I got to the miserable apartment Ben and Maddie were in—I'd given her plenty of money, but I suppose her gin was taking most of it—I was not only horrified at the conditions they were living in, but I found one of my children wasn't there. Ben told me how you'd gone missing, for over a year by that time. I took Ben and Maddie home, and Constance took them in and became their mother. And I have spent these years searching for you, Tilda. I was sure you were dead. Johanna was never seen again. I was sure she was dead, too.

"I searched every orphanage in the city and beyond. Ben and Maddie had gone out many times, before their mother vanished, and asked questions at orphanages. There was no sign of you.

"Nothing. For years, nothing. And then one day we found that tintype of you displayed in our church. There you were, the very image of Maddie. We've been on a mad search ever since. Eventually it led us right here. It led Ben to do something he never should have done. Or if his version is correct, and it was a misunderstanding, then he scared you so badly that you thought you were being kidnapped. I find myself believing both of you are telling the truth."

Tilda's jaw went tight. Carl was telling a very good story. She knew they were going to let Ben go. "And if you stay, I'll never know a moment's peace because you might *misunderstandingly* kidnap me again one day."

Carl shook his head. "No, I am not going to try to take you back to New York City. You've grown into a strong woman, a woman who has the marriage and the life she wants. You've made your own life here, and you've done a splendid job of it. I just want to know you. Maddie wants to know you. I hope one day I can convince you—that young, arrogant sinner no longer lives in this old man's body. I hope I can convince you that I love you. I have loved you and prayed for you for years. I want to be your father."

Tilda stood there silent. She had no idea what to do. She came up beside Josh, and their eyes met. Hers full of confusion, his strong and sweet and kind. He took her arm as if to hold her steady.

Closing her eyes, she gathered her thoughts to the extent she could. "I'm going to need time to trust you. Because I really don't. Ben can spin whatever tale he wants, but he *did* kidnap me. He made sure to take me out the side of the house that no one sees. I didn't know that because he knocked me unconscious—"

"I did not," Ben interrupted.

And since she'd been unconscious, it was a little hard to contradict him.

"He brought me to town, carried me onto your train, and locked me in his room."

"It wasn't locked."

Carl gave Ben a fierce look and shook his head.

Ben gave his father a look of desperate love, and again Tilda felt pity for her brother.

"Like I said, I need time to trust you. I won't be alone with you or Maddie." Then she had a notion. "I suppose it's true that you are my father." She glanced at Maddie. "That *we* resemble you. All of us have such dark hair and eyes. Mr. Cabril, are you by any chance of Spanish ancestry?"

Josh's hand tightened on her arm. She'd surprised him with her direct question.

"Spanish, yes. My ancestors have been in America since

before the Revolutionary War. I'm very proud of my roots. We lived in Florida when it was a Spanish territory."

"Is Cabril a Spanish name, then?"

"Actually, it was shortened. Our family's original name was Cabrillo."

Josh and Tilda exchanged looks, their eyes wide.

"One of my ancestors was a Spanish conquistador. In fact, he was a sailor who explored the coast of California hundreds of years ago."

"Three hundred," Tilda said quietly.

Carl furrowed his brow. "What?"

"I was a sailor myself before I settled down to ranching," Josh said. "There will be saltwater in our children's blood, Tilda. We'll raise them up as landlubbers, though. I'd like to keep them close to home."

"I'm not sure what to do next," Tilda said, looking at Josh.

Nodding, Josh turned to Carl, then to Ben. "I suppose we have to tell them."

Tilda's shoulders lifted and dropped. A very slow shrug, but she knew he was right.

They turned to face what had to be said.

Twenty-Five

Brody had done two weeks' worth of work in half a day. He was weary to the bone. By midmorning they had Cord helping with minor medical care, and Mayhew was acting like a receptionist, keeping order in the small front office.

The Mayhews refused to come at first because they were fascinated by the artifacts, but they'd stopped in to talk about the armor and never escaped.

Gretel didn't invite them to come and eat lunch at the ranch house. Instead, during the only lull they'd had all morning, she arrived with her husband carrying a large basket loaded with fried chicken and a platter of biscuits. Zane, trailing after them, lugged a bowl of mashed potatoes and another of gravy.

"Where are the children?" Ellie asked.

"I got Harriet to stay in the house while they napped. She's there if Michelle needs anything, but Michelle and the baby are asleep, along with my two and Harriet's little one. The woman's watching over a sizable brood. God save her if they all wake up at once."

"How's Michelle?" Brody finished drying his hands with

a towel, then led the way to the small table in the examining room. Mayhew and Cord followed the delicious scent. The Westbrook men drew the table away from the wall and rustled up two more chairs so that all four of them could eat together.

Zane set the bowls on the table. "Michelle is perfect. You took good care of her, Brody. You too, Ellie. Thank you both. I reckon delivering a baby will slow her down for a bit, but she's already been up and dressed today. She's staying inside, though, with the baby."

Rick handed over the chicken and said, "I'll go make sure everything's in order at the house."

"I'll be right along, *Liebling*." Gretel put the biscuits on the table, turned and left.

Brody dashed upstairs and came right back with plates and utensils.

Zane said, "We got a telegraph from the man Michelle contacted about the armor. He'll be here tomorrow sounds like. Someone's gonna have to pry themselves away from doctoring to talk to him. If you don't, I'm afraid Michelle will insist on doing it. That woman needs to take care for a few days." Then he left the room.

"We haven't even seen the artifacts yet," Ellie said to Brody.

"Well, here's something no one's seen yet." Mayhew reached into the inside pocket of his suit coat and drew out a brittle sheet of paper. "I found this just this morning. We discovered two matching pieces of armor that looked like one piece at first. When we pulled them apart, we came upon this paper. It was wrapped in oilcloth. I've looked over your papers, Brody, and I'm pretty sure it's your grandfather's handwriting."

Brody gasped. "Who was it said Grandpa must've found all that armor, dug it up, maybe found any gold that was among the bodies, then buried it all again? This proves it."

Mayhew nodded. "Could be. I haven't read it yet. I unfolded it and saw it's a fairly short note, and it was written in your grandpa's hand. At a glance it made little sense. The note is to your father."

Brody said, "We'll copy it out to keep from ruining this fragile paper." He carefully smoothed out the note and read it through to the end. "This is Grandpa's handwriting, all right, but I have no idea what it all means.

"Frasier,

"Herd there ain't much gold but plenty of madmen. I didn't want that for us. Saw these mountains and thought of the old country. Wanted it. Looking fer land, I found treshur. Nuff fer us all. Got my notes sent to you. Goin' back fer more. Leavin this here lessen somethin happens to me. Sent haff the map to the man who stood me for my claim. Only fair he gits haff. Mayhoo Westbroks, a good man. I found what's here cuz of him. Got all the gold out."

Solo yo sobrevivo
Yo solo sigo
volveré a mi barco
a donde La Río está muerto

38.151294647218755, -120.45130425641777

Brody had read the note aloud except for the last part. "Spanish again, in Grandpa's hand but printed out as if he'd copied it. And what's this string of numbers?" He passed the note on to Ellie, who knew a little more Spanish than he did. Which wasn't much.

She studied it for a bit, then looked up at Cord and Mayhew. "Do either of you speak Spanish?"

They both shook their heads.

"We'll take this to Michelle—she knows the language well." Ellie sounded uncertain.

"We'll let her sleep another hour or so," said Brody, "then take her the note."

"What about the numbers?"

Ellie looked at Grandpa's note again. "*Solo* means 'one' or 'alone.' That's in there twice. Maybe he was the last one alive. I think maybe *barco* is 'boat' or 'ship.' *La Río* is the river, like Dorada Rio, which means 'Golden River,' and I think—" Ellie hesitated—"*muerto* means 'death.'"

Brody thought he heard the whole table swallow.

Cord said, "The river of death?"

They all looked up, each of them a little afraid of what they'd heard.

"My grandpa wrote this note, went hunting for the river of death, and then he died." Brody rubbed one hand over his face. "It would be superstitious to let this scare us, right?"

No one answered him.

The outer door slammed. "Doc? I cut my arm!"

Shooting to his feet, Brody didn't even pretend it wasn't a relief to have to attend to something else.

———✧———

"You've found evidence of Captain Juan Cabrillo? Out here? No, that can't be right. I know my family history well, especially surrounding old Captain Cabrillo. It's said he might have gone as far north as the Columbia River in Washington State, but he died on Santa Catalina Island at the end of his only voyage up the coast."

Tilda had told him most of the story. But she hadn't mentioned the gold nor how much armor they'd found. Let him think it was just the littlest shred of evidence. At least for now.

"We found a reference to Cabrillo," Josh said. "It's our guess one of his ships got separated from the armada he sailed with and ran aground, maybe in a storm? There was one reference to thick fog. We just don't know. But we found proof someone was near our ranch three hundred years ago, someone who had a connection to Captain Cabrillo."

"And you're a direct descendent of Cabrillo?" Tilda felt a little dizzy. "I thought I knew a lot about him. My father was a history teacher, and I was allowed to read his books. The history of the West stuck with me in particular. I can't remember knowing anything about my name, yet it must have been lodged in my head somewhere."

Carl blushed and lowered his eyes. "I called myself Carlo Cabrillo when I was with Johanna, your mother. I always knew my heritage, but my family had Americanized the name long ago. My real name is Carl Cabril."

"Another lie then?" Tilda's jaw tightened.

The sheriff had gone out once he was sure Josh felt all right with that. Josh's cowhands were sitting outside on the boardwalk, listening for a shout for help.

"And you've found artifacts?" Maddie's eyes lit up. Giving Tilda a shy smile, she said, "I love history, too."

Tilda wondered if Maddie had ever considered being a teacher.

Tilda felt the first real spark of a connection with her sister. She still had trouble trusting them, but she fully believed in forgiving others. Of course, God gave her common sense, too. Loving and forgiving your enemies surely wasn't the same thing as trusting your enemies, was it? She'd have to pray about that. Eyeing Ben, who was sitting behind bars, she knew she was going to have to pray really hard.

The afternoon was as hectic as the morning. Ellie could hardly remember anyone getting sick before Brody had come.

He still refused to charge anyone for his services because he wasn't staying much longer. Just until they found what was at the end of Mayhew's map. He had written to Dr. Tibbles in Boston several times, informing him of the delay and promising he'd be back soon.

Ellie had accepted she was moving to Boston, and they both wondered if his brothers would agree to come along. Thayne and Lock visited the doctor's office after school and helped out, pestering Brody about his coming to look over the armor. When things finally quieted down, they all headed for Michelle's laboratory, which Ellie liked to call the "invention shed."

As they walked, Brody told his brothers about their grandpa's note Mayhew and Cord had found. To give Michelle some peace, they decided not to eat at the ranch house tonight. Ellie had run upstairs during a lull in the hectic day and put a stew on, so supper was ready and waiting for them.

They eagerly planned to spend the evening studying Grandpa's odd note with the Spanish words.

"We'll need to go over those pieces of armor very carefully in case anything else is hidden among them," Brody said. "Cord found the note Grandpa left tucked between two pieces shoved together that looked like one piece. What if there are more notes to be found?"

"Maybe we should go see Michelle first, have her read the note and figure out the Spanish." They all thought that to be a good idea.

Thayne reached Michelle's shed first and opened the door. Michelle kept the building locked, but they'd gotten the key from Zane.

Just as Thayne swung it wide, hoofbeats pounded into the yard. They turned to see Josh and Tilda riding in.

Josh saw Ellie and waved. "We've got news," he called. "And we want to see the armor, too."

"Not as badly as we want to see the new baby," Tilda said.

Josh told them Ben's lawyer still hadn't arrived and that Carl Cabril was indeed a descendent of Captain Cabrillo.

Tilda said, "I fear Ben is going to be set free. Carl does an excellent job of muddying the waters, which doesn't lead me to trust him any more than his son. Ben almost sounds believable when he denies he did any of the things I know he did."

"There's something about Carl. He says he's a believer, and he says it with real conviction." Tilda dismounted. "But the way he talks to Ben . . . I suppose a man who makes a fortune in New York City has to be tough and smart. He has to be excellent at bossing people around. But I don't like the way he treats Ben. I don't know quite what to make of it. Oh, and he said he's staying. Moving permanently to California. He's looking for a house to buy in Dorada Rio. He aims to send Ben back to New York to run his business there."

"He must trust Ben to give him so much responsibility," Brody said.

She shook her head. "At least if Ben goes back east, he'll be far away from us. I wonder if Sheriff Stockwood has a way to check with the New York police to confirm he in fact gets to New York and that he stays there."

"I'll ask the sheriff about it, Tilda," said Josh. "What Ben did was a crime, pure and simple. A serious crime. If he gets away with it, you'll be left to live in fear that he'll show up and do it again."

It was now Brody and Ellie's turn, and they told about finding the note and the new Spanish language clue. The former one about Captain Cabrillo had helped them find some of the treasure, so the new clues might be helpful.

"Let's go examine that armor, every nook and cranny of it." Josh looked through the door and smiled. "The boys... that is, your brothers are beating us to any new discoveries."

Gretel yelled out the back door that they were all invited into the house for supper.

Ellie told her they had supper going at their own home, but Gretel wanted them there and said she'd fetch the stew and see it was chilled for the MacKenzie family to eat tomorrow.

"Zane and Michelle want to know what's going on. You'd better join us before Michelle brings the baby over there to help examine armor."

"Thank you, Gretel. We'll be there."

Josh was the last one inside.

Tilda gasped. "I've never been here before. I only vaguely heard it called the invention shed. I had no idea it was so large and so loaded with strange equipment. What is she inventing in here?"

"I can barely keep up with what she's working on," Josh said. "She seems to be making improvements to trains mainly. Let's go look over the treasure. We can talk about inventions later."

They got to work. The armor had been cleaned since arriving at the ranch. After Michelle sketched a diagram showing the placement of the pieces, each suit of armor had been disassembled to some extent and wiped free of dirt and debris. There were a surprising number of pieces to a suit of armor; the whole collection of artifacts was laid out in front of them.

"Can I see the note you found?" Tilda asked.

Ellie nodded. "Do you understand Spanish?"

"Not a word, and now that I know I have Spanish heritage, that seems a shame. I'm just curious."

Brody had copied his grandpa's note onto a new piece of paper to protect the original note, which was very fragile from age. Tilda read what she could of it as Josh came up to look over her shoulder.

It was his turn to gasp. Josh jabbed a finger at the page. "Why did he write down latitude and longitude coordinates?"

Everyone turned to stare at him.

Brody strode straight for the paper. "Is that what that string of numbers is?"

Josh shrugged. "Sure looks like it. We used such numbers for sailing all the time. That way we knew our location."

"So they tell us a location. An *exact* location . . ."

Ellie came to Brody's side and looked at the numbers. "Can you tell us then where the coordinates point to?"

"You said your grandpa was a sailor just like me. It's only natural he'd be able to figure the location. I'd need to spend a little time making calculations on a globe or a map. But yes, I think I can tell you where on the map they point to."

"Brody, you and Ellie brought back his original mining claim, didn't you?" Tilda stared at the paper, her brow furrowed.

"We did. I left it in the house last night. We can get it when we go in for supper."

"With those two things combined, we ought to be able to ride right to the end of that map." Josh smiled at Thayne and Lock, who were listening with rapt attention. "We can go snap up the rest of the treasure tomorrow if you want."

Brody took Ellie's hand, his expression solemn. "And then I can go back east. I have to go, Ellie."

"I knew that when I married you. We can build a good life there, Brody. And with the train, we can come home to visit."

Brody looked at his brothers, and Ellie held her breath. "I want you to come with me. But you're adult men—or getting close to it. It's your choice."

Thayne watched with sharp eyes. Lock scowled.

"I want to be with you, Brody. I want our family to be together. I'd go with you—after we find the rest of Grandpa's treasure—but I can't leave Lock behind. He needs me more than you. I'm old enough to be out in the world on my own, and I've known youngsters Lock's age who were taking care of themselves." Thayne turned to his little brother. "Will you go east with us, Lock? Then Brody can work for his doctor until he feels his debt is repaid. Maybe I'm old enough to go to medical school myself. I'm a little shy on education, so I don't know how easy it'd be for me to get into college. But I'll do the work I have to do to get in, even if it takes a while."

Lock was silent.

Ellie watched the boy, because despite his protest, he was still a boy. Lock studied his brothers, then looked at the armor. He was close enough to a shield to run his hand over the old iron, pitted from age. This was the one that had been hanging in a tree. It was rusted and much worse off than the ones they'd dug out of the ground. Lock leaned closer. "What's this?"

All of them turned toward the shield. There was a small space where the surface wasn't ruined.

"It looks like some letters carved into the shield." Brody leaned closer. "It says *solo sigo*." Brody's eyes met Lock's. "Those same words are in Grandpa's note. He must've copied it off this shield. It was probably readable thirty years ago."

They all considered it quietly, and then, one by one, they smiled.

Lock slapped Brody on the back and said, "I'll go with you, but I like it out here in the West. Can we come back like Thayne said, after your debt is repaid? We only have the three of us since Pa died, but now, with Ellie and all the Harts, we'd be surrounded by family. I like the idea of that."

"I like the idea of that, too," agreed Brody. "I think Ellie's going to miss her family a lot. I'll write Dr. Tibbles and tell him we'll be there before winter settles in. I'll tell him I'm willing to work for him for one year. With my help, he can spend that year finding someone else to partner with him."

Legends of Gold

Ellie felt unshed tears burn her eyes. She was so in love with Brody that she would willingly follow him anywhere. But only now, when they spoke of returning, could she admit to herself how much she would miss her family.

Lock stepped over to Brody and extended his hand. Brody caught hold and shook his hand thoroughly. Thayne, standing nearby, rested his hand on top of theirs. The three of them, for once in their life, in complete agreement.

Lock turned to Josh. "Can we go treasure hunting tomorrow, then? You think we can finish this up in a single day?"

Josh said, "Tilda needs to be on hand to testify at Ben's trial. Can we wait until that's over? We'd like to go with you. I think the trial may take place tomorrow, but if not, it should be soon."

Brody nodded. "We'll wait. Hopefully it's not for too long. We're ready to finish this and return to Boston."

Ellie's heart stumbled a bit as she wished for a longer delay. But she kept her mouth firmly closed. Michelle had a new baby. She wanted to watch her grow up.

"Once the trial is over," Tilda said, "I'd prefer to get back out in the wilderness again."

Josh smiled at her. "I'd say you're starting to like Maddie."

Tilda nodded. "It's a fine thing to have an unexpected family that's truly mine. I want to know her."

"If Grandpa found all that gold like he said he did, I suppose there ain't no rush." Lock exchanged a glum look with Thayne, who dipped his chin.

Josh stepped to Tilda's side and pressed a hand to the middle of her back. She leaned against him and sighed.

Ellie thought of how much she enjoyed leaning on Brody.

And he leaned on her, too. Being married was a wondrous thing, even if you had to leave your family far behind.

"And maybe," Lock said, "we don't have to go out there in a mad rush and find the location on Cord's map and Graham's mining claim and wherever that row of numbers Josh called 'tude'-something takes us. Maybe we can just settle in beside the treasure, dig mighty slow, and ponder our lives for a bit."

Josh said quietly, "Longitude and latitude."

"Maybe we can spend time out in the wilderness memorizing those words," Tilda added.

"Let's examine this armor more closely, all of us," Ellie said. "Just in case there are more carved words somewhere or another hidden note. But be very careful—we don't want to damage any of it."

"And whatever we find, we'll turn it over to the men Michelle contacted. For research." Tilda frowned. "But they get to examine it, not *take* it. What we do with this treasure is a decision *we* make, no one else."

Everyone nodded in agreement.

No one seemed overly excited about searching for treasure now. Ellie thought that Lock accepting the absence of more gold doubloons had taken most of the thrill out of the hunt. One more search for the treasure should end it. One more day for a treasure hunt—after Ben Cabril's trial. And after that she'd head for Boston with her husband and his brothers and leave the rest of the Hart family and the ranch far behind.

She wondered if she'd ever see her family again.

She wondered if this was how Josh had felt when he went to sea.

Twenty-Six

"We the jury find the defendant not guilty." Fatty, who was cranky about serving on the jury when it was lunchtime at his diner, groused. "But only cuz you told us he'd leave the state."

The judge slammed his gavel down. "We've agreed to that condition as a requirement for not locking you up, Mr. Cabril. Which means you're bound by this court to leave the state forever. California is done with you, you kidnapping polecat."

Ben, standing to receive the verdict and sentencing, glared at the judge. "Forever? No. I want to come back after Tilda calms down and realizes I didn't mean her any harm."

Tilda wasn't very experienced with legal matters, but that seemed pure stupid to talk to a judge that way. On the other hand, he'd been found not guilty, so she hadn't expected that he'd receive any sentence. His lawyer had called it a plea deal. He'd only been found not guilty because his lawyer had promised he'd go far, far away.

"I don't cotton to the idea of you walking away after you hurt Mrs. Hart." The judge rapped his gavel again. "If you don't agree to the deal you made, then I'm going to instruct the jury to find you guilty—which they were inclined to do. After that I'll sentence you to a few years in San Quentin. That's where we usually send kidnappers, if we don't hang them."

Ben, scowling, sank back into his chair. "If I could convince Tilda to let me come back here, would you allow it?" he asked.

The judge narrowed his eyes. "Get out of this state and stay out. For all I know, you might threaten Mrs. Hart in some way and get her to cooperate with you out of fear. No, you're out. Go home."

Ben turned to his father, his shoulders slumped.

Carl was sitting in a chair right behind his son. "We'll come back east and visit, son. You've helped me run the company for years. You've got a talent for it. We'll come and see you in New York."

Tilda wasn't sure how she liked this outcome, but she had to admit that urging others to hang her brother didn't sit right. Having a family was turning out to be confusing.

The whole trial had been annoying. As anticipated, Ben's lawyer had shown himself to be a smooth talker, with Ben acting contrite before the judge and jury, apologizing for "upsetting" his sister, and so he'd gotten away with the kidnapping.

When it had been her turn to be questioned, Ben's lawyer made her sound like she'd slept through the whole thing because she was tired, not because she'd been knocked out by Ben and his partner. Then, in her disoriented condition upon awakening, she'd leapt from the train when all she'd needed to do was ask politely to be taken back, to say she'd changed her mind about leaving the man she'd gotten engaged to only days before.

"The train arrives midmorning most days," the judge continued. "Until then, Cabril, you're to be held in jail. When the time comes, the sheriff and his deputy will escort you to the train when it's ready to pull out. And don't forget, you're paying for your own ticket."

That had been part of the sentence: to pay for a ticket, food, and lodging, and for a deputy to ride all the way to New York and back. One of the deputies seemed eager for the adventure.

It took longer than Tilda liked, especially with those reckless MacKenzie men champing at the bit to get back to their treasure hunt. She took a moment to marvel at how western her thoughts had become.

When the jury filed out of the courtroom, but before Ben could be led away, Tilda said, "Wait, Ben, before you go, I'd like to talk to all of you."

Sheriff Stockwood turned to her and nodded. Seeing that Josh was right there, the sheriff said, "I'll step over there." He gestured to the back of the courtroom. "Give you a few minutes with your family, Mrs. Hart."

It struck a tender place in her heart to hear "your family." Until Josh, she'd never had one, never believed one existed. Now here were three people who shared blood ties with her.

Tilda went to Maddie and rested a hand on her arm. Speaking to all of them, she said, "If you're staying in Dorada Rio, F-Father"—she forced out the word—"I hope we will get to know each other. My family . . . the Harts attend church every Sunday. Maybe you can join us for worship." She turned to Maddie. "Finding out the connection to

Captain Cabrillo, and realizing I'd heard that name before, makes me believe my memories of you all are still there. Maddie, I feel a special kinship with you. I want to come to know you better." She paused and looked at Ben. "If you write to me from New York City, I promise to answer your letters."

"Tilda, I-I . . ." He shook his head and looked down. "I thought I knew best. I believed if I could get you back home to New York City, you'd find Father and Maddie waiting for you with open arms and end up being happy. But I . . . um, I took that choice away from you. Hearing you were getting married made me desperate to get you away while you were still free. I was a headlong fool. I do want your forgiveness and your trust. I will try and earn that through my letters."

Ben reached up, slowly, cautiously. Tilda felt Josh tense beside her, but he didn't interfere. He touched the scar on her forehead with the tip of one finger. "It really was awful when this happened. I'm glad we found you. No thanks to any of us, you're a woman who's made a good life for herself."

Tilda managed a lopsided smile. "No five-year-old should be left in charge of two babies. I'm glad I found out the story of my scar."

"I'll write. Maybe I'll get a tintype made of myself and send it to you."

Carl gave his son a hug and said, "Ben, I've made you doubt me. I made you believe my love is only as good as your behavior. That's something I need forgiveness for. I'm going to try and let go of my tyrannical ways."

"Not tyrannical, Father. Bossy maybe, but you're no tyrant." Ben stepped back, offered a hand to Josh, who shook it. Ben gave Tilda a nod, but seemed to realize a hug might be a bit too much. He kissed Maddie on the cheek. "I think there'll be time to visit me before the train leaves in the morning. I'll see you again, baby sister." He turned away. "I'm ready, Sheriff Stockwood."

The sheriff came and escorted Ben out of the courtroom.

Tilda managed a quick hug with her father, then a longer one with Maddie, before she and Josh headed for home.

They talked about leaving tomorrow to wrap up their treasure hunt only to be met by Zane, who said, "No treasure hunt for a while. We've had an outbreak of fever at the orphanage, and Thayne's among the sick. Several of the cowhands have whatever it is, too. Brody says it could be measles. He and Ellie aren't going anywhere for a while. We all have to wait. We contacted those arckil . . . uh, archolage . . . the men who hunt old relics Michelle sent for and warned them back until the fever clears up."

Josh took Tilda into the house, where they found themselves unwelcome because Michelle didn't want the fever to affect the baby. Everyone got kicked out.

Brody agreed to let them have his room because he and Ellie were staying at the orphanage until the sickness had passed.

Tilda scowled. "We're never going to find that treasure."

"If it's measles, most of us have had it. It went through the ranch last year. About five of our hands were affected, and most of the children got it then. When I was a youngster, our whole family had it. If Brody's right, it'll be contained mostly in the orphanage."

"A lot of them will have had it, too. It swept through the orphanage in New York when I was there, so I've had it as well. That'll be true of the street children—they tend to get sick whenever there's an outbreak."

"Brody will have a lot of miserable little ones, but hopefully the sickness will run its course soon enough without any serious trouble."

"Two weeks, as I remember." Tilda looked toward the mountain and gasped. "Is that snow?"

Josh turned to look at the colorful trees to the east and, beyond them, the snowcapped peaks. "Snow comes down in feet up there, not inches. And we're into the fall season. Whatever snow falls now is going to stay around till spring."

Tilda felt like kicking something, maybe Ben. "We ran out of summer days."

"It depends on where that map leads. The higher elevations get plenty of snow. Ellie said Graham MacKenzie's Spanish note mentioned the 'river of death.' She isn't the best at Spanish, so she was going to ask Michelle about it. But baby Leah was fussy last night, and she didn't come down."

"I wanted to see her." Tilda heard the self-pity in her voice, but she'd really wanted to see little Leah. Michelle and Zane had named her Leah because it reminded Michelle of her father, Liam Stiles.

Josh took her hand and walked with her to the doctor's office. "Since I'm not leaving you alone for a moment until that deputy gets back to say he left your brother in New York City, you'll either ride the range with me when I need to go to work, or we'll hide in the doctor's office and call it a honeymoon."

Tilda smirked, then laughed out loud. "We get a honeymoon because there's measles at the orphanage? That sounds like the kind of honeymoon I'd get."

Josh got her inside, then leaned down and kissed her thoroughly. "If I have a say in it, it'll be very romantic."

She kissed him again, and all she felt was too much to hold inside. She rested one hand on his cheek and whispered, "Have I told you I love you, Josh?"

A smile crept over his face. "I don't believe I'd heard that from you, no."

"Well, I do. It seems like it all happened too fast. But I love you with all my heart."

He drew her close, his eyes shining, his smile fading to something else. Something deeper and warmer. "I love you too, Tilda. I think I fell in love with you while you were sitting on my lap on our ride home from Dorada Rio the day I met you. I spent every minute after that trying to figure out how to get you to marry me."

"You did a good job of it, Husband. I went right along with all your figuring without even thinking of saying no."

When he'd stopped kissing her, she said, "You're right. I'm thinking we might just manage the most romantic honeymoon two people ever had."

"And after this outbreak of whatever's ailing our students passes, we'll get to that treasure. If snow comes to the lowlands, or the map leads up a mountain, then we'll go in the spring. I mean, if there's no more gold, digging up artifacts that have been buried for three hundred years can wait a bit longer."

"Maybe if we have to wait out the winter, Brody could go back east and then visit next spring. Then we go on one last treasure hunt together."

Josh kissed her again. "We can spend the winter getting to know your father and sister. We can help tend Michelle's baby, and if the men she contacted about the artifacts turn up, we can spend time studying with them."

Holding Tilda's hand, Josh led her through Brody's doctor's office to a back window. "Just look at that snow come down."

"How can that be happening? It's a warm day here." Tilda and Josh stood at the window with their arms around each other, gazing at the mountains in the distance. "It's not just the peaks either—the snow is covering everything."

He held her closer as if she'd just complained of the cold. She hadn't, but she didn't protest his nearness. Instead, she said, "We can't just settle in here and hide from the work of caring for the sick children."

"Nope, we can't. And we still have cattle to round up for the drive to San Francisco."

The sun sank lower as they stood watching the weather, casting the Two Harts in a wash of bright orange.

"I'm wondering if maybe this is the first time we've had a quiet moment since we got married."

Josh gave her a sound kiss. "I've got a keen memory of a few moments we had alone."

"Yes, I remember them, too." She drew back and looked deep into his eyes. "I don't think we have time for quiet moments right now."

He chuckled. "Maybe not, but we can hide away for a day or two, I think. We have time for everything, Tilda."

Right now, though, all they had time for was love.

Epilogue

Lock hadn't come down with measles until a full week after the outbreak started, and he was among the last to get well. When finally he was over his fever and rash, he stepped out of the doctor's office where he'd been recovering for two weeks. It was the second week of October, and autumn had fully come to the Two Harts Ranch.

And winter had come to the Sierra Nevada Mountains.

Lock looked to the east and howled, "No! We can still go. We can still get in the treasure hunt before spring, as long as the map stays at lower elevations."

"Those are some big *if*s, Lock," said Josh, who was waiting outside the doctor's office in the balmy autumn weather. Tilda was there, too.

Thayne hadn't been hit as hard by the measles and had gotten well fast. He'd then worked at Brody's side caring for eleven sick orphans, three sick cowpokes, the children of those cowpokes, one of the mothers, and little Caroline. Thankfully, most everyone was on the mend now, but it had been a harrowing two weeks. Nearly all the healthy folks had helped to care for the sick. Those not caring for them got ready for the cattle drive, which would begin just as soon as the last fever broke.

"I told you we should have mentioned the snow." Thayne sat on the boardwalk outside the doctor's office. He looked at Brody and rolled his eyes.

"I wanted Lock to concentrate on getting well. I was afraid if he got upset by the snow, it might set him back." Brody rubbed one hand over the back of his neck in a gesture that reminded Josh that his brother-in-law was still new at this doctoring job.

Ellie patted him on the back. "Telling him earlier wouldn't have changed a thing. He wasn't up to going, and none of us was available to go with him."

All five of them turned to study Lock.

Tilda said, "We've studied those notes thoroughly, and Michelle has translated the Spanish. It sounds like your grandpa found all the gold the explorers left behind." Mayhew Westbrook, who'd returned to Sacramento for the winter, had checked on the gold coins' value. "Mayhew found a man who's willing to pay a shocking amount of money for the coins. If you MacKenzies decide to sell them, Mayhew will handle it for you. He also said he'd like to come back when we go treasure hunting in the spring."

Cord had remained at the Two Harts, moving into the bunkhouse. Josh and Zane had hired him on for the winter. He was a skilled rider and able to do farm chores and carpentry work. But mostly he wanted to learn to be a cowboy. He'd shared his dream of finding his own land and settling somewhere to farm or maybe ranch. But he had scant roping and branding skills and the like, so he planned to spend the winter learning.

"Lock, now that the measles is about finished," Brody said, shoving his hands deep into his pockets, "after talking it over with Ellie, we're heading back east. I've written to Dr. Tibbles and told him I'm hoping to come out west again next spring, but I'll be there to work for him over the winter. I'm hoping Ellie and I can move back here for good after we spend the winter in Boston." Brody bent forward, and he stared at the ground. "I still want you and Thayne to come with us, but you can choose. If you do come, you can spend the winter in school."

"And, Lock," Josh said, "if you do stay, no one is going into those mountains until next spring. We had a man ride in hunting for work just yesterday who said they've had over fourteen feet of snow in those mountains. Right near where Cord's half of that map takes us."

Lock winced. "Can the train get through?"

Josh shrugged. "Usually."

Brody studied his brother with kind eyes, sad eyes, as if he already knew Lock would choose the Two Harts and California and MacKenzie's Treasure.

There was a long silence as Lock showed about the second flash of maturity in his life. Finally, he gave a big sigh and said, "We'll come back in the spring? You promise?"

Brody made sure to look the kid in the eyes before answering, "Yes, I promise. You have my word on that."

Lock nodded. "All right then. I'll go along. I like being with my brothers." He gave Ellie a smile. "And my sister."

Brody went to Lock and clapped him on the back. "We're leaving on the train next Monday morning. You're the last to have your fever go down. I want you to have three days to rest up, gather your strength. I'll watch over everyone else for that long, too."

Ellie came up to her little brother and hugged him tight. Thayne rose and slung an arm around Lock, and Ellie pulled him into the hug. Brody wrapped his arms around all of them.

Josh caught Tilda by the hand and drew her away. They started walking toward the house. Michelle had allowed them back inside as soon as she was convinced Josh and Tilda weren't going to get sick.

"Did I tell you all of Michelle's family is coming here in the next month? The Stiles family, all five of them, will stay a month or more because Jilly has some building to do. We've got two more cowhands who want to marry, and we promised them their own cabins. And those archeologists will be visiting as soon as we let them know the measles is over. We'll stay in the house, and they can sleep in Ellie and Brody's place while they're here."

"My father wants to study the artifacts, too. He and Maddie are coming out to help with the research."

"Seems we've got our lives all mapped out for us. We're mighty lucky to never have to waste a minute doing our own thinking."

"Yes, and you said the man is called by the Bible to do all the thinking in the family."

Josh flinched. "Did I say that?"

She laughed, then leaned against his side. "You did. But it doesn't look like either one of us will have to waste time on that."

They'd left the MacKenzies behind but hadn't reached the house yet.

"You can come along on our cattle drive. We can stay in San Francisco for a few days. The work slows down after the drive." Josh stopped and turned to face his wife. "So we won't be greatly missed. Michelle has talked with her ma, and we can stay in the Stiles house in San Francisco and go see the ocean, maybe ride on a trolley car." He leaned down, slow as can be, giving her plenty of warning about what he was doing. "Then we'll come back and decide whether to build our own house or stay with Zane, and we'll settle in." He kissed her.

Tilda stood on tiptoes so that her lips could meet his, wrapping her arms around his neck. Then, pulling back the barest of inches, she said, "Wherever you go, I'll go. Wherever you are is my home."

Josh smiled. "I don't need to go on a treasure hunt, darlin'. I'm holding my treasure right here in my arms."

Read on
for a sneak peek at

Riches Beyond Measure

BY MARY CONNEALY

BOOK 3 OF
✧ GOLDEN STATE TREASURE ✧

Available in the fall of 2025

March 1875
Two Harts Ranch—California

Cordell Westbrook dropped a lasso over the head of a skittish spring calf. It was branding time at the Two Harts, and Cord was now a cowboy. At last.

Grinning, he leapt off his horse, landing next to the bawling calf. He flipped it onto its side, hog-tied it, and held it still while Josh Hart, his boss and friend, made quick work of branding the little heifer.

The poor little heifer.

But Josh was fast, and Cord had gotten mighty skilled at this. He untied the critter's feet as Josh freed the lasso from around her neck, letting it run off to its outraged mama to be nuzzled and fed and comforted.

"That's the last one," Josh said. He stood and watched the milling red-and-white Hereford cattle settle down. "We got ourselves a great calf crop this spring."

Cord scanned the herd while he coiled his rope, appreciating all he'd learned since arriving at the ranch. These days he knew what he was looking at. Good, sturdy cows with calves that were shedding their shaggy winter coats, revealing the shiny coats beneath. The cows had survived the winter well without any worrisome weight loss. The weather in this Californian valley wasn't all that harsh, and yet it got cold often enough.

Cord understood all this to mean, to his absolute delight, that sure enough, he was a cowboy. "This is so much better than being a banker," he declared. "I can hardly believe I lasted so long in that office."

Josh clapped him on the back. "You're a solid hand, Cord. You've got a job here on the Two Harts for as long as you want."

Nodding, Cord walked over to his ground-hitched horse. The well-trained animal stood patiently despite the noise and commotion and smoke all around him.

"I've always wanted my own place, Josh. I'd like to stay on longer at the Two Harts if I can, but the plan is still to buy my own land and settle down. Build something of my own. Even Grandpa Westbrook has accepted that now."

He hoped.

The sound of steady, clopping hooves caused him and Josh to turn to the north just in time to see a chuck wagon pulled by two brown Morgan horses moving toward the branding site. They were driven not by the bunkhouse cook as was usual but by Josh's pretty sister, Annie Lane. Cord wondered how such a beautiful widow had managed to stay single for so long. As she drew closer, Cord saw Annie's five-year-old daughter, Caroline, tucked up beside her ma.

They were a pair, those two. Dark hair, deep brown eyes, red roses in their cheeks. Annie leaned toward being a solemn woman, and Cord knew she'd loved her husband. She'd watched him die from a gunshot wound and still carried two bullets in her own flesh. That seemed reason enough for her not to risk her heart again.

Annie pulled the chuck wagon to a halt, and Josh slapped Cord on the back, a little harder than he had before, jolting Cord back to awareness of his surroundings. He then glanced at Josh. It did near to a physical injury to have to take his eyes off Annie.

As if sensing Cord's thoughts, Josh rolled his eyes and then headed for the wagon. But Annie was already off the bench seat and on the ground, helping Caroline alight before any man could reach her.

"Did Casey go to the south pasture?" Josh asked as he stepped to the back of the wagon and brought down the back gate to unload the food and other supplies. Plenty of hungry cowhands stepped in to help. They had a full crew today. The ranch boasted several pastures, and all of them held spring calves ready to be branded.

Josh and his brother, Zane, had hired a new bunkhouse cook just a few weeks ago to help their longtime cook, whose knee was giving him trouble again.

Annie tucked stray hair behind her ear and shook her head. "Neb went south, so Casey got pulled into helping make lunch for the orphanage and school. And Tilda had an extra-long morning class because whatever she hit on teaching today kept the whole class enthralled. Your wife has a rare gift for teaching."

"She does indeed." Josh smiled at the mention of his wife. "I like sitting in on her classes too, although I don't get much chance to do so." He leaned down and kissed his sister on the cheek. "Thanks for bringing our food out. We just got done with this pasture, so you timed it perfectly. We're all starving!"

Suddenly, a strangle rumble had all the men stepping away

from the wagon, most with their food already in hand. An earthquake. Which was normal enough in a place like California. Nothing to worry about—that is, if it was a small one. And with no roof overhead to collapse on them, they just had to wait it out.

Then the shaking turned rougher than any Cord had experienced before. Nevertheless, the men started eating, their feet spread wide for greater balance. Apparently, nothing would interrupt lunchtime.

Annie drew Caroline close and said, "I hope they got all the children outside back at the ranch."

"I'm sure they did," Josh reassured her. "Zane stayed around today since Tilda's pa is coming out. I don't like it when there's no one to watch him, even if he's turned into a man Tilda and I trust. Mostly." Josh hadn't yet settled into having a father-in-law close at hand. Especially a meddling father-in-law who Tilda, raised as an orphan, hadn't known existed until just last fall.

The quaking worsened, and Annie pulled Caroline tight against her own body. The earth rolled in a way unlike anything Cord had seen, and he'd grown up in California. "Look at that! The ground's moving like waves."

Everyone turned to gape at an incoming ripple. Then a deeper rumble was felt by everyone, and a crack appeared in the ground.

"Step back!" Cord rushed to Annie's side to pull her away from the oncoming rupture. But he wasn't quick enough. A crevasse appeared right between Annie's feet.

Annie screamed and jumped toward Cord, losing her tight grip on Caroline. Fortunately, Josh was there and so grabbed his niece, who shrieked in terror.

The ground collapsed under Cord just as he caught ahold of Annie, a narrow slit that kept widening. Cord clawed at the edge of the crack with one hand while holding on to Annie with the other as she plunged downward.

Mustering all his strength, Cord managed to push Annie up and out of the crack even as he slid down deeper. Then someone grabbed ahold of his hand. Before he knew it, a whole crew had him. They dragged him out of the collapsing ground and well away from where he'd been falling.

But the shaking and rumbling went on, causing the men who had him to fall as they scrambled backward.

With an awful creak, the chuck wagon sank into the widening crack. Cord took one look at the vanishing wagon and hollered. Josh sprang into action, passing Caroline to their foreman, Shad, before pulling his knife from its sheath. He ran to the horses and slashed their reins, setting loose the Morgans before the earth could swallow them up.

Cord got to his feet, rushed over, and caught the terrified horses' reins. Then, as Cord was leading the animals away, the earthquake turned violent and tossed him to the ground again. Somehow he held on to the horses as they dragged him along, Cord clinging to the reins more out of habit than anything else. Finally the pair of Morgans halted. Everywhere, the men were sprawled on the ground.

The sound of thundering hoofbeats alerted Cord and the others to the cows and horses charging away from the crack that was swallowing the still-smoldering fire, along with a couple of the Two Harts branding irons.

At last the shaking stopped.

Shad brought Caroline to Annie, who remained sitting

on the ground. She hugged her terrified, sobbing daughter, soothing her with quiet shushing sounds.

"We've got to get back to the ranch. There'll be damage for certain." Josh looked around and began snapping off orders, rattling off four names. "You four are lightest. Ride the Morgans double back to the ranch house, rounding up enough horses for the rest of us wherever you can find them. One of you bring them here to us. The others should stay and help at the ranch. There may be injuries. In the meantime, we'll walk as fast as we can for home."

Cord thought of Brody MacKenzie, who'd traveled back east to partner with a doctor to whom he owed money. It'd sure be nice to have a doctor around the place right now. The doctor in the nearest town, Dorada Rio, would most likely be needed there after such a quake. That left them with Zane's wife, Michelle. While she was a knowing woman, she had a baby to tend, and the simple truth was she was no doctor.

Cord could only hope and pray that there were no serious injuries at the ranch.

The four cowhands rode off for home. Before they'd gone far, the ground started trembling again, this time less violently. Even so, they all froze and swayed, looking in all directions for a dangerous new split in the ground.

The powerful aftershock stopped soon enough, and after it did, they quick hoisted their saddles and slung them over their shoulders. They grabbed up the remaining branding irons and bridles, whatever hadn't been swallowed up by the earth.

Though they were miles from home, they set off on foot toward the ranch house regardless. Cord sure hoped they wouldn't have to walk the whole way. Then again, considering what they'd just endured and the possible chaos they might find when they arrived home, he felt very grateful to be in one piece.

Annie decided to make Caroline walk, although her instincts told her to carry her daughter. But they had a long way to go, and Caroline had gotten too heavy to lug any farther. At least the girl was finally calming down after the scare of the quake.

Of the eight of them left to walk, Caroline was probably the most tireless, judging by the little girl's constant motion all day every day.

Occasional aftershocks, small tremors in the ground, kept them all on edge as they walked.

They hadn't gone far when Bo, one of their cowhands, came riding back. He was leading three horses. "I'll bring back more if I can find them," he said. "We saw a couple ahead of us, both still running, no doubt headed for the barn. Shad and I both set our riders down so that I could get back to you fast. He'll try to catch more horses."

"Annie," Josh said, saddling the closest horse as Bo rode off, "those of us who can should ride ahead. There's going to be lots of work to do back at the ranch."

Annie nodded. There would be work for her as well, but if any of the buildings had collapsed, a lot of it would be heavy work, and the men needed to get on with it.

Josh jabbed a finger at five of the men. "You're with me. We'll all ride double. Cord, that leaves you out here with Annie and Caroline. More horses will be coming soon."

Josh mounted up and galloped away with all the men except Cord.

They walked briskly along, Cord toting his saddle and bridle. "Do you think he picked me to stay behind because he knows I'm still the most useless of his cowhands?"

Annie surprised herself by laughing. Not much made her laugh since Todd had died. "And he left me behind for the same reason."

Cord turned to her and smiled.

"I'd say you are doing a decent job," she said. "Between Josh and Zane, when it comes to ranch work, neither of your bosses is real worried about anyone's tender feelings. If you were poor at your job, you'd sure know it by the way they tore the hide off you."

He nodded. "You're right, Annie, because they've done that to me a few times before. Your brothers are competent teachers, but they aren't exactly tactful. As for myself, I prefer straight talk. Anyway, I'm going to have my own place one of these days. Nothing, I suspect, as impressive as the Two Harts, but I spent four of my growing-up years on my grandpa's farm, and that way of life suits me rather well."

"Mayhew Westbrook owns a farm?" Annie knew Cord's grandfather had gone back to his mansion in Sacramento for the winter. He'd cleared out when Michelle's family—five of them—had turned up to see her new baby and filled the ranch house.

Not long after that, Brody and Ellie MacKenzie had taken Brody's younger brothers with them all the way to Boston on the opposite side of the continent. Brody had a doctoring job waiting for him there with a partner by the name of Dr. Tibbles, the man Brody was indebted to.

Thayne and Lochlan—the scamps who'd run away from New York City in search of treasure—had lied their way onto the Two Harts Ranch and left mayhem wherever they went. They'd only agreed to go with Brody to Boston on the condition that when it was determined Brody had fulfilled his promise to Dr. Tibbles, they'd then head back to California.

The men had already found some of the treasure they'd hoped to find, though Annie was convinced that a lot more treasure remained hidden out there, and it was just waiting to be discovered. . . .

Mary Connealy writes romantic comedies about cowboys. She's the author of the BROTHERS IN ARMS, BRIDES OF HOPE MOUNTAIN, HIGH SIERRA SWEETHEARTS, KINCAID BRIDES, TROUBLE IN TEXAS, WILD AT HEART, and CIMARRON LEGACY series, as well as several other acclaimed series. Mary has been nominated for a Christy Award, was a finalist for a RITA Award, and is a two-time winner of the Carol Award. She lives in eastern Nebraska with her very own romantic cowboy hero. They have four grown daughters—Joslyn, married to Matt; Wendy; Shelly, married to Aaron; and Katy, married to Max—and seven precious grandchildren. Learn more about Mary and her books at

MaryConnealy.com
facebook.com/maryconnealy
petticoatsandpistols.com

Sign Up for Mary's Newsletter

Keep up to date with Mary's latest news on book releases and events by signing up for her email list at the link below.

MaryConnealy.com

FOLLOW MARY ON SOCIAL MEDIA

Mary Connealy   @MaryConnealy   @MaryConnealy

Be the first to hear about new books from Bethany House!

Stay up to date with our authors and books by signing up for our newsletters at

BethanyHouse.com/SignUp

FOLLOW US ON SOCIAL MEDIA

   @BethanyHouseFiction